THE BRATVA'S CHRISTMAS BUMP

AVA GRAY

BLURB

One night.

One mistake.

I slept with the wrong man.

Maxim Krasnov — *Bratva prince.*
Cruel. Inked. Deadly.

He took me in a **club bathroom.**

Now I've seen him **execute a man.**

He should've killed me.

Instead... he **claimed** me.

Forced a **ring** on my finger.

Marked me as **his wife.**

His father wants me dead.

The Bratva doesn't leave witnesses.

But **Maxim doesn't follow rules.**

He breaks them.

He breaks *me.*

What he doesn't know—

is that I'm already carrying his secret.

A baby bump born from sin and snow.

And this Christmas,

when **blood stains the snow in New York,**

will he protect **his heir...**

or execute *its mother?*

Author's Note: A scandalously steamy age-gap Christmas mafia romance where danger, desire, and a forbidden baby bump collide under the glitter of winter lights. No Cliffhanger. HEA Guaranteed.

1

HOLLIE

"Hollie, where are you? The Lays arrived ten minutes ago and they keep harping on about the live music performance from my daughter, but you're not here!"

Mom's voice crackles in and out as I weave through the surge of traffic filled with people in exactly the same situation as me. We're all trying to get home for Thanksgiving, and every single person in each of these cars is as late as I am. Grimacing, I tighten my grip on the steering wheel and with a pounding heart ignore the blare of a furious horn behind me as I cut in front of a white sedan.

"I told you not to make promises like that." Not that she ever listens. "You knew I was fully booked tonight and you started dinner so early."

"Don't act like this is my fault," comes the indignant reply. "Far be it from me to expect you to choose your family over your job on Thanksgiving. No one *else* works on Thanksgiving."

"That's because everyone is having a dinner as fancy as the one you have prepared and everyone wants live music to complete the atmosphere. Which is exactly where I come in."

"And despite knowing what I had planned, you fully booked yourself anyway!"

I'm not winning this argument. I've lost track of how often I've told her to stop volunteering me for things without my knowledge or tried to explain how this time of year is exactly how I make the majority of my income, but all Mom sees is my letting her down again and again. At least I give her decent stories to tell her friends about how her daughter ruins the holidays.

"I'm thirty minutes away, maybe longer with traffic."

"At this point, you're so late, why even bother!" The line crackles and dies, leading to a momentary pause. Then my playlist resumes and Christmas music floods my car. The familiar tang of guilt rises like a burn in my chest. She's right, to an extent.

Tiffany, my boss, presented me with a last-minute opportunity at one of the city's most elite restaurants. A chance like that is rare and the money was far too good to pass up. I made more money in that two-hour session than I'm likely to make all week. Given how fleeting this career is, my entire financial year rides on the success of the holidays. Gigs pick up around Halloween, then it's a straight shot of monetary heaven all the way through to the New Year. Around eighty percent of my income happens in these few short months, and yet my mother always acts like it's brand-new information to her.

Deep down, she means well. This isn't the most secure job in the world, and I could settle into a permanent contract with a hotel or restaurant, but I prefer the freedom of choosing my own clients. Every night can be different, if I'm lucky. Besides, Tiffany would spiral without me.

Settling back in my seat, I focus on the road as the world grows so dark and the city becomes so quiet that I soon feel like a lone fish swimming through the abyss. Where I was once surrounded by like-minded drivers hurrying home, suddenly, the streets are empty and quiet as I head further out of the city toward the small town where my parents live. Christmas Carols fill the car and with them comes a bead of excitement. After Thanksgiving, it's the home stretch to Christmas, my favorite time of the year. Between the food, the lights, the snow, and the sheer joy that exists within festive music, I'm set up for a good run this year.

In fact, this year might be *the* year for me. I've been saving to leave New York for a long time, and if my plans pan out this year, this might be the last time I'm late for Thanksgiving.

As I drive through the dark streets, a passing shadow amid buildings containing the laughter and light from families finally together, a soft crackle rises from my phone, interrupting my soft humming along to the music.

Low battery.

Shit. Did I bring my charger?

Keeping one eye on the road and a single hand on the wheel, I cautiously begin rummaging around in my glove compartment seeking out the familiar smooth charging cable. Nothing. It's not in the dip next to my seat, either. Dragging my hand back from the passenger seat and into my lap, I rummage around past my makeup, emergency toiletries, and wallet, but there's no charger to be found. The only place it could be is in my violin case, but there's no reason for it to be there.

Did I forget it?

A memory suddenly bursts to the forefront of my mind of placing the charging cable down on the sink in the restaurant bathroom then being interrupted by a breathless manager begging me to start my set early.

It's still there.

"Shit." Puffing out my cheeks, I tuck my hair behind my ear and floor the gas. All I need to do is make it home and I can charge up there.

Three seconds after I speed up, something loud clunks in front of my car and a vibration moves through the whole chassis. Alarm spikes through me like a clap of thunder and I tighten my grip on the steering wheel.

Did I hit something?

Another clunk rises up from my car followed by a spluttering and chuffing sound, then with a long, low groan, there's the painful sound of something snapping. With another splutter and something akin to a wheezing gasp, my car dies and rolls to a stop, haphazardly parked against the sidewalk where I have enough sense to guide it as it slows.

"No way," I whisper to myself as the lights on my dashboard flicker and die. The warmth blasting out of the heater is the next to go and within ten seconds, I'm shrouded in darkness inside a rapidly cooling car with no other soul in sight.

"You've got to be kidding me!" Snatching my phone from its hands-free stand, I gaze out of the window and try to take in as much of my surroundings as I can.

The outskirts of the city are dark and quiet. A couple of orange streetlights sparsely illuminate the sidewalks on either side of the road. There are a couple of parked cars covered in a light dusting from the earlier snow shower showing they haven't been moved since, and all the businesses up the street are closed and shuttered. Aside from the dark, ominous alley to the left of my car, it looks like I'm alone.

It should be safe to get out.

I tightly clutch my phone in my hand and ease out of my car, scanning around me as I do so. There are too many stories of women being snatched or attacked just for being in the wrong place at the wrong time. My heart begins to race and each breath trembles out of me while I hurry to the front of my car and pop the hood. A useless endeavor because as soon as it lifts, I realize I have no idea what I'm looking at. There are enough knobs and tubes to confuse me instantly, and my heart sinks.

Mom is going to kill me.

The biting November air wraps its long, cold arms around me, seeping through my short coat and biting at my bare knees above the hem of my boots. Any warmth lingering inside me quickly fades even as I stamp my feet on the frozen ground and peer down at my phone while quickly scrolling through my apps for my mechanic. Getting anyone on Thanksgiving is painfully unlikely, and I'll have to eat whatever extra charge they throw my way for making them work, but it'll be better than facing the wrath of my mother for letting her down.

Again.

The number dials with a tap of my trembling thumb and I press my phone to my ear. The street remains dark and empty, so dark, in fact, that I catch the twinkle of stars above me somehow not swallowed by the light pollution of the city.

Beautiful.

The line clicks and a rasping voice comes across the line. "MacMillan's Break Down."

"Hi! Oh, thank goodness! My name is Hollie Wolfe. My car has broken down on the corner of..." I pause and peer around at street signs, but nothing jumps out at me. "Hold on, I'll check my—"

Click.

Did they just hang up on me?

Lowering my phone, my heart sinks as the empty battery image flashes up on the screen and then fades to darkness.

"No! There's no way! Not now! Oh my fucking God, this is turning into a nightmare!" As panic rises inside me like an overboiling pot, the sound of a car engine freezes me to the spot.

A sleek black sedan pulls around the corner and crawls slowly down the road toward me. Every orange streetlight reflects off its black tinted windows as it slowly drives closer and closer to me. Something about the car plus the looming dark alley beside me turns my frustrated panic into a spike of cold feet, and reflex takes over. I duck down behind my car and throw a hand over my mouth.

What are the chances it's someone who can help me? Low, given this neighborhood. But what other choice do I have? Walk back into the city and try to find a place willing to let me charge my phone? Or sit here until daylight and hope everything looks less scary in the daylight?

Neither choice sits well with me, and I mentally kick myself for not being more proactive with my battery life. If I wasn't rushing around so much, this wouldn't have happened.

I huddle next to my car's front wheel and wait for the car to crawl past and out of the street until a soft squeak of brakes greets my ears. They're not driving past.

They've stopped.

Given the state of my own vehicle parked at an angle with the hood wide open, there's a chance they've seen it and decided to help me, so I place one hand on my wheel and try to nonchalantly act like I know what I'm doing should anyone come around my car and spot me.

No one does.

Rising from my haunches, I peer through the window of my own car to spy on the sedan that's parked exactly opposite me in front of a closed restaurant.

Vinny's Pizzeria.

Three men in dark clothing have climbed out of the car. Two stand at either end of the vehicle while the third pulls up the shutter to the restaurant. Seconds later, the neon sign bursts to life with red and white colors when the third man opens the door and heads inside.

Then a fourth man climbs out of the car, and my frantically pounding heart screeches to a painful halt in my chest.

I *know* him.

He stands a good head taller than the other two men, illuminated in the glow from the pizzeria lights. His shoulders are almost as broad as he is tall, and alarmingly thick muscles flex along his thick arms as he raises one hand and points to one of the other men, briefly engaging in a conversation I can't hear. Even in the brisk November air, he only wears a white T-shirt that looks seconds away from bursting at the seams across his thick, broad chest. Those arms are entirely covered in tattoos. There are far too many to count from this far away, but the ink weaves an intricate pattern over all his exposed skin, telling a story that vanishes under his clothing.

His large hand moves to caress the thick, neatly kept medium-length beard that hugs his thick, square jaw, then he turns and strides into the restaurant. My last glimpse of him is as he runs that same hand through his jet black hair. The two men left outside turn and follow him in, returning the street to its eerie silence.

I'm still frozen in place, staring after him in a mix of awe and disbelief.

Two months. I've spent two months trying to track him down and then he just drops right back into my lap like this? I can't lose this chance, and if I'm lucky, he'll be kind enough to let me charge my phone. If I'm *super* lucky, he'll even be able to help me with my car.

Ensuring my car is locked, I dart across the street and catch a glimpse of my reflection in the window. It's enough to make me quickly run my fingers through my crimson hair to try and look less haggard as a nervous flutter enters my heart. The last time I saw Maxim, those massive arms were wrapped around me like two warm logs and I was soaring higher than I've ever been in my life.

Despite my relief at finally finding him again, there's a note of frustration too. How can someone just vanish after a night like that? I roll my eyes faintly while hauling open the door to the pizzeria and heading inside.

The short entranceway opens up into a humble eating area with six tables all covered in the same checkered cloth. Salt, pepper, and chili flakes stand proudly at the center of each table while I weave through them toward the voices in the back of the restaurant.

I'd recognize the sexy gravel of Maxim's deep voice anywhere. It's replayed in my dreams often enough.

Raising both hands, I push through the red double doors into the kitchen with a small smile fixed on my face and Maxim's name on my lips. But just as the doors slip from my raised fingertips, a deafening bang rings out in the kitchen and I jump out of my skin.

Frozen in place, I'm just there to watch as the severely beaten, bruised, and bloody body of a man flops to the ground like a dead fish and lies there with wide, unseeing eyes fixed upon me.

Above him stands Maxim holding a smoking gun in his right hand.

I've spent two months searching the city for Maxim.

And he's just murdered a man in front of me.

2

MAXIM

An ear-piercing shriek fills the kitchen as blood spreads out in a circular pattern from the body at my feet. For the first few seconds, I gaze at the body, unsure how he could be making such a noise with a bullet between his eyes, but as shoes squeak on the kitchen tiles around me, it clicks.

The body isn't screaming.

Someone else is.

Turning on my heel, I glimpse a woman with her face warped by terror and her mouth open in an almost perfect O shape. Then she whirls around and flees from the kitchen in a flurry of deep crimson hair.

I don't need to speak. My guards lunge after her in an instant and vanish through the same door she's just fled.

"Who is she?" I lock eyes with my head of security, Rex, and frown. "You told me this place was on lockdown."

"It was—it is," Rex corrects himself. "No one has been in or out of here except me since we closed." He shakes his hand once and flexes his fingers, fighting to ease the throb there from the last two punches he delivered to our captive.

"Clearly not."

"I'll deal with it." Rex takes a step forward, but I stop him with a raised hand.

"No. I will."

Beyond the double doors, furniture clatters, wood splinters, glass salt shakers smash, and the woman's screams of terror mingle with the alarmed grunts of my men. One woman can't be that difficult to subdue, surely?

My answer comes a second later when Toto and Stu drag the woman, kicking and screaming, back through the doors. Toto has his arms around her middle and has lifted her from the floor, but her arms and legs flail out in all directions. She thrashes so hard that her crimson hair covers her face. Her fingers are like clawed hooks, seeking out contact with anything that will save her while her feet jerk and thrust in all directions to keep everyone away. Stu surges forward and grunts in pain as her foot collides with his stomach. Toto wrenches her around to one side and leans over just as Stu's hand snaps back.

Before I can stop him, his open palm collides with her face with such force that her head snaps to the side like the crack of a whip, and she instantly goes limp while the echo of impact rings around the room.

"Stop." Anger rises in me like the ignition of a furnace, and

Stu barely contains the second strike. Our eyes meet, and he glares at me for a second while massaging his stomach.

"You said get her."

"I did. I didn't say *hurt* her, did I?"

"Kind of implied, Boss," Stu mutters. "She's violent."

"She's *scared*," I correct sharply. "If that wasn't clear, then perhaps you're losing your edge." A thinly veiled threat exists within my words. Those who lose their edge are not welcome around me. I need everyone on top of their game, not just for my survival but for their own. The trust that exists between all four of us is fragile, given how often this world shifts on a dime. An extra dollar in the wrong person's pocket can spell the end of a dynasty.

Stu's jaw flexes back and forth as if he's wrestling with something he doesn't dare say, then his shoulders slump. "Sorry."

Toto blows out a loud breath to free himself from some of the woman's red strands of hair caught in his stubble from her struggles. "What you wanna do with her, Boss?"

"Take her to the office."

"We're not killing her?" Rex's raised brows catch my eyes as Toto moves past me, dragging the motionless body with him.

"No."

"Maxim, you know the rules—"

"I'm acutely aware, thank you."

"No witnesses," Rex presses. "Your father will—"

"I know *exactly* what he will want." I cut through Rex once more. "I know his rules. And I'm telling you, no."

Rex sighs and crosses his arms over his broad chest. "So we're playing it like this?"

"Yes. We are."

"Fine. What about him?" Rex jerks his head down to the dead body on the floor. "We have to clean this up. You also have to make an appearance at your father's Thanksgiving, and you ordered me to remind you not to miss dinner with the girls. We don't have time to babysit."

Rex is right, as always. We're on borrowed time as it is, but the thought of killing an innocent woman for stumbling into the wrong restaurant curdles my blood. Moving past Rex, I follow Toto's path into the office and pass him as he leans against the doorframe.

"Take Stu and clean up," I order curtly.

Toto nods once and dips out of my sight.

He's placed the woman on the worn fabric couch situated parallel to the office desk. Her head is to the side covered by her hair, one arm crosses her abdomen, and her legs rest askew on the armrest.

A short, pleated skirt ruffles around her golden brown, bare thighs. Black knee-high boots hug shapely calves and her woolen coat lies open, showing a floral blouse that hugs tightly at her chest and flares out toward her waist. A silver pendant rests around her neck, coiling into the hollow of her collarbone. Approaching, I lightly grasp the bottom hem of her skirt and straighten out the fabric to cover her thighs, then I lower to my haunches and very gently start pushing strands of her thick, wavy hair away from her face.

It's as red as a Christmas bauble. More and more of her face reveals to me, and just as I tuck the last strand behind her ear, careful of her glittering earring, familiarity hits me.

I know her face.

The soft slope of her nose with the little bump in the bridge. Her lips with her upper lip being fuller than her lower. Her apple cheeks are so soft and round when she smiles, only now, one carries a rapidly bruising handprint courtesy of Stu.

I met her some time ago before I had to leave the country on business. Back then, her hair was a deep blue and she'd crammed her delicious body into a silver dress that rode up her thighs with every step she took in these gorgeous black heeled pumps.

But what was her name?

It sits on the back of my tongue, a distant thought that refuses to come forth no matter how long I stare at her peaceful face. I know it and yet it escapes me. I slowly reach forward, expecting her to wake up at any second, but she doesn't stir as I press two of my thick fingers to the slope of her neck to check her pulse.

It's there. Strong and slow.

As I count just to ensure everything remains normal, it's alarming how easily my entire hand could seal around her throat and crush the life out of her without my having to even break a sweat. She's as small and lithe as I am tall and broad. And her presence here is alarming.

No one should walk in on us, least of all someone I've had previous contact with. Is this some kind of setup or an honest to God mistake?

Following the law set out by the *Pakhan*, my father, I should torture her to be sure this was just an accident and then kill her. They won't find her body until the river thaws, and by then, any possible evidence will have been eaten by the ice and the current. That's how Dad deals with everything. If it bothers him, he gets rid of it. No exceptions.

I can't do that. Not now. Not ever.

Happy that she's alive, I return to Rex out in the kitchen. The body of my target has been removed, leaving behind a pool of blood that Toto is in the middle of cleaning up.

"I want this kitchen deep cleaned," I say as a spattering of blood on a nearby cupboard door catches my eye. "Top to bottom. This place has to look brand-new before we reopen, understand?"

Rex, with his arms still crossed, nods. "And her?" He nods past me to the open office door. "You know what we should do."

"I do. But I'm not going to."

"Why?" Toto peers up from amid his scrubbing. "We've done it before."

"Toto, when was the last time you pulled the trigger on someone who didn't explicitly deserve it?"

His lips part and his boyish face melts with confusion as he struggles to recall an exact time. Like a fish gasping for air, his lips part repeatedly and then he leans back onto his knee. "I ain't got a clue."

"Exactly. Until I know exactly why she walked in here, she doesn't *deserve* anything," I say, and I lock eyes with Stu as he walks back through those double doors rolling one shoulder to free it from an ache.

"Igor won't be happy," Stu comments, wrinkling his nose and causing the scar on his cheek to jump.

"Let me deal with my father. If nothing comes of this and she is innocent, you will owe her an apology."

"Sure," Stu replies easily. "*If.*"

"Take her to my penthouse. From there, we'll find out the truth and keep her quiet."

"No!" Her voice rises up from behind me. "You're not taking me anywhere!"

We all turn. She stands in the doorway of the office on trembling legs, brandishing the desk lamp clutched between both her hands. Despite the evident fear in her stunning, crystal clear green eyes, her brow is pinched in anger and her lips set in a straight line.

"Let. Me. Go."

It takes balls to face down four members of the Mafia with a desk lamp, I'll give her that.

"If you can make it past all four of us," I say casually, "then you're free to go."

"Really?" She and Toto speak in unison. Toto earns a slap on the back of the head from Stu.

"You idiot," Stu mutters.

"You mean it?" the woman challenges again.

"Sure. And I'll make it easy for you. None of us will even move."

Her eyes dart back and forth between the four of us and I see the wheels turning behind her eyes. She's trying to find the path of least resistance between us, a path that doesn't exist given the close build of the kitchen and the amount of space I alone take up.

"How do I know you'll keep your word?" Her voice trembles and she takes a wobbling step forward. Her grip on the desk lamp becomes so tight that her knuckles become almost translucent.

"I always keep my word."

She scoffs weakly, trying to appear stronger than she actually is. "Shit like that doesn't mean anything between strangers."

"Then make your choice. Either you're going to my penthouse or you're trying to get past us. Decide."

Her lips part. The lampshade quivers in her grasp and her chest rises so rapidly, it's a wonder she's getting any air with how she pants. There's a moment of silence broken by Stu popping his gun. The sound makes her jump, but it spurs her into action. She sprints from the doorway and reaches Rex first, who watches her with a mildly amused smile. He doesn't move and he doesn't try to reach for her either, so she slips past untouched. Next is Toto, still kneeling on the tiles next to the stain. He also doesn't move other than sliding his bucket of water out of her path so she doesn't trip. Each victory gives her confidence, but I'm next.

And she's not getting away.

She tries to run past me, hair flying and cheeks vibrant from the adrenaline rush of success, but she doesn't make it. I sweep my arm out, and she runs right into it with a pained grunt as all the air bursts past her lips. With one motion, I sweep her right off her feet, and the desk lamp slips from her fingers, then she collides with the fridge next to me as I shove her into it and crowd her in with my entire bulk.

"You said you wouldn't move!" she gasps as gigantic tears flood her eyes.

"I didn't. My feet are exactly where they always were."

"Please let me go. I didn't see anything, I swear. I won't tell anyone anything, please!" She dissolves into terrified sobs and tension coils around my beating heart.

"What is there to tell anyone if you didn't see anything?" My head tilts to the side. "I don't like liars, and we both know what you saw. So beg all you want. The only place you're going is my penthouse."

3

HOLLIE

Despite my vocal protest, I'm thrown into the back of the sleek, black sedan and handcuffed to the door. Maxim doesn't join me. He just gives me one last cold look and slams the door in my face, then the car starts moving and I'm dragged away from everything I've ever known.

What the hell is happening?

Over and over, that gunshot rings in my ears, followed by the sickening thud of that body hitting the floor. His eyes, open and unseeing, pierced right through me and they repeatedly flash up every time I close my eyes. Tears come swiftly after a few minutes of wrestling with the steel cuffs to no avail, and I sob into my hands.

I've never seen someone die before. Sure, it's been on the news and in stories, but to see it with my own eyes sets a chill deep in my soul that I can't shift. For two months, I searched for Maxim and seemingly, it's the biggest mistake of my life.

He's going to kill me.

I don't see why he doesn't just do it now. Why drag this out? Whisking me across the city like I'm some kind of package and acting like it's *my* fault for witnessing the murder and not his for committing it in the first place. And those men around him? They were as calm as anything, like this is some kind of daily occurrence for them. Not a single one of them seemed horrified by the murder.

Thoughts of Thanksgiving and my mother collide in my mind, but it's too much for me to think about on top of everything else. That and my face hurts. I feel like I slammed face-first into a moving truck, but it was just a slap from that asshole.

Stu, I think I caught his name.

The car glides through the streets without a single stop, not even for any red lights that crop up on our path. It's either stupidity or arrogance, I can't decide, but as the drive continues, the turmoil in my gut worsens. Each breath scrapes against my throat, my heart pounds like a drum and shows no sign of stopping, my hands shake like I'm no longer in control of them, and nausea assaults me in waves.

Tears pour silently down my cheeks no matter how hard I try to stop them, but a sudden soft lurch of the car is the cork that pops it all. Bile rushes up my throat and I'm barely able to haul my hair out of the way before I'm throwing up all over the floor of this luxury car. The leather seats are ruined in seconds as another wave overtakes me, and what's left of my lunch burrito ends up staining the soft felt floor.

Oddly, I feel miles better by the time I've regained control of myself and I sag back into the plush leather seat, panting.

Holy. Shit.

Two minutes later, the car pulls to a soft stop. Ten seconds after that, the door opens and one of Maxim's men leans inside, holding a small silver key. His eyes widen when he sees the mess on the floor.

"Sorry," I say weakly, although I'm not all that sorry. "Your driving was terrible."

The man's boyish face breaks into a brief smile as he unlocks my cuffs, then he grasps my upper arm and pulls me from the car. Any urge to bolt down the street fades when I see two men clad in black framing the golden entrance into a building so tall I can't even see the top.

"Toto." One greets the man guiding me with a nod of the head.

"Toto?" I croak, wincing around the acidic taste lingering in my mouth. "Like the dog?"

He glances at me but doesn't speak while he drags me through gold-rimmed glass doors and into a marble foyer. Several red couches sit around a small glass table to my left, and a deep red carpet leads the way toward a wooden half-oval desk where a woman sits filing her nails. She doesn't even glance up as we pass, and I stumble over myself all the way to the elevator.

Toto doesn't release me until the doors close, and I immediately hug the wall furthest away from him.

"I'm not going to hurt you."

"Why, because you have a conscience?" I snap.

"No." His blue eyes lock onto mine. "I'm under orders not to."

Orders? What the hell is going on? "Do you always do what he tells you?"

"Yes," Toto replies simply, and half a second later, the doors glide open once more. I barely even felt us moving. "This is where you will be staying."

His arm sweeps out and on trembling legs, I step over the threshold, but Toto doesn't follow. I turn back to face him as he presses an unseen number on the elevator.

"You're not coming?"

"No."

"You're just going to leave me here?"

"You'll be fine," Toto says, and for a moment, there's almost something genuine in his little smile. Then the doors close and I'm left alone.

Hugging my arms around my waist, I stand alone in a short hallway. Black flooring leads to an open-plan lounge with white and blue furniture situated three steps down. Three couches surround a coffee table piled high with magazines and several unopened packets of blank printer paper. To my left, the black flooring leads to another hallway but just before the wall, a small kitchen is on my left and several tall potted plants surrounded by small glass stones are on the right. As I approach, the sound of trickling water catches my attention and I glimpse a small stream weaving between the plants filled with an array of colorful fish calmly swimming around.

My stomach cramps and after a few slow breaths, I sprint toward the smaller hallway and throw open doors until I find the bathroom. There are two bedrooms, a study, and then a bathroom at the very end, which becomes my haven as I sink to my knees and heave over the toilet. There's nothing left inside me to bring up. The cramping is just from stress, but I don't move from my hunched position until I'm certain the spasms inside me have stopped.

"Fuck." Groaning, I stumble to my feet and fiddle with the gold-tipped taps until cool water splashes forth. Splashing it on my face and neck, I gulp a mouthful directly from the stream and swirl it around my mouth, then spit it in the sink and straighten.

My gray reflection hovers before me in the mirror. Water droplets run down my chin, my mascara runs in rivers down my cheeks from my tears, and a bruise forms on my cheek from that asshole's blow. I look pathetic. A far cry from all the work I did to be presentable as soon as I made it home.

A soft, dry sob bubbles up inside me and I tear my eyes away. I can't stay here. I need to get help.

The elevator doesn't respond to my calls no matter how often I press the button, and despite the lavish layout of this luxurious penthouse, there isn't a phone anywhere. Not even a laptop, and the computer in the study refuses to turn on even after I spend ten minutes under the desk checking and following the wires to the sockets. It's like the entire apartment is working against me.

Frustrated, I retire to one of the couches and curl up around a cream tasseled pillow, determined to sneak a phone away from Maxim whenever he gets here. Taking a moment to myself, to sit and rest and process everything I saw, results in overwhelming exhaustion, and I close my eyes to fight off the growing throb of a migraine swarming my temples.

It feels like a blink but when I open my eyes, I'm lying down on the couch with cushions around my head and a thick, brown blanket draped over my body. It pools around me and is butter soft against my skin yet has a comforting weight that keeps me lying down as my sleep-addled mind catches up with the events that led me here.

The gunshot.

The dead body.

Maxim.

Metal clatters softly from beyond the couch, and I tear my attention away from the haphazard gold patterns weaving across the gold ceiling, slowly lifting myself onto my elbows.

Beyond the couch, Maxim stands in the kitchen with his back to me. He's topless and his broad, bare back shows an equally intricate pattern of tattoos as his arms. He's absolutely covered in ink. From this distance, they seem like nonsense, but as I slowly stand and approach, more detail comes clear. There's everything from flowers, birds, animals, flames, to a large dragon perched on one shoulder. A few stars and a cluster of flower petals are visible at the base of his neck, and they ripple and weave as if caught in a breeze as he turns toward me with a silver spoon dangling from his mouth.

As soon as our eyes meet, anger surges up inside me and I storm forward until my body hits the island counter. Slamming both hands down, I glare as much hatred toward him as I can.

"Let me go!"

"I know you." Maxim removes the spoon, and his gravelly voice would be like honey to my ears if I weren't so twisted up.

"No you don't," I snap.

"I do. You had blue hair when we met, but I know." He brandishes the spoon toward me and it bobs lightly between his fingers. "Are you hungry?"

His question catches me off guard and I falter, hovering back a step. "Huh?"

"Are you hungry?" He steps to the side, revealing several pots bubbling away on the stove. "I'm making curry."

"You can cook?"

"Why does that surprise everyone?" His blue eyes crease at the corners. "Yes, I can cook. I won't ask a third time."

"No."

"Are you sure?" He turns back to his cooking, but not fully. He's angled as if every part of him is keeping an eye on me. "It's good."

"I bet it's poisoned."

Maxim scoffs. "So what if it is? I'm eating it too."

My lips part but no sound comes out. So quickly, he engaged me in a light conversation and I almost forgot what the hell was going on. "I'm going to walk out of here."

"No, you're not."

"Just watch me."

"You can try." He swivels back to me. "The elevator is biometrically coded. It won't work for you."

"What if there's a fire?"

"Then you'd better hope I don't succumb to smoke inhalation."

"Stop!" I throw my hands up. "Stop talking to me like you know me! You've kidnapped me! Dragged me across the city after I saw you murder that poor man! You're twisted and sick, and if you don't let me go, then I'll make you regret ever bringing me here!"

Maxim seems unaffected by my outburst and suddenly, his dark brows lift. "Hollie."

"What?"

"I remember now. Your name was Hollie."

Slowly, my hands lower and something else twists in my gut. Nerves. "You remember?"

"It took me a second because you look so different, but yes, I remember. We were at Leviathan. The club."

"Mhm."

"And now you're here. In my line of work, that's too much of a coincidence, so tell me, Hollie. Are you going to tell me who you work for or am I going to have to drag it out of you?"

The soft patter of rain rises up against the floor-to-ceiling windows lining the lounge. As the tantalizing aroma of the curry fully invades my senses, my shoulders slump and confusion mingles with the upset in my chest.

"I have no idea what you are talking about."

"You walked in on something you never should have seen," Maxim states flatly. "That's a problem for me."

"Then you'd better go ahead and kill me because I'm never going to forget your murdering some poor man in cold blood."

4

MAXIM

S he isn't shying away from me. That's a start. She's either very bold or incredibly stupid. Typically, in situations like these, the burst of confidence fades after a few minutes and the gravity of the situation sets in.

Then again, typical situations like this don't involve my penthouse or curry at three in the morning. If she were anyone else, she'd likely end up in one of our facilities having her teeth pulled out until we learned every detail about her life and then, if she wasn't deemed a threat, we'd get enough dirt on her to destroy her life if she ever talked.

Instead, I had her brought back here because I remember her, and something about the genuine fear in her eyes cut through me a little. Innocents, true innocents who make up the majority of this city, are left unharmed when my orders are followed.

Orders often overruled by my strict, cold-hearted father. In truth, my home is currently the only place in the entire city where she's safe and she doesn't even know it.

Turning back to the sauce bubbling merrily in my pan, I stir slowly to ensure all pieces of chicken are evenly coated. "People who walk into my business are one of two things—either nosy enough to play with their lives or they're working for someone else who is happy to risk their life in order to get any kind of information on me. So, which is it?"

Glancing over my shoulder, Hollie has eased into one of the tall, high-backed chairs against my breakfast counter. "Why are you talking like that?"

My hand pauses. "Like what?"

"Like you're some kind of spy or something."

A brief grunt of humor escapes me. "Not a spy. But your life rides on your answer."

"You're not serious."

"Deadly."

Her face pales slightly and she brings both of her hands together, clasping at her knuckles. "I wasn't doing anything. I don't understand this at all. I just..." Her lower lip trembles. "I want to go home."

"If you satisfy me, it might be possible."

"*Satisfy* you?" A flicker of alarm crosses her eyes.

"With answers," I add. Poor word choice. "Tell me what you were doing there."

"I..."

Her brow creases and debate seems to rage inside her, so I turn back to the food and continue to cook until her small voice drifts through the air once more.

"My car broke down across the street and my phone died. I saw lights in the pizzeria, and it was the only place in the entire block with life, so I walked in hoping someone could lend me a phone for a mechanic or a charger. That's *it*. That's all I was doing, I swear. And why are you interrogating me? You *murdered* someone! I watched you! And I'm next, right? If I don't play your little game?"

Her voice rises and rises until it starts to crack and she's babbling breathlessly. "I have people who will miss me, you know. People who will look, and they won't stop looking, so unless you plan on wiping out my entire family line, you will let me go. Because my parents know people. And my boss? My God, you do not want to piss her off. She's like a hornet in a helicopter when she's pissed and she will track me down and make your life a living hell if you do anything to me!"

Listening to her patiently, I dish up the curry into two bowls and face her. Placing one down in front of her, I then lean back against the opposite counter and cross one leg over the other while I dig in. "It's simple, Hollie. You don't know what you saw."

"Are you telling me that as some tricky way of telling me what to say if the cops come knocking?"

"No. You *really* don't know what you saw."

She gapes at me and pushes the bowl away. "There's no way you're telling me that poor man deserved everything you did to him? And why am I even trying to discuss morals with a cold-blooded killer and kidnapper!"

"Have you been harmed?"

"Yes." She turns her bruised cheek toward me and I wince inwardly. "Did you forget what your brute of a friend did to me?"

"No. I hadn't forgotten. I am sorry that happened. It wasn't supposed to."

Her hands return to being clasped tightly. "*Oh*, that makes it alright, then."

With a trembling sigh, the telltale signs of her adrenaline-fueled confidence are fading. Her hands shake more visible, she's constantly chewing on her lower lip, and rather than glaring at me, she's scanning her surroundings for any way out. Not that she'll get far if she does run.

Before I can say anything else, my phone buzzes from its current home face down on the counter next to the stove.

"Hello?"

"Maxim!" My father's voice barks in my ear and it takes all my strength not to wince at the volume. "Tell me what the fuck you are doing playing house with a witness?"

Stu. That bastard.

He's always been a bit of a problem but constantly insists it comes from a place of concern to stop me from ending up on my father's chopping block. I fail to see how his tattling on me to the *Pakhan* is saving my neck in any regard.

"We have a problem and I'm dealing with it."

"You know exactly how to deal with it." Dad's almost clawing his way through the phone and burying in my mind. "So deal with it. Kill her and move on. I don't have time for this."

With a click, the call ends as abruptly as it started, and I bite back a sigh. Hollie's watching me with large, saucer-like eyes and her hands have moved to hug the bowl for its warmth.

"Are you going to let me go now?"

Setting my phone down on the counter, I draw another phone from my pocket. This one is in a purple butterfly case and Hollie recognizes it immediately. Her hand flies to the small pocket on her skirt, then her brows lift in alarm.

"You stole my phone?"

"It took you this long to notice it wasn't there anymore."

"Give it back!"

I lazily scroll through the device as Hollie half rises in her seat and then thinks better of it. Her passcode was painfully easy to crack with Toto's help.

"Your parents, Susan and Martin Wolfe, correct? Cute. You take a lot of family pictures. Warm. Wholesome."

All attitude has faded from Hollie's face, replaced by open fear. "Please..."

"Cute dog. Such an important part of the family and always such a tragedy when they pass. Although nothing compares to the loss of a parent now, does it?" Through her contacts and linked pictures, I scroll until her phone buzzes with a message. "Tiffany says Happy Thanksgiving. She's your boss, hmm? The hornet in the helicopter?"

Hollie nods weakly. "Mhm."

"And all these other names? Steven. Charlie. Rebecca. Francis. Andre. Kirk. Quite the list."

"Clients," she chokes out. "Please. Please don't hurt them."

Our eyes meet. "You care that much about your clients? I suppose I also care about where my money comes from."

"No, my family." Tears bead in the corner of her eyes, striking me with the force of a punch in the chest. "Please don't hurt my family."

Lowering her phone, I walk toward her until only the counter exists between us. She seems so small huddled on the stool with fear glistening in her damp eyes, and her knuckles have turned white with how tightly she grips the bowl.

"I'm sensing there is a deal to be made here, Hollie."

She nods rapidly. "Mhm."

"What did you see tonight?" Her voice is barely above a whisper, so I tilt my head. "What was that?"

"Nothing," she chokes out. "I saw nothing."

"Really? Tell me what happened."

"M–My car broke down and I–I couldn't call anyone. My phone died and I..."

She's wrestling with herself to get the words out, and I feel disgusting but I can't pinpoint why. I've done this dance a thousand times before.

"I was alone and I didn't know what to do."

"Then, Hollie. Tell me." Setting her phone down on the counter, I slowly slide it toward her without lifting my fingers. "How did we meet?"

Her eyes are like the biggest emeralds I've ever seen in my life. "Your car pulled over after seeing me parked and you offered me help?"

"Are you asking me or telling me?"

"T–Telling you."

"Good. I'm sure your parents will be happy that you weren't alone, Hollie. But if I need to stop by and tell them myself, we might have a problem. Are we understood?"

She's shaking so much it's a wonder she's even still on the stool. "I understand. I do. Please, I understand."

"Good." Straightening, I leave her phone next to her on the counter. "Now eat. I won't have anyone thinking I'm a bad host."

She stares at me as if I've just sprouted another head right in front of her.

"Please. Eat."

Hollie snatches up the spoon and shovels food into her mouth before I can blink. It's good that she's eating, but I can't shake the guilt eating away at me. Is our previous tryst a few months ago really a good enough reason to treat her differently from anyone else in this position? She caught my eyes back then and while alcohol warmed and influenced both our decisions, I can't deny that I was more than a little sad when we stumbled out of the cubicle and I lost her in the sea of clubgoers, never to be seen again.

Now she's in my kitchen with tears clinging to her lashes while shoveling down curry like her life depends on it.

Maybe my wording did give that implication. I return to my own meal and eat slowly, angled away from her so she doesn't feel like I'm watching her even though I'm in tune to her every move.

Gradually, her eating pace slows and the worried wrinkle between her brows eases out as if she's actually enjoying her meal. In my experience, anything like what happened tonight is enough to build up an appetite even if you're stressed.

Just as I'm sweeping my spoon around the last of the sauce, a soft female voice carries through the apartment.

"Elevator in motion."

Hollie straightens up, her eyes upward. "Who was that?"

"Think of it as an Alexa," I say, setting my bowl in the sink. "Only way more advanced."

"Wow," she murmurs. "Like a smart kitchen?"

"Something like that." I leave the kitchen and approach the hallway. I'm not expecting any guests so unless it's Stu coming to apologize, I'm not in the mood to face anyone either. The demand for them to leave hovers on the tip of my tongue, but it doesn't see the light of day as the elevator doors slide open and reveal my father, Igor.

He strides toward me at such a pace that his open coat trails behind him along with his white scarf. The tassels flop back and forth with each powerful stride while a cotton turtle-neck stretches across his broad chest. His hair, as black as mine, is slicked up and back to make his forehead appear squarer and the short beard hugging his jaw has been dyed so dark that it looks like someone colored his jaw with permanent marker.

His dress shoes slap on the floor as he closes in, flanked by two of his personal security, and as soon as he reaches the lounge, he speaks like the snap of a belt.

"Where is she?"

Hollie squeaks in fright, but it turns into a squeal when Dad's left-hand guard pulls out his gun and aims it at her. The spoon clatters from her trembling fingers and she cowers, caught between sliding off the stool and not moving to try and prevent injury.

"Father—"

"Don't," he snaps. "I told you to take care of this and instead you're..." He casts his eye over me and the kitchen in disgust. "You're sharing a *meal* with her?"

I don't reply, but I stride forward and position myself between the guard and her, locking eyes with him and daring him to pull the trigger.

"Maxim," Dad barks. "We don't have *time* for this. There are enough distractions and I am up to my neck clearing up other people's messes. I do not need to handle yours either, understand?" He raises a hand, ready to signal the brutal and abrupt end to Hollie's life, but I refuse to move.

An unfamiliar, weak surge of panic rises inside me, its cause unknown. I barely know this woman. The fact that she's hot is in no way reason enough for me to throw my life and reputation on the line to protect her, but something keeps me rooted to the ground, steadfast between her and certain demise.

"You can't kill her," I say in a voice that barely sounds like my own.

Igor's fingers hover in the air. "You dare tell me what I can and cannot do?"

"You can't kill her because I'm going to marry her."

5

HOLLIE

"You can't kill her because I'm going to marry her."

I gape at Maxim's back in utter shock. There's no way I just heard that correctly, right? *Marriage*? To a man I barely know? A murderer who just casually stood in front of me and threatened the lives of my family and everyone I've ever known just to force me into silence?

"What?" Maxim's father sounds just as shocked as I feel, but before the conversation continues, he suddenly grabs Maxim by the arm and drags him down the corridor toward the office. After the door slams with both of them inside, their voices immediately rise, but they're muffled enough that I can't decipher any of the words.

My heart pounds. What little comfort I earned from the rather tasty curry melts away in the presence of the two new stony-faced guards who eye me with curious disbelief.

"Marriage," says the one with the blue silk tie as he lowers his gun.

"A wedding," says the other with the red silk tie.

I can't speak. This night has been a whirlwind. Did I crash my car? Maybe I actually died and this is some alarming purgatory where my morals and values are being tested in the face of some really terrible decisions.

I'm supposed to be home. This late, I should be filled with turkey and my Mom's amazing creamy, cheesy mashed potatoes. I should be relaxing on the couch watching Dad trying to help Mom to bed after one too many sherries.

Instead I'm here, trapped in this nightmare.

"What did you say to him?" Blue tie moves closer to me, rolling his shoulders as he approaches and fiddling with the cufflinks on his suit.

"Are you some rich heiress or something?" Red tie asks, approaching slowly from the other side of me.

"Nah," blue tie scoffs. "I know all the rich bitches this side of the river and there ain't any that look this good."

Red tie snorts and his beady gaze starts wandering down over my body. A sickly, cold chill creeps across his skin as if led by his gaze until his eyes lock onto my thighs and I'm suddenly highly conscious of the skirt I chose.

"Gotta be that sweet slit between your legs, right? I always knew it would take a special pussy to make Maxim settle down," red tie remarks. "Gotta be one dazzling cunt."

"You're disgusting," I snap hotly, shifting on the stool and keeping my legs pressed closed together.

"She doesn't deny it." Blue tie smirks as he gets closer. "What did you do? Suck him off in the car? Spread your legs while he was cooking? A meal after sex always tastes better, don't you think?"

My cheeks flare hot while my heart pounds harder and harder. I feel like a gazelle cornered by hyenas while the lions are busy elsewhere. With nothing to defend myself, I try to act as confidently as I can while looking them both in the eye.

"Why don't you go ask Maxim? I'm sure he'll be more than happy to give you an answer."

"Maxim," red tie scoffs. "He's a puppy dog. Dude doesn't kiss and tell. But his bitches, on the other hand?" Whatever he was going to say next dies as a subtle voice buzzes in his ear. He lifts one hand and presses on his in-ear speaker, then he grimaces. "Shit. Boss!"

In a flash, they're both heading down the hall and I sag on the stool like my puppet threads have been cut.

This is *awful*. How is it I feel safer with the murderer than I do with those two disgusting men? Tugging the hem of my skirt down as far as it will go, I glance toward the opening leading toward the elevator. Biometrically coded, he said. No escape. One wrong move and it's my family that will suffer.

What the fuck am I supposed to do?

The guard's rapid knocking on the door is quickly answered and a short, sharp conversation occurs. Then Maxim reappears with his gaze fixed down on his phone, but he looks up the moment he's close to me.

"You good?"

I nod, speechless. What use would it be to tell him what happened when those same guards were seconds away from shooting me? Whoever they are and whatever criminal shit they're involved in is beyond me, but I know one thing for sure.

I don't want to die.

I just want to go home.

"I have to go," Maxim states, though it's unclear who he's talking to.

"This isn't over." His father appears behind him, flanked by his two smirking guards. "Did you listen to anything I just said?"

Maxim locks his phone and slides it into his pocket, then he moves to a built-in closet in the wall and removes a T-shirt. It's black with red fall leaves drifting in a light pattern across the back and down the sleeves. Despite how large it looks in his hands, it fits like a glove and looks seconds away from ripping by the time he slides it over his bulky torso.

"I heard you, but I made myself clear. Hollie and I are engaged. We were engaged before tonight and the whole reason she was there was because I told her the wrong time. She saw nothing, do you understand? Nothing."

The lie spins from him like silk and my mouth runs dry. He's painting out a life story for me and I have no idea what it is.

"But I have to go," Maxim continues. "There's trouble at one of the clubs."

"Let me keep an eye on your *fiancée* then, until you make it back to finish our conversation," his father says abruptly, his tone as icy as the wind outside.

My heart punches painfully up into my throat. Staying with him sounds terrifying, and with how his guards ogle me like I'm a piece of meat, I think I'd rather die.

"No," Maxim says, much to my immense relief. "She's coming with me. Right?"

I blink, and Maxim's intense blue eyes are locked onto mine, but his expression is unreadable. It's almost like he's giving me a choice, and while a choice between two awful things is hardly a choice at all, I choose him.

"Yes," I say, unable to stop my voice from trembling.

Suddenly, my hand is engulfed in Maxim's fist. He pulls me from the stool and strides down toward the elevator at such a pace, I have to jog slightly to keep up. His grip, despite being firm and almost dwarfing my entire hand, is warm and oddly gentle, like the touch of a friend rather than that of a captor.

Once the doors hiss closed, I jerk my hand away and he releases me without complaint.

"The men you surround yourself with are disgusting," I snap, huddling away from him against the side of the elevator.

"We can't choose our parents," he replies without looking at me.

"But you choose your guards, right?"

That catches his attention and one dark brow arches as he looks at me. "What happened?"

Telling him the truth might be the smartest option, but this hellish night leaves me entirely unwilling to engage any longer than I have to, so I look away and focus on the gleaming floor numbers on the elevator. "Nothing."

Whether he believes me or not is unclear, but he doesn't press the issue and I don't offer any more information. Outside, one of the men from the pizzeria greets us but it's not Toto.

"Stu." Maxim's fist suddenly flies out and collides with Stu's face, sending him sprawling flat onto the ground like he was made of air. The powerful sound of skin slapping skin rings in my ears as I stare down in shock.

"I deserved that," Stu groans from his heap on the sidewalk. "You know why I did it, though, right?"

"Yeah. Your loyalty is mis-fucking-placed. And you owe her an apology." He's pointing at me, and I'm more confused than ever.

Stu doesn't appear surprised and he climbs to his feet while massaging his jaw. Then he looks at me, and I weakly brace for the next disgusting onslaught from one of these men.

It doesn't come. Instead, Stu grimaces and indicates briefly to my face. "Sorry about that."

"What?" My brain short-circuits and after blinking rapidly, the situation isn't any clearer. "I don't... understand."

Maxim turns to face me as he opens the rear door. "My father speaks in violence between those close to him," he explains. "I hate that approach. Stu never should have laid a hand on you."

"Does that really matter when you're holding me hostage?" I challenge, glaring at him. "Will you hit me if I run right now?"

"No," Maxim replies easily. "I bet I'd reach your parents faster than you."

There it is again. That same threat, although it's much clearer this time. Narrowing my eyes, I glance back at Stu, who is still massaging his jaw. "For a man who doesn't speak through violence, you sure could've fooled me." With that, I slide into the car and huddle in the back seat.

Thankfully, I'm not handcuffed this time and I focus on the passing buildings while we weave like silk through the streets of New York. I've never been out in the city this late. It's like another world. Feels like my entire life has crashed into another world, at this rate.

"I punched Stu because he didn't trust me, to an extent." Maxim's voice is soft despite the gravel undertones. "He didn't think I could take care of myself."

"You're built like a brick house," I scoff. "Why would anyone think that?"

Maxim doesn't reply.

Sighing, I glance over at him and bite into the offered conversation. "How does punching him build that trust?"

"My father thinks Stu is still a mole for him so occasionally, Stu has to give him tidbits of information. Sometimes, that info has to be juicy enough to keep my father satisfied. Other times, he genuinely thinks he's helping."

A mole? He speaks less like they're street criminals and more like they run some kind of organization.

"I knew he would use you as a juicy piece of information and I was fine with it. What I wasn't fine with was his not warning me that my father was on his way to visit me."

"So you punched him." Sounds like ego aggression to me.

"Yes. My father would be suspicious if I didn't react to Stu's betrayal in some way. Better my fist in his face than my father's blade in his spine."

Oh. "You hurt him to save him?"

"Yes."

"Why are you telling me this?"

"I'm hoping you will understand."

"Understand what?"

"Everything."

Rolling my eyes, I look back out the window. I'm too tired and stressed to play around with riddles right now. Maxim doesn't press the conversation so we settle into silence for the rest of the drive. Not once does he move closer or try to reach out and touch me, and once again, the vehicle moves as if red stop lights don't exist. Either we're super lucky and it's green all the way, or no one in the group gives a shit about road safety.

We pull up outside a nightclub called Plumme. The name blinks at me in gold and neon pink letters that throb in time to the low thump of music drifting from inside.

"Can I stay in the car?" I ask as Maxim opens the door. I could tell him I'm exhausted, that being on edge for so long is draining me, but ultimately, I'm tired of being herded from place to place like a sack.

"No."

"But—"

"I said no. Come."

"I'm not a fucking dog," I snap while dragging myself from the car before he can do it for me. Maxim looks at me like he wants to say something, but he thinks better of it and heads inside the club. I follow with Stu by my side.

We're immediately swallowed by thin smoke that creates a haze over the entire club. A black corridor with sparkles adorning the walls resembling stars leads us to a single red door, where a thick, tall bouncer stands guard. He grimaces slightly and immediately waves us through.

Inside, the club is filled with shining black stages scattered around the floor below the small entrance balcony we walk onto. I count six at first glance. Each one has a shining silver pole and is highlighted by a personal spotlight shining down with soft, golden light. Beyond the mini stages, a long, large stage hugs the back wall, adorned with thick red curtains held in place above the stage by silver cords.

Silver confetti drifts about the smoky haze covering the room, and those who aren't in the middle of getting a lap dance or a drink at the bar to the far left are huddled around some commotion in the center of the room. Maxim takes the curved stairs to my left and makes a beeline for the huddle. The crowd parts around him like the sea and as the scuffling men break apart due to a punch, Maxim immediately tackles one of the men to the ground.

I wince as they hit the floor and someone screams in alarm. The two other men groggily climb to their feet. One is dressed in the same red suit as the bouncer we passed at the door and he heads toward the third man who wobbles back and forth, waving what appears to be a rhinestone-covered cane. It matches the outfit of a nearby woman. Her rhinestone-encased bikini glitters in the light, and a miniature top hat is affixed to her curls on top of her head. The crowd ducks and sways as the man swings the cane, then he brings it down hard on Maxim's back.

My stomach flips and the man is quickly tackled back to the ground by the second bouncer.

"He's fine," comes Stu's voice. He's watching, and something about my face must have enticed him to give me that reassurance, so I quickly frown.

"Sure," I mutter. "I don't care."

Remaining on the balcony, I watch as Maxim and the bouncer subdue the two drunken, angry men and drag them through the crowd toward a sleek black door next to the large stage. They vanish through it and the crowd below slowly dissipates. Dancers return to their poles and patrons resume drinking and flashing money at the stages.

"So he owns a strip club?" I look over at Stu, and he winces.

"Harsh way to look at it. Is that what you think this place is?"

"What else would it be?"

Gazing back over the railing, I see that Maxim reappears with the bouncer. The two drunken culprits are nowhere to be seen. Maxim claps the bouncer on the shoulder and for the first time since I saw him in that restaurant, he smiles. In an instant, the intimidating face with the sharp jaw and harsh, narrow eyes melts into something soft and unrecognizable. He's more like the man I met at the bar all those months ago.

The man I spent so long looking for.

As he passes a stage, the rhinestone-clad woman darts down effortlessly in her six-inch heels and throws her arms around Maxim's neck, planting a bright red kiss on his cheek. "Thank you! Thank you!"

Something cold and sharp rises in my stomach.

Am I... jealous?

No... I can't be. Can I?

6

MAXIM

Xena presses up against me in a cloud of sweet perfume and glitter and places a brief kiss on my cheek. "I knew you'd come!"

"Didn't I say I would?" With one arm around her waist to support her after she threw herself at me, I gently lower her to the ground while she pats my cheek.

"It's Thanksgiving night. No one thought you'd escape dinner with your father to come and sort our problems."

"Dinner was a bust."

"Oh, no!" She pouts. "Wanna vent about it? I get off in twenty."

"Nah, I'm good."

"Okay, honey. Let's get you some ice for your knuckles, though." Xena winces as she takes my hand and turns my palm face down to study the rapid swelling and bruising across my knuckles. "Did you teach him a lesson?"

"He won't be back. Tell me what happened?"

"Sure!" She pops her gum between her teeth and leads me toward the bar, teetering on eye-wateringly high heels. "Nancy was giving that first guy a dance, the usual. He wanted a private session so after forking out the cash, she took him through the back, but the other guy, the one with the squint?" She motions to her own thickly lined eyes as she hops over the bar. "He left Candy's room and followed them into Nancy's. Started going at her and they tried to double team, which is when Leo threw himself into the mix. I think that's about when I called ya. The fight spilled out here, and we did everything we could to stop them from leaving until you or the cops turned up."

"You called the cops?" Perching on a barstool, I flex my knuckles with a wince while Xena scoops a handful of ice into a towel and wraps it up.

"Nah, but I was worried one of the guests would, y'know? Luckily, I think we're fine. Here, honey. Put that on your knuckles."

"Thanks."

"Course. Leo alright?"

"Mhm. I'm sending him home."

"And the customers?"

"After what you described, I'll take care of them properly." It only takes a few seconds to fish my phone out my pocket and text a few words to Toto. "They'll be dealt with before sunup."

"Thanks, honey."

"I told you. You need me and I'm here."

"You can't spend all your days running after little old me and my girls. You do enough for us already."

"I don't care." My eyes meet hers. "After what happened to—"

"Ah." She raises one long, perfectly manicured hand. "Say no more. I understand. You gotta do what you gotta do."

"Thanks, Xena."

"Course, honey."

"Speaking of, actually. I need a favor."

She leans both hands on the bar and smiles. "Sure. Whatcha need?"

"Witnesses for a wedding."

"Oh?" She tilts her head, yet somehow, the miniature top hat doesn't move. "What for?"

"I'm getting married."

"Married?" Her mouth falls open and she lunges for me, pinching my cheeks like I'm a child. "No way! Who is she? What's the deal? When do I get to meet her?"

"Maybe in an hour, if you and some of the other girls can be my witnesses?"

She leans back with her hand on her cocked hip. "A shotgun wedding? Honey, I am all over that!"

"Help me!" A yell suddenly rises from the crowd, but her voice is so familiar that nothing other than dread fills my stomach. "Please, somebody help me!"

Concern floods Xena's eyes and she darts past me with impressive speed in her heels, colliding with Hollie a few feet away.

"Chick! Calm down, I'm here. What do you need?"

"Please!" Hollie grips Xena's bare arms and gasps. "He killed someone right in front of me and now he won't let me leave! He's keeping me prisoner, please, you've gotta help me!"

"Who, chick?" Xena's eyes widen in alarm. "You're safe here, honey. You're safe. Ain't no one gonna hurt ya, I promise."

"Him!" Hollie points at me with one trembling hand. "It was him."

Xena follows her hand to me and immediately, her demeanor changes. Instead of comforting Hollie, she pulls back, much to Hollie's visible alarm.

"Xena, meet my fiancée," I say as I stand. "She's a little fragile."

"Chick..." Xena sucks on her teeth and eyes Hollie as she stumbles away from me.

"Please! Why won't you listen to me? I saw it! Call the cops or something, please! I just want to go home, but he threatened my family and kidnapped me. Please, you don't understand. He's a monster!"

"No, chick." Xena scoffs softly. "Sounds to me like you don't understand."

"What?" Hollie gapes at her and suddenly becomes rooted to the spot as I approach. "Are you insane? He's a murderer!"

Xena rolls her eyes and stomps past me, pausing to place her hand on my arm. "I'll rally some of the girls for you. How many do you need?"

"Three. Can you meet me at the chapel in an hour?"

"Sure thing, honey."

"What the fuck?" Hollie gasps hoarsely.

Disappointment swells as she darts away from me. Rather than chase her, I return to the bar and order a beer while Stu watches from the balcony above. To her credit, Hollie tries her best. She tries to talk to every single dancer and even a few patrons, but most guests here are far too ashamed to be caught here to actually bring the cops when there's no longer any serious danger. Every girl gives her much the same reaction—concern that melts into understanding or irritation when she points out me as the demon in her life.

I am the demon. Deep down, I know that this is hard for her. But my father was abundantly clear. Hollie is a liability— which she is painfully demonstrating right now—and she needs to be silenced for good. He offered to kill her or sell her so far away that nothing she says will ever matter, but I refused. Spinning the lie that we became engaged *before* tonight will be hard to sell if she reacts like this in every public setting.

But it's the only way to save her life and in turn, protect me if she runs her mouth to the wrong person. She reminds me of a cat caught in the grasp of a vet.

My beer is drained by the time Hollie, exhausted, makes it back to my side with fury burning in her defeated eyes.

"What kind of man are you that not one single person here cares that you're a murderer and a kidnapper?"

I spin in my stool, brushing the now-damp towel away from me. "You're judging me on two small actions."

"Two pretty horrific actions," she spits, her voice trembling.

"Hollie. I wanted to make this as simple as I could for you, but you're making it incredibly difficult."

"Oh, I'm the problem?" she yells hoarsely. "Maybe you should have kidnapped a quieter girl then!"

"Did you forget what I said?"

She looks me right in the eye. "You're doing everything you can to stop your precious daddy from killing me, so no, I don't think you'd kill my parents either!"

Hollie's on the right train but careening down the wrong track. I stand and catch her arm, keeping my grip firm even as she violently tries to jerk away from me. "I never said I would kill your parents to get my way," I say, bringing my voice down low. "Where's the fun in that? Keeping them alive is much more beneficial."

Her eyes widen as she catches on to my threat, but where I expect more snapping fire and pushback, she suddenly relents and defeat floods her eyes and posture. Even her struggles cease, and she stands there, limp, as if she'll fall over the second I release her.

She's right. I am a monster. Being viewed this way due to my size, my bulk, or even how I present myself has never been an issue. So why is it suddenly one now? Why do I want to shake her until she opens her eyes and realizes I'm trying to help her?

"Hollie—"

"Whatever." She cuts me off, her gaze down to the floor. "If it's so fucking important, sure, let's go get married."

I tell myself it will be worth it as we drive a few blocks to the chapel. It's not far and this late at night, Stu called ahead to wake up someone capable of performing a brief ceremony. Luckily, it's someone on our payroll so if Hollie decides to act out again, it won't cause any problems. Keeping her quiet won't be much of an issue once that ring is on her finger and I'm protected by spousal privilege in the eyes of the law, but until that moment, every second is a risk.

Inside the chapel, Hollie follows me to a small room fitted with a single mirror and a small couch.

"What's this?" She doesn't look at me, but she walks to the middle of the room.

"For you to get ready?"

"Huh?" She spins on the spot. "What's wrong with what I'm wearing?"

"This has to be believable and the outfit you're wearing doesn't scream pre-planned wedding, does it?"

"What are you, a wedding expert?" Her eyes narrow and she mutters something under her breath, then crosses her arms over her chest. "Fine. What is it?"

"This!" Xena pops up at my elbow, making me jump, and she holds one of the dancer costumes aloft. It's a string of fabric barely constituting a dress, and I bite back my own surprise.

"You're kidding." Hollie's face turns pale.

"It's the most respectable thing we had," Xena exclaims. "What, are you too good for it or something?"

"There's no way in *hell* I'm wearing something like that!"

7

MAXIM

The struggle is evident on Hollie's face but she has no choice. If I want my father to buy that she was my fiancée long before tonight, then this needs to look like a pre-planned ceremony, and part of that includes a different dress. If what Xena has brought can be classed as a dress. I can't work out the shape from the fabric dangling from her fingers. She looks at me with a question in her eyes, so my lips twitch and I turn back to Hollie.

"Put the dress on."

"No," Hollie replies sullenly. "I'm not some toy for you to dress up."

Snatching the fabric from Xena's hand, I throw it in Hollie's face and she catches it on reflex. "If you care about your family's Thanksgiving not ending in a bloodbath, then you'll put the damn dress on. Xena? Help her."

With that, I storm out of the small room, leaving Stu guarding the door, and I don't stop until I make it outside the chapel.

The cold air swirls around me like fog, icicles forming in my lungs as I breathe deeply, the chill creating an ache in my chest. Hands on my hips, I groan and briefly close my eyes.

"Maxim." Rex's voice appears beside me along with the familiar tang of cigarette smoke in the air. "You wanna explain to me what the hell you're doing?"

Opening my eyes, I fix him with a glare. "I don't have to explain anything."

"Hey, I'm on your side!" He raises one hand in mock surrender, then with his cigarette balanced between two fingers, he taps my chest with his thumb. "But you're spinning one hell of a lie here, and for what?"

The urge to lash out dies quickly, replaced by a numbness that weighs me down and slumps my stature. "I'm making it up as I go along."

"Why do you want to save her so badly?"

"Do you really think I could continue to do what I do if I let my dad kill her? How can I preach that I do things differently if I let an innocent woman end up on the six o'clock news? All the women in our clubs would lose trust in me like that." I snap my fingers in the brisk air. "And it's already hanging by a thread after..." I can't say their names. I should, but something about it makes my throat close up, so I look away toward the few stars fighting to be seen through the city's light pollution.

"I get that." Soft embers from his cigarette drift up into the air as he draws on it, followed by a cloud of smoke. "But marriage? That's one hell of a way to save a life."

"It was spur of the moment. I had only just got talking to her and he waltzed in with all these threats, and you know those two fucks he travels with?" I glance sidelong at Rex. "All I saw was that they now knew her face and no matter where we sent her, there'd be a chance that they found her. This way, she's protected not just by us, but by our traditions. No one can hurt her."

"And she can't hurt you either." He inhales deeply, ending his cigarette in a flare of gold. It slips from his fingers, and I watch it drift down onto the icy sidewalk.

"Exactly. Spousal privilege."

"Listen." Rex's hand lands heavily on my shoulder. "We're on your side, you know that. Even Stu, for all his idiotic actions. But you gotta keep us on the same page because your father will dig."

"I know. I know. I'm sorry."

"The world will weep tomorrow waking up to learn a Mafia prince got married at..." He checks his watch. "Five in the morning."

"Romantic, right?"

Rex snorts out a laugh. "Sure. Alright, give me the details."

Turning to face him, the corner of my mouth twitches. "You remember the girl from the bar a few months ago? The one in the silver dress?"

Rex frowns as he searches his memories, then he half nods. "Vaguely. From your description more than anything else."

"That's her."

"What?" His brow jumps up to his hairline. "Jesus... Maxim."

"I know. I know what it looks like. We never run into the same person twice in this line of work without it being a death sentence, but I believe her. This is just a really bad night."

His eyes narrow and his mouth twists but Rex doesn't speak. Instead he sighs. "Alright, so that's what we're going with? You two met a few months ago at a bar and the love blossomed from there? She's just very spicy and very angry at you."

"It's also only half a lie which means even if he does go digging, Dad will find shit to back it up."

Rex puffs out his cheeks and rubs one hand up and down his torso. "I hope she understands what you're doing for her."

"Nah. Less she knows, the better, for her and her family. She hates me. Understandable. Thinks I'm a murderer."

"You are."

I send him a withering glare. "Sure, but what she saw and what actually happened are two different truths."

"Then tell her."

"Did you hear what she did at the club? I'm not giving her more information to spout to anyone who will listen. It's one thing to have her begging for help when she thinks I'm a killer, but if she started giving out details? I'd become the Mafia prince with a loud-mouthed wife, and she'd become a bigger target while making me look like a fucking fool."

"You're already a fool." Rex snorts. "But I understand."

"Thanks. You have my back on this, right?"

Rex is momentarily offended. "Dude. Did you not hear me?"

"Alright," I scoff softly, amused. "Just checking."

"*Just checking*," Rex mimics with open mockery. "Fucking hell."

"Boss?" Toto's voice joins the fray, and we turn to him in the doorway. "They're ready for you."

"Alright!" Rex slings his arm around my neck and drags me back into the chapel. "Let's get married!"

Inside, there are no fancy seats or pews, no aisle for anyone to walk down. This late at night and on such short notice, there's only the officiant standing next to his makeshift altar looking half asleep. Next to him stands Stu who has his gaze fixed on Hollie.

Thanks to Xena's magic, she's been poured into the costume provided and despite the pain of the situation, she looks absolutely beautiful.

The bra is adorned with diamonds and pearls, featuring a string of diamonds that loops up around her neck to create a sparkling choker. Strings of pears and diamonds pour down from her breasts and across her abdomen to connect to the absolutely tiny white mini skirt that's really more of a thick belt than a skirt. Walking up from behind, I fight to keep my gaze away from the alluring swell of her ass cheeks peeking out from underneath. Sheer white stockings connect to a glittering garter, hugging her shapely legs all the way down to where her feet are covered by white six-inch heels.

Guilt warms my abdomen so as soon as I'm close enough, I shrug my suit jacket off and drape it around her shoulders. She flinches at the contact and fixes me with a venom-filled glance, but she doesn't refuse the cover-up.

"We'll only need you in the full thing for the pictures," I say in a low voice as I stop next to her.

"Whatever," she hisses out of the corner of her mouth. "Get this over with."

It's not how I envisioned my wedding would happen. I always dreamed of meeting someone who could look past the intimidation of my size, my bulk, my accent, and my family and fall in love with me. The real me. Then we'd have a small, beautiful wedding at a country house surrounded by color and nature.

Here, the most colorful thing is Xena's outfit as she stands just behind me with two other girls from the club alongside Rex and Toto.

The officiant is being paid too much to care about any of this and quickly reels through the traditional vows like he's reading off a shopping list. There's no romance, there's no warmth or love in his words or Hollie's as she flatly repeats what she's asked to say. I try to meet her eye, clinging to a small hope that she will understand I'm doing this to help her, but she refuses to look at me. Her anger burns as hot as embers in her words and at one point, she looks like she's contemplating making a break for it.

But she doesn't. By the time I slide a ring onto her finger provided by the officiant, she sounds cold and defeated.

We're married within fifteen minutes and then whisked off to the picture booth in the next room. Placing one arm around her waist after she shrugs off my jacket, I jerk her against my torso and her hand flies to my chest to push herself away.

"Remember," I say despite the guilt burrowing deeper in my chest. "These pictures have to sell it. If I'm not happy then—"

"Yeah, yeah," she cuts in, her voice trembling despite the hatred licking at her words. "You'll pay my family a visit."

"Exactly."

For three minutes, Hollie melts into a completely different person. Her smile grows warm and full of life, her eyes sparkle with happiness rather than tears, and she presses so close against me, it's reminiscent of our night together all those months ago. She caresses my face, molds her body to mine, and even drapes back on my arm for one sexy picture with her leg raised.

It's equally the longest and the shortest three minutes of my life. As Xena gives a thumbs-up from the camera, Hollie shoves me away with as much force as she can muster but due to my size, I don't move. She wobbles away from me in those heels and crosses her arms over her body.

"Can I get dressed now?" she snips at me.

"Yes. Xena, can you help her?"

"I don't need help getting dressed!"

"Girl, I know that skirt is so far up your ass you're gonna need a hook to extract it yourself, so yeah, I'm helping you,"

Xena remarks, amused. With a wink at me, she trails after Hollie with Stu in tow.

"How do they look?" I approach Rex, who flicks through the pictures. Over his shoulder, I glimpse what could be a happy, excited couple who were so in love that they just couldn't wait for a proper wedding.

"Pretty decent," Rex says, turning to face me. "I'll put the word out and make sure these just *happen* to reach your father."

"Thanks."

"You good?" Rex's face twists as he eyes me, and I nod.

"Tired."

"It's been the longest fucking night," Rex agrees. "You wanna go home?"

"Not yet. We should at least celebrate."

After Hollie redresses, we head back to Plumme. It's quieter and emptier than before and as soon as we enter, Hollie is swamped by all the other girls.

"Oh my God!" one squeals, taking Hollie's hand between both of hers. "I heard about it but I didn't think it was real!"

"Let me see!" Gasps another. "Oh, it's so pretty, although Maxim, where the hell is the rock?"

"I was in a hurry," I say as I reach the bar. "I'll get a proper rock."

"You better!"

"Girl, how did you do it?" comes a third voice. "Don't take this the wrong way, but I've been trying to taste that for years and you just swoop in and take him just like that?"

"He'd never look at you," snaps a fourth voice. "I honestly never thought he'd settle down. Not because of work but I mean, a guy with a heart that big? How do you close yourself off to just one person? You must be quite the catch!"

They all surround her, laughing and giggling while complimenting her and the ring, asking for details of the ceremony and how we met. Xena pops around the bar and uncaps a beer for me but as she places it in my hand, I glimpse Hollie's reflection in the mirror behind the bar.

She looks tired. Worn down. But there's a hint of enjoyment on her face as the girls bustle around her like chicks eager for a feed. Maybe this kind of attention is a good thing.

"Your first night as a married man," Xena says quietly. "How does it feel?"

I drink my beer slowly and wince. "Tell me I'm doing the right thing."

She frowns and leans toward me. "Honey... I know you have your reasons. When I married my wife, we also did it quick and dirty. In the end, your reasons matter more than the ceremony, more than the guests, more than anything else. So yeah, I think you're doing the right thing if your reasons are just."

Our eyes meet. "Thanks."

"Sure thing. Chick?" she calls over my head. "Bride, you want a drink?"

Hollie's answer is drowned out by my phone buzzing in my pocket and my heart sinks. The wheel never stops.

"What is it?" Rex appears next to me, hand on my shoulder.

"Trouble," I sigh. "We gotta go."

"Dude, when did you last sleep? Can't it wait?"

"No." Rising from my stool, I flash Xena a thankful smile then turn to the crowd. "Toto, take Hollie back to the penthouse."

Whines rise up from the girls as if I'm taking their new toy away and Hollie steps away from them. "Let me call my parents."

"No."

She pulls her phone out of her pocket. "You changed the passcode, you fucker. Let me call my parents!"

I meet her angry gaze steadily. "After your display when I first brought you here? I'm not letting you call anyone until I know I can trust you."

8

HOLLIE

Despite Maxim's seemingly insistent request to have me taken back to his penthouse, Xena insists on not letting me leave until she's seen me eat something, so we linger at the club for another couple of hours.

The entire place feels like a dream. I clutched at freedom but not a single person here cared to help me. Any concern anyone had melted away when they learned my captor was Maxim. What kind of man has this many people afraid of him that they wouldn't do a single thing to help me? That they'd instead spend all their time and energy on helping him lock me into a marriage against my will?

Though for people who might be afraid of him, they all get along like the best of friends to the point that I'm beginning to feel like I'm the unreasonable one when Toto escorts me back to the car after a meal of chicken tenders and fries. I've lost complete track of the days, haven't slept in so long, and I cling to the faint hope that someone I recognize will see me and give me the out I desperately need.

But I see no one.

I'm escorted into the car and the door closes, locking me in a bubble of silence with only my turbulent thoughts for company. Toto drives around long enough that exhaustion is about to pull me under when we finally make it back to the penthouse.

"Why'd you take so many detours?" I ask as I climb out of the car with Toto holding the door open.

"Policy."

"*Policy?*" I meet his eyes. "What kind of organization has a policy like that?"

He squints at me while leading me toward the building. "You really have no idea who we are, do you?"

"Should I?"

He doesn't reply. Instead, he walks me right up to the elevator but doesn't follow me inside.

"You're not coming?"

"My place is here."

"What if I escape the elevator?"

"If you manage to bypass the biometric instructions and escape, then I'd let you go. Anyone who can do that deserves to have their escape."

"I'm a woman of many tricks."

"Then I'll see you when you make it out."

The doors close and silence entombs me once again. Toto speaks to me like we're friends and his words weave through my mind while I absently press buttons on the elevator's control panel. They all light up to my touch, but it doesn't stop the rapid pull upward.

Should I know who they are? Is Maxim some kind of celebrity? No, not with this kind of attitude. He must be something else. A criminal? Maybe he's in a gang. That would explain why he has so many people around him who are loyal to him and don't blink an eye when he kidnaps people.

I bite back a yawn when the small speaker box crackles under my fingers after I've pressed every single button. The elevator stutters softly and then comes to a halt. Hope rises inside me that I broke some secret code and the doors will open out onto another floor, but it's Maxim's dark penthouse that greets me when they open.

Shit.

I'm so tired.

My parents must be worried sick about me. Then again, they haven't texted me. Mum might have taken her last comment literally and really not wanted me to go. Pulling my phone from my pocket as I trudge inside, my thumb hovers over the *Emergency Call* button.

If I press it and explain my situation, how quickly will the cops get here? How quickly can they protect me and my family from a murderer? Given Maxim's all-knowing persona, probably not fast enough. With a deep sigh, I slide my phone back into my pocket. It's useless until he tells me the new passcode because there's no way I'd be able to crack it with a guess.

Maxim's penthouse is dark and quiet. Water bubbles from the small plant-filled pool near the windows and a neon-green light flashes occasionally from the microwave in the kitchen, bathing the entire lounge in a sickly green light. Low voices rise up from down the hall near the bathroom, and my heart starts to race.

Did Toto drive me around for so long that Maxim is already home? I didn't hear the elevator woman speak so maybe he doesn't know I'm here. The last thing I want to do is spook a man with a gun so taking a deep breath, I walk toward the hallway and try to think of something to say. Mostly, I want to sleep, but I'm so strung out that I doubt I will drift off here until I'm past the point of exhaustion.

Creeping closer, the tones become clearer. That's not Maxim's voice. Who is that?"

"I don't care," drawls the deep, slow tones. "Do you understand how much money I have riding on this? My son should already be there, so why are you calling me?"

Son?

Wait... Igor. Maxim's father is still here? My stomach sinks as the faces of his two guards roll through my mind and suddenly, a pang lances through my chest. Can I go back downstairs to Toto?

"Listen," Igor snaps. "I want those Italian fucks dead, you hear me? I've given them chance after chance but those guns were fucking terrible. I put down three guards after their hands got blown off due to their faulty equipment, and no money is going to be enough to cover the loss, you hear me? So kill him."

Silence follows and I'm frozen in the hallway. One wrong move and the floorboards beneath me might give away my presence. The last thing I need is this man thinking I'm eavesdropping on him.

"Oh, him?" A dry laugh escapes Igor. "That Irish bastard was singing like a canary. I've got them exactly where I want them. I didn't spill all my blood over this city just for some Irish twat to swan in one day with a misguided claim for power. He might have the manpower, but he sends his people in like fodder, and I mop the floor with them. So listen, the next time he steps out of line, I want you to take his daughter. Skin her alive and record the whole thing, understand? That should put him in his place."

Skin her alive?

"Listen, I don't have time for you to dance around this," Igor snaps. "I'm too preoccupied with Maxim's latest fucking project. Did I tell you he wants to marry that girl? This little street rat waltzes in and ruins everything." A pause. "I'll kill her before that happens."

The weighty ring around my finger tells a different story. What the fuck have I walked into? I need to get out of here.

Or at least not get caught awkwardly hovering in the hallway listening to every twisted thing coming from that bastard's mouth. My thumb strokes over the ring snug around my finger as I creep back down the hall and past the innocent fish bubbling away in their watery haven. Thankfully, nothing creaks to give me away and once I reach the elevator, I touch a few buttons.

"Access denied," comes the soft, melodical woman's voice from somewhere above me.

"Now you speak," I hiss as she announces my presence to everyone else in this damn penthouse. As I turn and walk slowly down the hall, it hits me. Maxim never actually told me how to get in touch with him, or anyone else, for that matter, but I want to. The thought of facing Igor by myself is a hundred times more daunting after listening to his tirade through the door.

This time as I reach the lounge, the lights flicker on and Maxim's father strides down the hallway, visibly relaxed until he spots me. His expression sours immediately.

"Where's my son?"

"I have no idea," I answer honestly. "He left me some hours ago."

Igor shrugs on a heavy woolen coat while flanked by only one of his creepy guards, the one with the blue tie, and nods. "Come with me."

I step aside as he strides past me, assuming he's talking to his guard, but he gets halfway down the hall and turns back to me. "Don't make me drag you because I will."

My racing heart pounds faster and faster. Curling both hands into fists, I swallow around the rising lump in my throat. "Maxim told me to stay here."

Igor snaps his tongue against his teeth and before I know it, blue-tie has his hands painfully gripping both my arms while dragging me into the elevator.

"Hey! Let go!"

He shoves me hard up against the rear wall while Igor presses a button and we instantly descend. Just as we reach the bottom, Igor turns to me. "I don't repeat myself. The next time I have to ask you twice, you'll be obeying after he breaks your legs, understand?" He points to blue-tie who watches me with a cold expression.

My heart's beating so fast that the edges of my vision pulse with darkness. Each step I take feels lighter than the last and my stomach twists into so many knots that the lingering, comforting warmth from my last meal fades.

The lobby's empty. I desperately glance around, looking for Toto, but even the person from the front desk is missing. There's no one around when we make it outside and soon, I'm back in a car next to Igor while blue-tie drives us through the city.

"I don't know what you did or how you did it," Igor speaks in a flat tone.

I want to speak but my mouth won't work.

"You put some kind of spell on my son, didn't you?" He fixes me with a furious glare and I can't look away. "He has a habit of picking up pet projects and forgetting where his loyalty should be. I entertain it from time to time because it keeps him happy, but this? You? Hardly fitting for a Mafia prince."

Wait, a *Mafia prince*?

Like the flick of a switch, it suddenly all makes sense. The men in suits. The expensive cars and the penthouse. No one blinking at the murder or caring that I needed help. Maxim's in the Mafia, seemingly running it right under his father. This has to be some kind of joke and before I can stop myself, shock has a soft scoff escaping me.

"You think it's funny?" Igor snaps, and I flinch as he raises his hand. "I've worked far too hard and far too long for my plans to crumble just because he took pity on another street rat, so we're going to make a—what the fuck is that?"

I flinch away from him again, but he's fast for his age. He captures my hand in a vise-like grip with his nails digging painfully into the soft flesh of my wrist. Holding my hand aloft, he stares in disgust at the single gold ring around my finger.

"It's a ring," I manage to choke out. "We're already married."

"Fuck!" Igor yells so loud that the car swerves when his guard gets a fright. "That stupid fucking son of a bitch!"

He's crushing my hand in his grip. Every passing second grinds the small bones inside my palm together and the pain flares sharp and hot. I start to struggle, but he seems completely unfazed.

"Let me go!"

"Does he have any idea what the fuck he has just done?" Igor glares at me as if I hold the answer.

"I don't know," I gasp as tears bead in my ears. "You're hurting me, let me go!"

"Do you have any idea what this fucking means?" Every word is spat at me with intent to wound and hurt, and he drags me an inch closer over the seats. "You don't understand a thing, do you?"

"No," I gasp, fighting with all my strength. "Let go!"

He does, and I lunge back against my seat, gasping and cradling my hand.

"Idiot son of mine," Igor growls. "That" —he points at the ring— "Were there witnesses?"

I nod silently.

"Fuck. Do you realize that marrying him grants you all the protection of being a Mafia wife? Did he explain any of that to you? Does he think I have guards to spare? He's forcing me into a fucking corner because how will it look if I don't spare men to protect his new bit of tail? Fucking hell."

Protections? I don't feel an ounce of that since they are the ones I need protection from.

"Did you see something?" Igor demands. "Did you see something you shouldn't have?"

"I have no idea what you're talking about," I gasp, shrinking away from him.

"Spousal privilege. Do you know what that is?"

I nod hastily. "So, what's the problem?" I gasp. "Anything I know, which is nothing, is through Maxim, so I wouldn't be able to tell anyone anything." Communication between a husband and wife is protected. Everyone knows that.

Is that why Maxim married me? So I can't tell anyone about what I saw? And even if I did, it wouldn't matter. The cops wouldn't be able to listen.

"It matters," Igor snarls. "Because I had plans. Maxim has a wife lined up, and it would be the cherry on top of a perfect deal until you came along."

"I didn't ask for this," I hiss. "Just stop the car and let me out. I–I'll disappear and no one will have to know! I won't talk to anyone, I won't bother anyone, I'll just leave and vanish and —ack!"

Igor's meaty hands are suddenly around my throat, and I choke violently with how quickly he cuts off my air supply. There's so much pressure rising in my face that heat flares behind my eyeballs while my chest throbs and my heart stalls.

He slaps me once, then clamps that hand over my mouth and nose.

Something unlocks inside me and I fight. I fight like a wildcat caught in a trap. I hit him with all my strength, kick him with everything I can muster, scratch his arms and pull his hair like my life depends on it.

Because it does.

Suddenly, my shoe slips off in the struggle and blue-tie immediately yells in pain. The car swerves dangerously and dislodges Igor from my body. The moment his grip slackens, I suck in a deep breath and attack his face, clawing and scratching at his eyes until he's the one yelling. He slaps me again, then we're all suddenly launched forward as blue-tie loses control of the vehicle.

I don't wait for him to fix it.

My seatbelt snaps free and I open the door and throw myself out onto the cold, hard road where I land with a grunt and roll several times thanks to the momentum of the vehicle. Car brakes screech, but I'm already on my feet.

With one shoe, I turn and sprint, gasping through tears and throbbing lungs.

And I don't look back.

9

MAXIM

"Hollie?"

No one answers. My penthouse is completely dark and silent.

Fighting a yawn, I head toward the bedrooms hoping that she chose one and climbed into bed without a second thought, but every room is empty, bathroom included. Even the home gym and balcony are abandoned, leaving me with a rising, uncomfortable worry in my gut.

Where the hell is she?

I'm in the process of putting a call down to the lobby when the elevator doors slide open and I'm face-to-face with a breathless Toto. I glance up briefly, confused why the announcer didn't tell me the elevator was in motion, then fix Toto with a glare. "Where the hell is Hollie?"

"She's not here?" he gasps, sagging against the elevator frame. "Shit."

"What do you mean, *shit*?"

"Why didn't you pick up your phone?" Toto waves one hand while still struggling to catch his breath. "I sprinted all the way to the club because you wouldn't answer, and Stu was there telling me you were already on your way here, so I sprinted all the way back!"

My phone lights up showing twelve missed calls from Toto. "Fuck. I must have slipped it onto silent. What the hell happened?"

"Your dad didn't leave. I sent Hollie up here as you asked, but when I was down there, I saw that fucker Yannis or whatever his name is. So I followed him and realized your dad was still up here, but by the time I got up here, he was gone and so was Hollie."

"Motherfucker—" Unlocking my phone, I delve straight into my tracking app. "When he called me to deal with the Italians messing with the warehouse, he told me he was back home. Fucker lied."

"Sorry, Boss," Toto gasps, finally managing to catch his breath. "By the time I got back down there, Yannis was gone too, but I got no clue where."

"It's alright. If Hollie kept her wedding ring on, I'll know exactly where she is."

"And if she didn't?"

Our eyes meet and the rest goes unspoken. I've spent the last two days doing everything I can to keep Hollie safe from everyone, including my father. Instead, he orchestrates a fight between us and a rival Italian family to draw me away from her, knowing I would never bring her along to such a violent altercation, and placing her firmly in his crosshairs.

"Got her," I say, pushing Toto lightly into the elevator with me. "Let's go."

Twenty minutes later, he pulls up on a disaster. My father stands in the middle of the road illuminated by the flickering headlights of one car. Another car, presumably the one he was in, is crashed just down the right-hand bank, resting against a tree with smoke rising from the hood.

"Where is she?" I bellow before I'm even entirely out of the car. "Where the hell is she?"

Toto follows me and Stu, who met us in his own car, flies out of his vehicle with his gun raised as my father's personal guards, Yannis and Frederick, move to position between my father and me. Several red claw marks streak down Dad's face and he clasps a bloodied tissue in one hand.

"Son, listen—"

"Don't!" I bark so loud that even in the dark, several critters squeak and flee in the darkness. "I swear to God if you've hurt her, then I'll do the exact same to you!"

"Watch yourself, Son. I was taking her to dinner," Dad snaps. "Decided it was time to get to know the woman you *married*."

I should be concerned by his tone, but his words don't hit with even a hint of truth.

"She attacked me out of nowhere. I told you she was suspicious, I told you that we should have killed her the moment she ended up at your penthouse, but—"

"*HOLLIE!*" I bellow her name at the top of my lungs,

striding right past my father and down the embankment toward the trees. "Hollie, where are you?"

Within minutes, Toto, Stu, and I are combing the woods while my father, despite his pathetic tale, joins in the hunt with his men. He delivers weak calls of her name in such a tone that it sounds more like a threat than anything else.

Twigs snap underfoot. Leaves crumple. Branches snap back and forth as they get caught on my clothing while I stride deeper and deeper into the woods calling her name until my throat burns.

I have to find her.

Given my father's presence here, I have to believe she's still alive. He wouldn't linger if he'd killed her.

Reception out here isn't the strongest and my tracing app constantly flickers in and out of connection while I stride as best I can toward a blinking dot on the map. The longer we search, the colder the world grows, and my worry spikes. Hollie wouldn't survive a night out here in the freezing cold, not after everything she's been through these last few days.

Around a log, I come face to face with Toto, whose face echoes the worry in my own mind. "What do you wanna do, Boss?" he asks in a low voice.

"Find her."

"Yeah, I know, but your dad—"

"Let me deal with him." My tone remains curt. "Finding Hollie is all that matters right now. But..." I hesitate and glance behind us where Stu is visible through the trees, purposefully keeping my father and his men illuminated with a flashlight. "Stay closer to them. If he's hurt her or scared her, then I don't want him close when I find her."

After a glance at my phone in my hand, Toto nods and redirects his search to loop back and meet with Stu. I continue, stomping through the woods toward the dot while my heart races faster and faster as if I've been sprinting the whole time.

"Hollie?"

Suddenly, a soft gasp rises from the darkness to my right. As I turn, twigs and leaves crunch and crackle as someone moves. Lifting my flashlight, I glimpse her crimson hair as she takes off sprinting and relief surges through me.

"Hollie, wait!"

"No!" She stumbles, but it doesn't slow her down. Branches and tree roots rise out of the ground to cut at my ankles and grab my clothes as I chase after her. It's like nature itself is mistaking me for the threat.

To her, though, I probably am.

It doesn't take long for me to catch her but when I do, she spins and throws a handful of dirt in my face. Blinded, I throw myself forward and catch her by the waist, then pull her backward as I stumble to regain my balance. She hoarsely yelps until both my arms are around her, then I trip and we both hit the ground with a grunt.

"Please," she gasps. "Don't hurt me again, don't hurt me!"

"Hollie, it's me. I'm not going to hurt you, I promise!"

Despite her trembling, something in her stills and she

slowly peers through her unkempt hair to meet my eyes. "Maxim?"

"It's me."

"Your dad—"

"I know." Cutting her off gently, I slacken my grip around her waist. "I'm sorry. I'm here now."

"He t–tried to—" She chokes suddenly, and through the reflection of my flashlight, I glimpse her tears. "He tried to *kill* me."

"I know."

"He said I was protected, then he tried to kill me! What the fuck, what the fuck, what the *fuck*? I want to go home. I want my parents. I want to go home."

Something unexpectedly heavy settles in my chest as I sit up, the freezing ground soaking its icy fingers through my jeans. "I can't take you home, but I can take you back to the penthouse. You're safe now with me. I promise."

"Safe?" She scoffs and rolls away from me, then slowly climbs to her feet while dusting leaves and dirt from her clothes. "Nothing about you is *safe*."

I climb up at a slower pace and step back so I'm not towering over her as much. "I married you to keep you safe."

"Does this look safe?" She gestures around us but freezes when my father's voice drifts closer. "You married me so I wouldn't go to the cops about what I saw, didn't you? You didn't do this to keep me safe, you did it to keep you safe, and your dad's trying to do the same thing by *killing* me!"

"Hollie, if I wanted you dead, then you would be."

"How is this any better?" A tear leaks down her cheek. "Please let me go home. *Please*."

"I can't. It's not safe."

Her face crumples. "I hate you."

"Hollie..." I step forward, and she doesn't move. "Marrying you is the only way to keep you safe, don't you see?"

"I don't feel protected. Your father dragged me into that car and tried to kill me. What about that is keeping me safe?"

"I made a mistake. I'm not asking you to trust me because you have all the reasons not to, but when you're with me, and from now on, you will be protected. It's how we work. It's how our entire world works."

"Because you're Mafia?"

Even with only a flashlight to illuminate us, her eyes sparkle like stars and that strange weight in my chest increases. "Yes. I am."

Her eyes close and the other voices grow closer. Toto is doing a great job of talking loudly so I can track them easier in the dark while I wait for Hollie to say something. Just as I grow impatient, she finally opens her eyes.

"Whatever. Killing me here or at your penthouse. What's the difference?" The defeat in her voice carries through the air like smoke.

"So you'll come back with me?"

She steps forward and hastily wipes away a tear. "Whatever," is her last response, and she remains silent all the way back to the road. Once we're back at my car, I call Toto and tell him she's with me. Less than five minutes later, Dad climbs the embankment with his goons in tow, followed by Stu and Toto.

"I found her, Dad." Our eyes meet and to my surprise, he doesn't say a word. He strides silently toward his second car and gets inside. Fredrick follows while Yannis moves more slowly. He fixes Hollie with an odd look, drags his tongue over his teeth, and slips into the driver's seat. They leave thirty seconds later.

"The fuck?" Toto stops near us, panting softly. "That's it? He just fucks off?"

Moving around Hollie, I open the door for her and help her into the car. After closing it, I face my men.

"I want eyes on him. This isn't over."

10

HOLLIE

"Let me look at you."

I'm far too tired to argue, so there's no resistance when, an hour later, we're back at Maxim's penthouse and he guides me into the soft, warm lighting of his bathroom. Just behind him, a large square mirror shows the state I've ended up in.

Small leaves and a few twigs embed themselves in my messy hair. Dirt streaks my face and clothes and there's a small tear in my top and a few small scratches along my bare arms. Around my throat, bruising rises from Igor's hands and my bruised cheek from Stu's blow darkens in color from Igor's own.

I barely recognize myself.

Maxim stands before me, a head taller and infinitely broader. His brows furrow as he looks me over. He dwarfs me with his miles of muscle and a height I could only dream of. Maybe I should be scared to be back here with him, but I'm so exhausted, I don't even feel it anymore. An ache rests behind my eyes that droops with every blink, and coldness seeps into my bones, creating a constant slight shiver despite the warmth of the air around me.

"He did this?" Maxim slowly motions to my throat, and I nod.

"What a great father you have."

He doesn't meet my eyes. "You don't need to defend him."

"I'm not," I mutter. "It burns when I swallow and I can still feel his hands around my neck. I'm not defending a damn thing. I'm just..." I'm tired.

"Come here." Maxim's hand gently grasps my wrist and guides me deeper into the bathroom where a gigantic oval bath is slowly filling with hot water and bubbles.

Steam rises, gradually erasing me from existence in the mirror. Maxim releases me once I'm next to the bath, then he turns to the sink and opens the lower cupboard. From there he removes a small red bag which, once unzipped, shows an array of medications.

"Are you allergic to anything?" he asks, glancing over his shoulder.

"No. Nothing I know of."

He pops two white pills out of a packet and lays them next to the sink. "Take these. They will help."

"With what?"

He rezips the bag and faces me. "Everything."

After ensuring the bath is at a good temperature, Maxim

steps out of the bathroom and promises me fresh clothes on the bed in the adjacent room. Then I'm alone.

The warmth radiating from the tiled floor and the bath is enough to make me sleepy. My defenses are low after the chaotic events of the past two days. I couldn't tell you what day it is, or what time it is. It was dark in the woods, and I almost made my peace with death until Maxim found me.

Eyeing the pills, I debate taking them. Drugging me would be fruitless since I'm already his captive. Maybe they really will help. I debate until I've removed all my clothes, then I pop the pills on my tongue and chase them with a mouthful of water from the tap.

Pain lances through my cold foot when I step into the hot bath, and I hiss through my teeth. Gradually, the pain leaves, and I sink down into hot water that encases me like a cocoon. Gentle vibrations move through the water from a machine within the bath, caressing my aching muscles and throbbing body.

When I close my eyes, I'm back in the woods running until I tripped and twisted my ankle. Hiding that's been easy until now. The heat of the water radiates against my bruised, marred flesh and as the cold within me melts away, the pain from the sprain flares up. But just as I register it, it begins to fade and within thirty seconds, I'm pain-free and completely mellowed out. The water runs like silk against my fingertips, the bubbles caress my skin with aching gentility, and the heat draws me down into a deep place of aching calmness.

"What did you give me?" I ask Maxim twenty minutes later after I've pried myself out of that heavenly bath and dressed in the grey tracksuit he laid out for me.

"Did it help?"

"Maybe."

"Then it doesn't matter."

"You expect me to trust you but you won't tell me what drugs you gave me?"

Maxim stands in the kitchen with several pots bubbling away in front of him. A mouthwatering scent rises from them and suddenly, my stomach growls loudly. Maxim turns to face me with a light smile playing on his lips. "If you didn't trust me, you wouldn't have taken them."

"Maybe I was hoping they would kill me."

"Were you?"

"Take a look at the past days of hell and you tell me."

Maxim grimaces slightly. "They don't have a name. They're a personal blend of some strong painkillers, a muscle relaxant, and something to calm the mind. You needed something to help you relax."

"So you can take more advantage of me?"

Maxim's hand pauses while stirring and he fixes me with such an intense, hard look that my breath catches in my throat. "I would never," he says with such power in his voice that I'm struck by a sudden wave of guilt. He starts walking toward me and stops a foot away.

"I would never touch you in any capacity, except to save you, without asking first."

I swallow, but the lump remains in my throat. "You touched me in the woods. And at the altar."

"All of which is part of saving your life. But now?" He steps forward. "You're hurt."

"A few cuts and scrapes."

"Not that. Your ankle."

The throbbing, a peaceful, distant thought in the back of my mind, flares suddenly. "It's fine."

"No, it's not. I saw you limping. Let me take a look."

"What are you, a doctor?" I fold my arms over my chest.

"Maybe I am. Would you let me look at it then?"

Irritation swells inside me because now all I can think about is my ankle, and the peace from the bath is fading. "Whatever."

"Is that a yes?"

Reluctantly, I nod.

Maxim suddenly grabs my waist with both hands, but his touch is incredibly gentle. He lifts me onto the kitchen counter, then kneels before me and slides his hands down my leg to my injured ankle. The swelling is light, but there's redness around the top of my ankle and across the bridge of my foot.

"It doesn't hurt," I say as if I've got anything to prove.

"Not all wounds do," he says softly. Maxim's thick, rough fingers slide over my fragile ankle joints and toes. The touch is soft enough to be soothing, and there's no pain as he carefully examines my ankle. His other hand remains just under my calf, supporting my leg while he looks..

"Is this part of the protection you promised?"

"If it was, you wouldn't have been injured in the first place."

"His murder attempt wasn't in your plan?"

Maxim slowly looks up at me. "I wouldn't have sent you back here if I knew he was here."

"But he's your father."

"And he's a hard, powerful man. We don't always see eye to eye on a lot of things. Where I see an opportunity, he sees a distraction."

"Which am I?"

Maxim gently applies pressure to the sole of my foot. "He sees you as a threat to the Krasnov name."

Krasnov.

I know that name. It appears sometimes on the news, often on the magazines that litter the hotel lobbies I spend my evenings in. Old money, I think. And a lot of jewels.

Blood money now, I presume.

"Do you see me as a threat?"

Maxim looks up once more. "I saw you for what you are. An innocent who stumbled into something they shouldn't have."

"So why not kill me?"

Maxim doesn't reply. He continues to examine my ankle, and when he's satisfied, he stands. An odd sense of loss follows and my foot tingles with the phantom touches he left behind against my skin.

"Your ankle will be fine after some rest. Maybe don't run for a few days."

"Fine." Maxim moves back to the tasty smells in the kitchen, so I swivel around on the counter and let my legs dangle over the other side. "Can I call my parents? They'll be worried."

"They'll stay worried. I can't trust that you will stay quiet."

"I thought the spousal privilege meant it didn't matter what I said?"

"You can still tell the world everything. It just means it can't be used in a court of law. But the damage you would do to my reputation, my family, and my business?" He shoots me a look. "So no, you cannot call your parents."

"I have no incentive to stay quiet," I retort, seeking to push his buttons in some way just to get his reaction. He doesn't rise to it, though. He simply continues cooking. Five minutes later, he presses a warm bowl filled with fragrant rice, chicken pieces, peppers, and a creamy red sauce that tangs on my tongue after two forkfuls.

"Good?" he asks from the opposite counter where he leans with his own bowl.

I ignore him and shovel the meal down like it's my last one on earth. One taste unlocked how truly ravenous I am for decent, good food, and within two minutes, the bowl is empty and my belly is full.

"More?"

I shake my head, lapping up a drop of sauce from my thumb. "No. I shouldn't."

"Drink?"

Our eyes meet. "Do you have soda?"

He nods and retrieves a can from the fridge. It's ice cold in my hands and the hiss when I crack the seal sends a satisfying shiver down my spine. "So, what's next?"

He pauses eating. "What do you mean?"

"I want to go home. You won't let me. I want to call my parents. You won't let me. You forced me to marry you, and now you're feeding me like we're friends after your *dad* tried to kill me."

He nods once. "Your point?"

"Are you just going to keep me locked up here until I forget what you did?"

His eyes narrow faintly, and the low light accentuates how thick his lashes are. "I'll deal with my father. He won't bother you again."

"I don't believe you."

"You don't have to. I know my intentions."

"But you don't know why you didn't kill me and get all of this over with."

"Things are more complicated than you know."

"How so?" I demand as he takes my empty bowl from me. "I want to go home. That isn't going to change. You murdered someone, and since you won't trust me, the only way to guarantee I don't talk is to kill me, which you won't do, so what kind of game is this?"

"You need rest." Maxim speaks with the softness of a lover, which infuriates me even more. How can this cold, dangerous murderer flip the switch so quickly and start caring for me with a heavenly bath and good food? How can he touch and talk to me like I'm not suffering because of him?

"I'm not tired," I snap stubbornly, draining my soda can as an act of defiance.

"Hollie. There's a lot going on, but all I can tell you is that our marriage is the best protection I can give you. I don't kill without reason."

"I saw what you did," I snap. "I saw that man. No one deserves that, and I don't deserve this!"

He sets his bowl down and fixes me with a small, polite smile. "You can take the bedroom at the end on the right."

That's it. Our conversation is over and I've learned barely anything. As infuriating as it is, I'm left to my own devices and with nothing else to keep the exhaustion at bay, I fold quickly. I barely make it to bed before my eyes close and I sink into a deep slumber wrapped up in blankets and pillows that are so soft, they likely cost more than my rent.

My dreams are turbulent. There's blood over everything and a darkness that extends no matter how far or how fast I run. Every time I feel restriction around my throat, Maxim appears and he saves me from it, but I always end up back in that darkness, running and running and running.

"*Hollie?*"

Suddenly, I have something to run toward. A light that

appears between the trees that promises warmth while guiding me back to civilization.

"*Hollie?*"

It glows brighter and brighter until, suddenly, I open my eyes to sunlight streaming in through the slatted blinds. They paint stripes over the walls and the ajar door of the closet where Maxim stands a good distance away. I immediately clutch at the blanket as my mind catches up and the events of the previous days hit me like a brick.

"What?" I croak, fighting the allure to return to sleep.

"As much as I'd love to give you more rest," Maxim says, "I need you to get up. It's time to leave."

"Leave?" Rubbing one eye, I prop myself up on my other arm. "What do you mean, leave?"

"I'm taking you to a new apartment."

"What for?"

"To keep you safe. Now get dressed."

11

MAXIM

"Has something happened?" Hollie stares at me groggily, fighting a yawn as she shifts beneath the covers. The bruise on her face has darkened a shade or two, and her hair sits atop her head like some kind of bird's nest, but she looks oddly adorable.

"My father has free access here, which means I can't leave you alone. I'd like to give you at least some freedom."

My comment appears to wake her up immediately, and her face relaxes into surprise as I exit the bedroom. I spent all night searching for a new apartment that would have everything I need, including the top-tier security I've come to love, just without the free access my father has. Until he faces me about what he did, I'm not leaving Hollie alone until I'm absolutely sure she will be safe.

Theoretically, that will come naturally as news spreads about my marriage. Once more and more people learn that she's my wife, she will become just as protected as she is threatened. A risk I have to take.

She joins me in the kitchen twenty minutes later dressed in the fresh clothes I had Toto bring from a local boutique. Unsure of her style, he kept it simple with flared jeans and a T-shirt to keep her comfortable. Her hair is tamed and neat around her face, her smile is small, and she's much more alert.

"Let me?" I approach her, and a frown creases her brows, then she nods despite the uncertainty in her eyes. Catching her chin, I lightly turn her face and inspect the bruising on her face. "Does it hurt?"

"Only when I talk."

"Is it bad?"

"Nah."

"And your ankle?"

She shifts back and forth slightly and the corners of her mouth lift. "Much better."

"Good. Hungry?"

"No, thank you."

"You should eat in the morning."

"I'm fine."

Releasing her chin, I step back to give Hollie her space and grab my phone from the kitchen counter. "It won't be a long drive."

"You're moving because of me?" There's a note of suspicion in her voice and my heart skips faintly.

I want to know her thoughts, what stories her fears might have concocted within her mind so I can soothe them. Building trust with her is going to be a challenge, and if she's completely unwilling, I face a tough choice. Keeping her locked up forever will become my only option if we can't find some middle ground.

"Well," I say as we walk toward the elevator, "I'm a busy man and ideally, I'd like you to be able to return to your life. Having a place to keep you safe only works if I can control who has access, and after last night?" My fingers linger on the call button. "I don't want my father having access to you at all."

Her head tilts, sending her hair cascading over one shoulder. Both her hands come together at her abdomen as she watches me. "But he's your dad. Isn't... I mean, is that going to be weird for you? I understand you don't want me to talk, but changing all of this just to keep me away from him..."

"Don't worry." The doors close with a soft hiss. "I had my issues with him long before you came along."

Hollie falls silent all the way down to the car, yawning occasionally behind her hand. Her phone sticks out a little from her jeans pocket which reminds me of her desire to contact her own parents. It wasn't difficult bugging her phone. But as soon as she talks, as soon as she spills anything, the damage will already be done. I'm lost on how to secure her silence outside of maintaining the threat that I'll kill everyone she talks to.

Once in the car, Stu's driving and we settle into an amicable silence weaving through the streets of New York. Hollie drums her fingers lightly on her thigh as she gazes out the window, watching the world. My attention remains on her despite the phone in my face and the constant encrypted messages flooding my phone about attacks from the Irish, threats from the Italians, and unrest among other Russian families under us.

Hollie shifts subtly in her seat once. Then a moment later, she does it again. Her drumming fingers increase and she moves her other hand over her abdomen. My interest peaks when distress warps over her face and our eyes lock as she takes a soft, deeper breath.

"I think I'm going to be sick."

"Stu!" Rapping my knuckles on the protective glass between us, I raise my voice. "Pull over."

"But we're in the middle of—"

"Pull over. Now."

He obliges and thirty seconds later, I stand at the mouth of an alley with Stu pacing nervously nearby while Hollie pukes behind a trashcan. I replay everything she consumed and reason the meal last night, plus her combined stress, must be taking its toll on her. People move around us like waves lapping at a rock, countless ants hurrying to get to work and go about their day. A few send judgmental glances our way when the sounds of Hollie's puking reach the ears of the crowd, but each look is met by my angry gaze and they all hurry on with their lives.

Five minutes later, Hollie appears at my elbow wiping her mouth. "Wow."

"How are you feeling?"

Sweat glistens on her forehead just below her hairline and her skin is slightly pale. "Kinda wrecked, if I'm honest."

"Was it something you ate, do you think?"

She shrugs. "Probably. I just get ill in the mornings sometimes. Stress, I think."

"Here." Stu approaches from the car with a fresh, unopened bottle of water and hands it to her.

"Thanks." The crack of the seal breaking cuts through the air, then she gulps the water down like she hasn't drunk in days.

"The apartment isn't far." I gaze out over the crowd and spot a small cafe in the distance. "How about we walk instead?"

"Boss—" Stu warns immediately, but he falls silent at my cutting glance. I know what he's going to say. Walking out in the open like this without our usual security detail is typically a death sentence, but putting Hollie back in the car doesn't feel right.

"We'll be fine," I assure Stu. "We can stop at that cafe over there and see if we can find something that will settle your stomach."

Hollie's visible relief warms my heart and she nods. "Sure."

The cafe is small and cozy with a long counter stretching from the door to the restrooms as the far end. The rest of the floor is dotted with several cute tables, each covered in a lace tablecloth and featuring different-colored birds, depending on where you sit. We choose the table furthest from the window with a cloth covered in bright blue and green birds. As we sit, Hollie races off to the restroom.

"You think she's making a call?" Stu asks as he sits at the next table. His cloth is covered in parrots.

"If she were, it would redirect to my own phone," I say. "Besides, I don't think she guessed the passcode."

"I've messaged Rex, by the way. He's pissed that we stopped here."

"Understandable."

"He says if you get assassinated, he'll bring you back and kill you himself."

Scoffing softly, I nod and relax back in the wicker chair that creaks dangerously under my weight. "I'd expect nothing less."

Hollie returns after a few moments and groans as she sits. "I feel terrible."

"Are you ill? Is there medication or anything I should know about?"

She leans heavily on the table and rests her chin on her upturned palm. "No. Strongest medicine I use is a special ointment for my hands."

"Your hands?" I glance down. Her hands look like regular, beautiful hands with short nails painted a light pink and the gold band of her wedding ring nestled around her finger.

"Mhm." She sighs deeply. "I'm a musician by trade, so I have to massage my hands a lot. And also keep them moisturized to stop wear and tear."

"You're a musician?" I barely know anything about her. This

woman who wandered into the wrong pizzeria has a whole life I know nothing about.

"Like a celebrity?" Stu asks.

"No." Hollie snorts softly. "I play parties. Hotel lobbies. Restaurants. That kind of thing. This time of year is my busiest time because everyone wants the charm of live music."

Past her head, several Thanksgiving turkey streamers weave between twinkling tinsel and sparkling drop lights of various festive colors. In all my years in fancy hotels and restaurants, I've never looked twice at the live musicians and yet they're such a core part of my experiences there.

"That sounds like a fun job."

She straightens up slightly and smiles. "It is. Hectic. And kind of strained when it comes to money, but it's so fun. My boss, Tiffany? She's got quite the knack for getting me gigs at some of the top places. And I'm great at being available at the last minute."

"Were you booked for Thanksgiving?" I ask as a waiter approaches us.

Hollie nods. "I was, yeah."

Over a pot of tea and some toast for Hollie's stomach, we discuss her musician life. She plays the piano and the violin, though her bashfulness keeps her reserved about the extent of her capabilities. She lists hotels and restaurants, and I'm familiar with nearly all of them. It strikes me that we've most likely crossed paths before in the past and never even noticed each other. It's a nice conversation, given the

circumstances, and ends when Rex calls me sounding like
he's about to have a brain aneurysm.

"Are you kidding me?" Rex barks down the phone. "You're
having coffee and tea while I'm tearing my hair out trying to
make this new place into a fortress for you? Do you not care
about me at *all*?"

Smirking, I finish paying the bill and we head outside. "Listen, Rex. I know what it looks like, but we really are on our
way this time. Just give me—"

"Miss Wolfe? Miss Hollie Wolfe?" An unfamiliar voice rises
up from behind us as we step out onto the street. Stu moves
around me, and I position myself between the voices and
Hollie, but my gut tightens like the snap of a rubber band
when we turn to face two police officers.

"Can I help you?" I ask, studying both faces. Neither of them
are familiar, and they both look young enough that they
might not know who I am.

"Sir, step aside. We need to speak with Miss Wolfe."

All eyes fall on Hollie who gapes at the officers, then she
looks at me and I see it in her eyes. That momentary hope
of freedom. One word to them and she'll be whisked away.
It won't matter that anything she says can't be used against
me. The stain of losing my wife to the police will be
enough to taint my reputation, and it's all downhill from
there.

Her family won't live to see another sunrise, and it won't be
by my hand.

"I'm Miss Wolfe," Hollie says, her voice strained. "How can I
help you?"

"Miss, are you alright?"

She nods quickly. "Yes, fine."

"Can you tell us what happened to your face?" As the officer steps closer, his presence invades my space as he tries to get closer to her. "Did someone hurt you?"

Hollie's lips part and a tense silence fills the cold air between us. Clouds of breath from all five of us collide and rise into the sky as Hollie struggles to find her words. "No," she says eventually, surprising me. "I slipped on some ice a few days ago and went down hard. Kind of embarrassing, really."

"What is this about?" I cut in, and one of the officers turns his narrowed gaze to me.

"Miss Wolfe's family reported her as missing since Thanksgiving. You can imagine our surprise to find you just out in the street like this. What happened?"

Hollie doesn't look at me. My heart stalls in my chest, and Stu subtly moves his hand to his waist for easy access to his weapon. One word from Hollie and this entire thing goes up in flames. A silence that lasts only a few seconds feels like it drags out for eternity as each officer shifts their weight.

"I..."

"Yes?" the officer prompts.

"I was in the hospital. Like I said, I fell and it was pretty bad. So I went to Accident and Emergency and they gave me some heavy-duty painkillers. The last few days have honestly been a little bit of a blur."

"And you haven't called home?"

Hollie laughs softly. "Well, my last conversation with my mother was her ordering me not to turn up at all because I was going to be late, so we're not exactly on speaking terms. This feels a bit far-fetched, though. I'm not missing."

"You understand that your father is very worried about you, don't you?"

"He hasn't called," Hollie replies smoothly. A lie, given how often her phone vibrates with calls. "I had no idea."

"Could you wait here a moment?" Both officers step back to their nearby squad car parked right next to my own vehicle, and they never take their eyes off us.

Keeping my attention on them and my lips close together, I speak. "You didn't tell them the truth."

"No," Hollie mutters.

"Why?"

"You made it pretty clear what will happen to my family if I talk, so what choice do I have? I don't want them to end up like that man."

Stu clears his throat and his eyes meet mine, but his silent question earns him a soft frown. As long as we remain relaxed, this shouldn't be a problem.

"Miss Wolfe?" One officer reapproaches after getting off his radio. "We're to escort you home."

"What?" Hollie's surprise matches my own. "Whatever for?"

"To reduce our paperwork. Our captain used to work with your dad, so consider this a favor to him."

Hollie's mouth opens and closes, then with a glance at me, she relents. "This feels like too much."

"Nothing is too much for the daughter of a retired police chief. So, should we follow you?"

Stu meets my gaze with an echo of the surprised horror in my chest. Hollie is the daughter of a police chief? How the fuck did my team miss that?

"You can follow," Stu agrees stiffly as he approaches the car. "Try not to get too close. Don't need those lights fucking with my paint job."

I climb into the car in a slightly concerned daze, and Hollie twists her hands together in her lap as we sit.

"You won't kill them, right?"

"Huh?" I glance up at her while furiously texting Rex with one thumb.

"My parents. For doing this. Please?"

"I won't." I shake my head. "You never mentioned your father used to be a cop."

She shrugs one shoulder. "Would it have made a difference?"

Painfully, yes, it would. Trapping someone like Hollie to save myself is one thing, but the daughter of a retired police chief? I'm basically placing myself into the lap of an enemy and hoping they don't bite. I don't answer her, choosing to remain silent while Rex blows up my phone with promises to find out how this was missed.

"A positive," I say softly as we drive, "is that my father will likely reevaluate his desire to kill you."

Hollie's fingers continue to twist together and she snorts. "Great."

Thirty minutes later, we pull up to a small house tucked on the edge of some forest in a small town not far from the outskirts of New York City. Pumpkins line the pathway to the door and a dusting of orange and yellow leaves cover the garden and blanket all the flowers in the flowerbeds by the door. Lights hang from the awnings and wind around the gutters, transforming the drainpipe into a sparkling beam of light. As the red and blue lights from the cop car light up the garden, the door flies open and an elderly woman charges down the pavestone path at alarming speed as Hollie climbs from the car.

"Hollie!" she screeches. "Oh my God, Hollie! Hollie!"

Hollie runs into her mother's arms and is immediately bundled up in her arms. By the time Stu and I climb out of the car, a man has joined the reunion. His grey cardigan strains around his generous abdomen while a smoking pipe hangs from underneath his thick mustache. Black hair streaks away from his forehead, and he lifts one hand to wave at the cop car, then fixes me with a steely glare.

"Who is this?" he demands in a throaty voice.

Hollie pulls back from her mother's hug. "Mom. Dad." She turns to me, and our eyes meet.

"This is my husband, Maxim."

12

HOLLIE

Telling my parents someone had died likely would have gotten a better reaction than the word *married*.

Standing in their lounge next to a roaring fireplace that washes my legs with waves of warmth, my father paces back and forth in front of the door leading to the kitchen, while my mother repeatedly switches between sitting and standing.

"Married?" she yelps upon standing once more. "You ran away and got married? Are you insane? How could you do this? How could you do this without telling us?"

"You're not in any position to be married," Dad retorts sharply. "That isn't something you do at the drop of a hat. How long have you even known each other?"

"A few months," Maxim replies from where he stands next to me, but whatever else he might say is silenced by a furious glare from my father. It's like his entire presence offends them and I understand it.

But I can't back out. Not now. Not if I want to keep them alive.

Thankfully, Maxim has enough sense to remain quiet. "We met a few months ago and hit it off," I explain, the lie flowing easier now. "When you know, you know, right? I mean you and Mom got married really quickly."

"Things were different back then," Mom gasps, sitting on the couch. "Things were more personal than they are now. Now it's all phones and electronics and secrets. How could you do this to me? You know how much I wanted to see you get married, how much your father deserved to walk you down the aisle. How could you take this away from us?"

I have no answers. Witnessing them being this upset pains me more than I can put into words because everything they're saying is correct. In an ideal world, things would have been very different and my parents would have been involved every step of the way. But this isn't a dream.

It's life and death.

"Mrs. Taggert's son did this," Mom weeps softly. "Her son eloped without a word and came back three years later with two kids and a divorce. God, it was shameful, and now this will happen to us. Hollie, I raised you better! What on earth were you thinking?"

My hands flex uselessly as I search for words. "It was... it was a romantic whirlwind, what can I say? We were in love and the timing felt right, the night was beautiful, and it was just... I can't explain it."

"Who was your witness, hmm? How did you even pay for something like that so quickly?"

"Well, Maxim's friends were there and he paid—"

"So you're the money bags?" Dad glares at Maxim but thankfully, Maxim remains silent like a shadow just out of sight. "Hollie, did you even sign a prenup or anything like that? Did you think about what this will do to your taxes? To your *life*? Do you understand your credit or anything?"

He's throwing blow after verbal blow at me and I scarcely keep up. But I do answer honestly. "No, I didn't and thought about none of that."

"Hollie!" Mom whines, and she's on her feet again. "How old are you, anyway?"

All eyes land on Maxim, and he clears his throat. "Thirty-six."

"What the hell are you doing sniffing around a twenty-five-year-old?" Dad nearly bursts a blood vessel.

"Don't start," I snap before Maxim has a chance to respond. "You both have a twelve-year age gap, so don't even think of pretending to be astonished at that."

"It was different back then," Mom whines.

I roll my eyes despite the way my heart breaks at their distress. "Hardly. If it's wrong now, then it was wrong back then, and you two need to reevaluate."

"Don't speak to your mother that way!" Dad halts his pacing.

"What way? She's the one who told me not to come home for Thanksgiving. She's the one who signed me up for things I didn't agree to. So I listened and didn't come home, and now that I'm here trying to share this with you, you're both acting like I've done something truly unforgivable! You can't have it both ways. You can't treat me like I'm an inconvenience or a place mat and then get mad when I decide to do my own thing!"

"You're our daughter," Dad remarks sharply. "We will treat you how we see fit!"

"And I don't need to stand for it! You can accept this and let things go back to normal or we can keep going in circles until you realize the real reason you both weren't included is because of how you treat me!"

They don't accept it. The argument continues and delves into the various ways this is disrespectful, the shame I've brought to them and the family, even the ruined food from Thanksgiving that was saved for me. Not once do they offer congratulations or even ask about Maxim as a person.

And I don't blame them.

Every raised voice, every hurtful word, and every tear that slips from Mom or me is the price I pay to keep them safe. If Maxim's threat against them wasn't enough, then the old stories overheard from my father as a child are. Tales of informants cut down because they talked too much, families slaughtered to send a message, and people disappeared, never to be found again. That's all from regular criminals.

Maxim is in the Mafia. I don't want to know the extent of organized crime and the harm they can bring to the ones I love.

So I face it all while feeling like the worst daughter to ever exist. My mother cries over the wedding I denied her, my father's fury rages at my reckless decisions and the strange man I've brought into their lives, and Maxim remains silent by my side.

All of it is worth it so they walk away from this without a single drop of pain.

By the time the world grows dark, things calm. My parents run out of things to say and we settle into a disappointed silence while the fire reduces to embers and tears finally stop.

"I think we need some time," Mom says from her corner on the couch. "You've really hurt me, Hollie, but if you promise to really focus on us at Christmas, then we can work on it."

"I'm sorry, Mom," I say earnestly. "But please try and be happy for me. This is my decision and my life. And I promise, everything and anything you need for Christmas, I am here. I promise."

"Him too?" She points at Maxim, who now leans against the wall near the window.

"Yes."

"I'll think about it, then," Mom says.

"Leave," Dad says stiffly, then he turns and moves into the kitchen and I never see him again. Staying will only increase the pressure, so I stand and try to meet Mom's eye, but she keeps looking away from me.

"Bye, Mom. I love you." Despite our troubles, it's true. She doesn't say it back.

Outside, the first touch of snow drifts through the air and soft, fat flakes float past my face and catch in my hair. The air is bitterly cold but pleasant against my faintly throbbing cheek. I bury my hands in my pockets and groan softly as the door closes behind us and Maxim and I stand in a growing winter wonderland. It's been snowing for a few hours, judging by the white blanket that covers the garden and the car where Stu is huddled inside his coat. The first snow of the year usually calls for a celebration. Mom and I would make hot chocolate and watch it fall, then come out here and make snow angels. Been doing that ever since I was a kid.

How different this year is going to be.

As I start to walk, Maxim stops me.

"Hollie."

"What?" I spin to face him. "Are you happy? Was my performance enough for you?" Anger flares inside me and I fight to keep it at bay. One wrong word, one wrong move, and it won't matter what I told them. He could decide at any moment to kill all of us.

"Your passcode is one, two, three, four."

I gape at him. "Are you fucking serious?"

"I'm surprised you didn't try it, actually."

Dragging my phone from my pocket, I unlock it with the simple code and let out a soft groan. "I can't believe it."

"Since you've lied to the cops and to your parents, I think you'll hold up your end of this. I'm happy for you to return to your normal life—under our protection, of course. As long as you maintain the marriage around anyone who asks, of course."

"So this is a reward for breaking my mom's heart?" Tapping the screen, I quickly set a new passcode and slide my phone back into my pocket. "Am I supposed to be grateful?"

"You're alive," Maxim replies curtly. "So are they. I would think you would be happy."

"You don't get it, do you?" Before I can stop myself, I prod his wide, solid chest. "You might have a fucked up relationship with your dad, but mine trusted me. Sure, they aggravated me and signed me up for things I hated and there might be a lack of respect about my work, but they raised me and they cared for me. And I just sat there and lied to their faces while denying them any detail of a wedding they both dreamed about for their only daughter. Do you even understand what kind of pain that gives me?"

"A pain that isn't comparable to what you would feel if you lost them," Maxim replies as if we're having a casual conversation.

"If you *killed* them, you mean," I snap, prodding him again and growing more irritated when he appears unbothered. "I hate this and I hate you! I get it, it's the cost of survival or whatever, but I'm allowed to be angry that it's shitty!"

Fighting to keep my voice low, I turn and stomp toward the car. Stu catches sight of us and straightens up. As we reach the vehicle, I turn back to Maxim and glare at him. "Ride in the front. I want to be alone."

His brows twitch but he nods quickly. "Alright."

"And one more thing," I snap as I open the door. "The next time you want to murder someone in cold blood, make sure I'm not there to witness it!"

13

MAXIM

Two days after the explosive encounter with Hollie's parents, I ride the elevator to the top floor of the Heart Memorial Hospital with Rex by my side. My phone rests in my hand with the CCTV from my new apartment displayed on the screen.

"That counts as stalking," Rex remarks.

"Does it when it's my own house?"

"Yup."

"Who are you, the morality police?"

"Maybe. With how things are going with your father, I might need to change careers."

I snort softly and watch Hollie as she busies herself in the kitchen making some pasta. "You couldn't be anything else, Rex. You love guns too much."

"Maybe." He leans up from the wall and peers over my shoulder. "What is it with this girl, anyway?"

I can't give him an answer. What started as trying to do the right thing is quickly morphing into something else. My silence drags on until the elevator doors open, and Rex doesn't push it, but there's a touch of concern in his eyes when I look at him.

"I won't be long," I say as I step out.

"I'll be right here."

The quiet corridor leads me past several private rooms, each one locked securely with access only granted to medical staff with the passcode. Reciting a number in my mind, I type it into the pad on the third door on the right and step inside as the door opens with a soft hiss.

Inside, warm yellow light floods the room. A soft breeze kisses the blinds covering the window and causing the lit candles on the bedside to dance with a little more vigor. In the single bed lies a woman, her head to the side and her attention fixed solely on the candles.

She's swathed in bandages and hooked up to more wires than I've ever dared to count. One hand rests across her abdomen above the blanket while her other rests underneath her pillow. Soft beeps rise from the machines next to her bed and music drifts from the small radio resting on the table at the foot.

I remain silent, watching her quietly until my presence finally catches her attention. She slowly turns her head and our eyes meet.

Pain squeezes through my chest and the weight that formed days ago with Hollie proceeds to increase like something has sat down on my breastbone and refuses to move.

"Maxim?"

"Hi, Zoe."

Zoe's beaten, bruised face breaks into a watery smile that lasts until the fat, healing split on her lower lip pulls painfully. One of her eyes is severely bloodshot and bruised, her cheek carries scars where knuckle dusters turned her bone to dust, and her patchy hairline shows promising regrowth amid the surgery scars across her skull.

"You came to see me?" she croaks, moving her arms around the bed to support herself as she attempts to sit up.

Her movements spur me closer, fearing she'll hurt herself if she tries too hard, so I take the seat next to her bed with a slow nod. "I did."

"You didn't have to do that." Her voice remains cracked and fragile even as she tries to smile at me once more.

Every time I see her, the list of injuries given to me by her doctor plays like a film reel in my mind. Broken ribs, punctured lung, ruptured kidney, countless lacerations, soft tissue damage between her thighs and a bite mark so severe on her shoulder, it's a wonder she didn't bleed to death. The list goes on and on, but I keep my face as light as possible.

"I wanted to," I reply softly. "How are you feeling?"

She waves one hand and swallows audibly. "Fine. The doctor says he wants to start weaning me off some of the good stuff, but I told him if he did that, I'd make sure he never got another good night's sleep with how often I'll press the call button." Her smile wavers and a deep sadness floods her eyes. "I don't want to feel any of this."

"Do you want me to talk to him?"

She shakes her head. "You've done enough for me, Maxim. More than I deserve."

"Don't say that." My hands clasp together as my elbows rest on my knees. "What happened to you is what you didn't deserve, and I'm *sorry* I couldn't stop it."

"Don't," she croaks. "You couldn't have known. No one did. We wouldn't have gone with him if we knew... if there was any hint..." Her eyes close and silence falls, as if speaking has exhausted her.

Less than two months ago, two men from a rival family swept into one of my clubs and lured out three of my girls with a promise of a good time and more money than they could dream of. It's not uncommon for rich men with more money than sense to pay obscenely for great sex. But they waited until all three of them had let their guard down and then they kidnapped them. For two weeks, I tore the city apart looking for them and when I found them, I was too late. Anna and Bea were gone. Zoe was clinging to life by a thread, and I never expected her to survive. They were beaten and raped, then left for dead.

My failure was immeasurable.

"Sometimes, I see his face," Zoe croaks, dragging me from my thoughts. Her eyes open once more. "I remember what he smelled like when he was over me, remember what he felt like when he was in–inside me. I remember Ana holding my hand telling me it was going to be okay, and I still hear the—" She gasps and tears flood her eyes. She reaches for me and I immediately take her hand. "I still hear the sound her skull made when he stamped on her over and over—"

"Zoe," I say as gently as I can. "We don't have to talk about this now."

"I do," she whispers, hastily wiping away her tears with her other hand. "Xena brought Harry to see me the other day, and I just..." She winces. "Do you have kids?"

I shake my head. "Someday."

"He's why I held on, my son. I think he's why I even survived. But seeing him... I couldn't touch him because I felt so dirty, and he didn't understand. He's only four. And I couldn't hold him. What kind of mother does that make me? He wanted to dance with me, but I couldn't do it. I can't."

"Zoe, it makes you a good mother. A strong one. You're hurting and you need to take the time to process and heal. Harry is being taken care of, I promise. So is your mother. I have people on them twenty-four, seven, they're in a safe place, and all of you will be cared for. Please be gentle with yourself."

She weeps softly, covering her eyes with her hands. "I don't want to feel anything," she whispers.

My head dips, and I stare at her bruised fingers intertwining with mine. "I came to tell you that I got one of them, Zoe."

Her hand lowers and she fixes me with a pained look. "What?"

"I found one. His name was Hector Popov. The Popov family are old blood but it seems they've forgotten the rules of warfare. Whatever. I found him, and I worked him over until he spat out the name of the second man who did this. Soon as I confirmed it, I killed him. He's dead, Zoe. He's never going to hurt you, or anyone, ever again."

Fatter tears flood her eyes and her lower lip wobbles. "And the other one?"

"I'm tracking him down. He won't be able to hide for long. The entire city's looking for him."

"What's his name?"

"Vincent Antonva."

"I don't... I don't know that one."

"Small family. Little rat dogs. We took them all out. He's the only one left with nowhere to go, and once I catch him, I'll make him suffer. I promise."

Zoe's hand tightens in mine. "You're a good man, Maxim."

Her words pierce my heart. If I were good, this never would have happened. If I were good, the women under my care wouldn't be fearing for their lives or struggling to do what they love. If I were good, two of my girls would still be here.

"I wanted to tell you face-to-face," I say, forcing a smile. "Is there anything you need? Anything I can do?"

"Sit with me?" she whispers. "Just for a little while."

I spend two hours with Zoe, making light conversation about anything unrelated to her attack. Mostly, we talk about her son and her plans to spend a portion of her savings on a villa for her family to live in. As much as she loves to dance, her future in her career remains shaky, but she's steadfast in providing for her loved ones. I deliver the news that I'm married while skipping on a few details. Zoe voices her displeasure at missing the ceremony, but it lifts her spirits for a little while.

I leave when the nurse comes to change her dressings, with a promise to return when I have more news.

Out in the corridor, Rex is buried in a magazine on a leather sofa but he rises the moment he notices me. "How is she?"

"Better. She's talking more. Full sentences this time."

"That's good." Rex grimaces. "Poor girl."

"She remembers stuff," I say as we step into the elevator. "She doesn't remember who, but she remembers the one who did this to her."

"Was it Hector or Vinnie?"

I shrug. "I can't show her pictures in this state. But when we nab the other cunt, maybe I can then. She's worried about her kid. And her mom."

"Shit." Rex drags a hand down his face. "What I'm gonna do to that fucker when I get my hands on him will be too grotesque to even write about in the papers."

"Get in line," I mutter.

Outside, the brisk air blows away the lingering hospital air. The weight in my chest eases a fraction, but not enough to allow me to breathe freely. Rubbing my chest, we walk toward the car while Rex kicks up a stone next to me.

"You know, did you think about telling Hollie the truth about what she saw?" he asks. "She might not give you such a hard time if she knew why you killed that bastard."

"I can't tell her. One, she's not part of this life. You've seen her. And if I tell her, all I'll do is terrify her while painting a picture of what people in this world could do to her. Including my fucking father."

Rex grimaces slightly. "True." He opens the door for me and shoots me a brief, sympathetic smile.

"Keeping her in the dark is the only way to keep her safe. Besides, one more dark detail and the fragile peace that's keeping her mouth shut might shatter. Then we're all screwed."

14

HOLLIE

Returning to work brings a comforting sense of normalcy that I cling to with both hands. The Elden Hotel houses some of the most elite people in the state and in my previous years of playing music in the lobby, I would get distracted by how regally dressed all these people were. The tips they left were just as obscene as their clothing.

This year's different.

After the explosive meeting with my parents on Sunday after Maxim's father tried to kill me, I focus on the music and *only* the music. The violin rests comfortably in my hands while numbing cream prevents the hidden bruises around my throat from flaring up. The bow rests loosely between my fingers and with my eyes closed, I play the next melody on the Christmas music list approved by the hotel manager.

Around me, golden lights twinkle on every single surface and to my left, a gigantic golden Christmas tree stands proudly, wrapped in elegant silver tinsel, baubles, and lights. A little too much gold for my personal tastes, especially since the manager poured me into a floor-length golden ballgown to emphasize that I really am part of the furniture.

But the money is good and with music in my ears, nothing else matters. I play my way through eighteen songs while appreciative guests drop tips into the snow globe basket near my stand. Some stand nearby and compliment my music, and anyone who gets too close immediately gets on the radar of the two men Maxim has guarding me.

Stu and Toto.

Ironically, they blend in well in a place like this. Money is clearly no object to Maxim, and the way he acts, I'd suspect a hotel as lavish as this is almost beneath him. That extends to both my guards even as they lounge in the lobby completely undisturbed by security. They watch me closely, but even they fade to the background as I play. Behind me, tall windows draped in silver curtains are coated in fake snow and above me, projectors create the illusion of an angel sending stars down to greet me.

Song after song plays until my fingers throb and my shoulder aches, but they're familiar, pleasant pains that I embrace as my last song draws to an end.

Sudden clapping catches my attention, so I scan the crowd as I lower my violin and catch sight of Tiffany, my boss.

A familiar, friendly face that immediately overwhelms me with the urge to run to her. Toto and Stu clock her a second after I do, but I reach her first and clasp her hands. "Tiffany!"

"Hollie, you've got some *insane* explaining to do," she scolds as she pulls me in for a tight hug. Her suit rumples but she hardly cares. "Not returning my calls? Ignoring my texts? Then you turn up here like nothing is wrong? Do you have any idea how badly I've been stressing that I'd have to rebook this gig and— oh, my God!" Clutching my hand, she notices the wedding band and drags my fingers to her face. "What is this?"

"Excuse me." Toto's hand lands on Tiffany's shoulder, but before he can pull her away, she turns to face him with a sharp glare over the top of her perfectly rectangular glasses.

"You'd better remove that hand unless you want to explain to the owner why all your fingers are broken and your membership has been revoked, young man!"

Toto gapes at her while Stu snorts just behind him.

"Guys, it's fine. This is Tiffany, my agent."

"You know them?" She looks back at me, visibly puzzled.

"Uhm... let me explain." After shaking off the guards, I guide Tiffany to the golden couches in the lobby and we sit. "I got married."

"I can see that!" She adjusts her glasses and winces as she keeps hold of my hand and observes the ring. "How cheap is this guy? I didn't even know you were dating!"

"The ring is only temporary," I say, though why I'm defending it, I have no idea. "And it was sort of a last... minute thing."

"Oh, my Lord." Tiffany would be clutching her pearls if she had any. "Hollie, what did you do?"

"I did nothing!"

"Are you in trouble?"

"No!"

"Do I need to call someone?"

She's tempting me. She doesn't know it, but each question coaxes at the truth I'm hiding deep down and it threatens to bubble over as her genuine concern washes over me.

"No," I say hoarsely. "I'm fine. Everything is fine. I just... I met someone and fell in love. Everything felt—feels right, and it just... it happened."

Her mouth drops open and she glances around. "Am I being pranked? Is this some kind of Christmas joke?"

"No!" Laughter rises within me. "I'm telling the truth."

Tiffany peers at me, then she glances at Toto and Stu hovering nearby. "Is it one of them?"

"No, they just work for him."

"Work for him?"

"Yeah, they're like... he's protective, so he has people keeping me safe."

"From what, muggers?" Tiffany's light laughter rings out at her joke. "There's some disconnect here, honey. He's rich enough for some bodyguards but not a decent ring?"

My thumb presses against the gold band. "It was a really fast wedding."

"You're telling me! I can't believe you didn't call. This is..."

She shakes her head and leans into me, clutching my wrist. "Are you on drugs?"

I immediately shove her away. "No! I chose this. Trust me, if you met him, you'd—"

"Met who?" Maxim's voice suddenly washes over me from behind like a warm blanket and my heart jumps.

I watch Tiffany's face. She glances up once, then does a double-take and stares with wide eyes and parted lips. Her fingers flex against my wrist and she continues to stare without a word.

Facing Maxim, I force a smile. "Maxim, this is my agent, Tiffany. Tiffany, this is Maxim." I meet her gaze. "My husband."

I could have knocked Tiffany over with a feather.

To his credit, Maxim looks very handsome. He stands in a black suit with a light blue silk shirt that's open halfway so his chest tattoos are on display. With one hand in his pocket, his suit sleeve is ruffled enough to show off a thick, gold watch. His hair is neatly combed with a slight side part where a few strands curl down and kiss his forehead with every subtle movement. Even his beard is trimmed neater than it was this morning. All in all, he looks devilishly handsome and his smile is gentle while he holds out a hand to Tiffany.

"It's lovely to meet you. I've heard a lot about you."

That feels like a faint threat and a shiver chills my spine.

"Wow," Tiffany gasps. "I–I mean you, too. Nice to meet you

too." She rises and shakes his hand. "You... I mean, Hollie, this is your husband?"

"Mhm." Standing, I brush my hands down my dress to smooth out the skirt. "Since Friday."

"Well, if you know, you know." Tiffany laughs, suddenly changing her tune while shaking Maxim's hand.

"Tiffany, I hope you don't mind, but I've come to take Hollie out to dinner. Am I interrupting?"

Tiffany waves her hand and laughs. "Not at all! Not at all. I just came to give Hollie this. Here, sweetie. Please call this number when you can. I got you another client."

I accept her card with a smile. "Thanks."

"Shall we?" Maxim's hand falls away from Tiffany and his blue eyes lock onto mine while he cocks his elbow.

I have no choice but to accept. As my hand loops around his elbow, my heart tremors from something that isn't fear this time. "Sure."

"Have fun!" Tiffany calls with a wave. "Call me later!"

Maxim whisks me away to a quiet restaurant two blocks away. The lighting here is dark and romantic as we sit at a table covered in a red tablecloth. Four white candles burn between us on a black holder, a green Christmas tree hugs the corner of the room near the bar, and it's swathed in red, blue, and gold Christmas decorations and tinsel. A large bird sits atop the tree with sparkling gemstone eyes observing everyone. Soft music plays, but I can't pinpoint the musician, and the lighting is so low in the restaurant

that anything beyond our table appears shrouded in darkness. The illusion of privacy is extreme.

Occasionally, a waiter appears to top up Maxim's wine or my
sparkling water, or to bring more plates of food, but other
than that, we're left alone.

I make it through three plates of utterly tiny dishes before I
speak. "Is this how a place like this makes its money? I bet
for the price of one of these tiny dishes I could get a full
meal from a burger joint."

"Would it taste as good?" Maxim asks as he eats his mysterious cube of meat, single rocket leaf, and swirl of sauce in
one bite.

My eyes narrow. "You can't be serious. You're built like a
truck and yet you're eating meals that look like they were
made for Thumbelina."

"This place is an experience as much as it is a meal."

"Do you hear how pretentious you sound?"

"Yes," Maxim replies, much to my surprise. Then he chuckles. "But the wine is good and the chef is a friend, so I make
appearances."

My brow twitches. "You're putting us through this for a
friend?"

"Wouldn't you do the same for yours?"

My lips part and my answer catches in my throat because
yes, I would. I have several times. "Maybe."

"Maybe?" Maxim picks up his wine glass. "You strike me as
someone very loyal. I don't think maybe is the answer."

"I didn't know you had friends is the most shocking part," I remark. "I thought you just had people you ordered around. Or hurt."

His eyes narrow. "That's your impression of me?"

"Can you blame me?" I tear my gaze away from the alluring bulge of muscle on his arm that rises each time he lifts his glass. "After everything that's happened these past six days?"

"It's been an intense week," he agrees. "How are you feeling?"

"Are you asking if I'm still thinking about telling the truth to the next person I meet?"

"No." Maxim sighs as if my answer irritates him. "I'm asking how you *are*."

"I'm fine."

"Really?"

"Don't pretend like you care."

Something akin to pain flashes in Maxim's eyes, but it's gone just as soon as I detect it. Maybe it was my imagination. As silence falls between us, guilt worms through my abdomen.

Why do I feel bad? If anything, today was pretty decent and normal. Maybe even better since Stu and Toto's presence kept away those guests usually eager to disrespect me by demanding that I change songs or just stop playing altogether.

One good day doesn't erase the past terrible five.

Still, something unsettling weighs down in my gut and I

wince inwardly. "Sorry," I murmur after a moment. "Long day."

"You're fine," Maxim replies easily. "No apology necessary."

"That's it?" I lift my gaze. "You're not mad at me for being a bitch?"

"I wouldn't call you that," he replies simply. "Given our situation, I think your responses are valid and understandable."

This man makes no sense. How can the monster who murdered someone in front of me and forced me to marry him be the same man who was so tender with my ankle, cooked me dinner, and now sits before me telling me my reactions are valid?

He's like a coin. Today's side is gentle Maxim, apparently.

"You're saying that like you're not responsible for the upheaval of my life."

"I'm responsible," he says. "I know that. But you're safe and alive."

"Until I say the wrong thing."

He lifts his glass and drinks once more. "Is there no part of you enjoying any of this? The food? The atmosphere? The new apartment?"

"I miss my apartment. And my car. What happened with that, by the way?"

Maxim sets his glass down. "Your car was repaired and delivered back to your apartment."

"But not to me."

"You don't need it."

"What if I want it?"

"Do you?"

I shrug. "I don't know. It is kind of nice being driven around." Admitting it feels like I'm saying I like being held hostage, but Maxim's expression doesn't change. "And the new apartment's nice. It's big."

Maxim nods. "I like space."

"Then you'll hate this weekend because my mom wants us to help her decorate the house."

"I have no problem with that."

"They want to get to know you. All of you."

Maxim shakes his head. "Again, I have no problem with that. Which reminds me." His head dips, and he rummages in his pocket, then he pulls out a small black box and sets it on the table in front of me. "Here."

I lower my fork. "What's that?"

"Open it."

The box is soft, black velvet and almost warm against my palm. Inside, resting on a white silk cushion, sits a ring. It's white gold, with seemingly liquid amber gold weaving across the top of the ring in the shape of a treble clef. In between the curls rest several diamonds and red jewels.

"Since music is important to you, I thought you would like it. A replacement for the other ring."

It's beautiful. More than that, it's *thoughtful*. He chose a ring that speaks to me as a person and I can't take my eyes off it. No one in my life has ever given me such a lavish or personal gift, and it almost hurts that this has to come from him. He stands slowly and moves around the table, then he kneels next to me. Despite his bulk, the usual intimidating aura from his muscular size is nonexistent and I struggle to keep my rising emotions in check.

"May I?"

I nod silently.

Maxim takes my hand and gently slides the gold band from my ring finger, then he slides the new ring into place. It nestles perfectly against my knuckle and the gems dazzle like a thousand stars have fallen to earth just to rest in my hand. It's lighter than the previous ring which Maxim pockets.

"Do you like it?"

I want to tell him yes. The urge sits heavily on the tip of my tongue because I more than like it. I love it. It's absolutely beautiful, but the words don't come. Our eyes meet and there's something puppyish about the hope flickering in his.

So I nod.

And he smiles.

Suddenly, it's too much, the swell of feelings that don't belong here. Maxim is a dangerous man. He's stolen me into this life. I shouldn't be feeling anything for him.

I rise abruptly, and Maxim stands back. "Sorry, I need to use the restroom."

Rushing away, I don't stop until the cool air of the restroom envelops me behind a locked door, and I grip the sink, panting.

Why is my heart racing?

I feel as giddy as I did as a teenager when my prom date brought me my corsage. Years of stress have been packed into six days, and now I'm here feeling like I have a chance with him? Gazing down, the ring twinkles back at me and my heart skips and excitedly beats again.

I can't listen to it.

He's dangerous. My main and only goal is to flee as soon as it's safe. I can't fall for his trap.

As I stare at the ring, music drifts from my phone within my purse. I retrieve it and answer it, fully expecting Maxim to be checking on where I am.

"Hello?"

"Miss Wolfe?"

"Mhm."

"It's Doctor Finfer. I'm calling about your missed check-up on Monday. Is everything all right?"

The ground drops away from me and I clutch the sink tighter as a wave of dizziness rises inside me like vomit. "Oh, no," I gasp.

"Oh, no? Are you alright? Are you having any trouble with you or the baby?"

My eyes snap down to my abdomen in the mirror, and sweat breaks out across my body.

In all the terror and strain of the past few days, I completely ignored the reason I was desperate to find Maxim in the first place.

"Miss Wolfe?"

I'm two months pregnant, and my sexy, mysterious one-night stand is a Mafia prince.

15

MAXIM

Thursday morning dawns with blue sky and bitter wind. It cuts through me like the slice of a blade as I stand on the balcony of my new apartment overlooking the city. Hot coffee warms my throat as I drink quickly to prevent the chill in the air from robbing my drink of its warmth.

I'm tired. This past week has been draining. Killing Hector was a highlight, but we've stalled in our investigation. Everything we know about the second bastard, Vinnie, is limited. New York City is a big place to hide.

I drink as my mind runs through every detail that bastard dribbled from his lips before he died. Apologies for the women he harmed and killed. Anger at getting caught. He even begged in the end, as if I would forget what he took from me and the pain he caused the people I care about. None of my girls will rest until Vinnie is found. None of my guys will either since everyone is working double on security detail.

I fight back a yawn, but before I make it back inside, Rex steps out onto the balcony to join me. "We've got something."

"On?"

"Vinnie."

"What?"

"An address. Stu's bringing the car around."

"Shit."

"Bad timing?" Rex gazes at me, his brows furrowed. "Want me to handle it?"

"I was going to spend time with Hollie today, but this is too important."

"How is she?"

"She accepted the ring last night. And dinner was... good, I thought. Until she went to the restroom. When she came back, she was different."

Rex's head tilts as the wind cuts through his hairline. "Do you regret what you did?"

"No. Killing her goes against everything I stand for. I just..." Shaking my head, I drain my coffee in one gulp. "It gets to me how she looks at me, and I don't understand why. I like listening to her, even when she's angry. I like her music. At the bar where we originally met, she caught my eye so quickly. Now she looks at me like..." Trailing off, my heart squeezes as if a fist has reached up from my guts and ensnared it. "She looks at me like my mom used to look at my dad."

"You're not like him," Rex cuts in immediately. "The fact that she's alive proves that."

"Does it?" With a final glance, I head back into the apartment. I'm met by warmth that chases away the bitter sting of the December wind within seconds as I walk toward Hollie's room. Ideally, I'd like to speak to her before I leave.

My soft knocks on her door go unanswered, so, daringly, I turn the handle and ease my way inside.

She's asleep. Her curtains hang closed over the window, but a sliver of light escapes through a crack and illuminates her face on the pillow. With the bruise fading from her cheek, Hollie almost looks like her old self. Both her arms wrap around the pillow she's sleeping on and one leg appears cocked upward under the blanket, bent at the knee. The blanket itself pools at her waist, giving me a glimpse of her bare back.

I should leave, but something keeps me there.

Admiration.

Concern.

A lick of desire.

Walking forward slowly, I pick up the end of the blanket and very gently cover her back up. She sighs and shifts against the pillow, tightening her arms a fraction, but she doesn't wake. She sleeps on, as peaceful as a baby.

That comforts me.

If she were at the point of no return, she wouldn't find sleep here with me.

All I can do is hope that in time, she will understand.

Leaving her room, I softly close the door and meet Rex back in the lounge. "Stay with her. I'll send Toto up. You both need to stick to her like glue, understand?"

Rex nods. "What are you concerned about?"

"My father. He called last night but I didn't answer. If he's about to make a move, I want her protected."

"Understood."

Stu and I arrive at Vinnie's apartment forty minutes later. It's small for an apartment, on the ground floor of a shabby block with cracked windows, peeling railings, and a front door that's not seen a lick of paint since its installation.

"He lives here?" Stu looks up and down the street. "This is on the edge of our territory. One block over and you're eating with the Irish."

"You think there's a connection?" I ask as we approach the door.

Stu shrugs. "Nah. Last I heard from your father's men is that the Italians are the biggest aggressors right now. The Irish have a lot of infighting to keep them busy."

"That doesn't mean they wouldn't have run with my girls."

"Sure." Stu leans heavily on the door and within a few seconds, the lock splinters free. "But it does mean they don't want your eyes prying too close while they fight out their own promotions."

"Hm." Inside, we're greeted with the sour stink of off milk and out-of-date meat. The source is the fridge. Judging by the piled-up mail that complains as we push inside and the lack of warmth within the apartment, Vinnie hasn't been home in a while.

"Vinnie?" Stu takes the stairs two at a time.

The clatter of doors being kicked open rings through the apartment while I inspect the lower floor with my gun clasped tightly in my hands.

There's no sign of him. The lounge, kitchen, and downstairs bathroom are empty. The back door leads to a backyard covered in untouched snow barring a few bird footprints and the pawprints of a local cat. Stu's footsteps thunder back down the stairs and he jogs into the kitchen.

"Place is empty, Boss."

"Figures. Bring a team in. I want this place picked apart until I know what color of underwear that bastard is wearing."

Two hours later, Vinnie's home is picked apart by the best team of investigators I have on hand. They've found more than I ever have and with it comes some semblance of the truth. Vinnie Antonva is really Vinnie Tetnova. The Tetnovas are a small family that presumably died out five years ago during a bloody territorial war between my family and another prominent Russian family, greedy for power. They challenged my father for power and lost spectacularly. So did all the other families that chose to back them. My father cleared them all out like bad garbage, but it seems he missed one.

"You think this is revenge?" Stu leans against the kitchen counter, flicking through a gross scrapbook discovered under the floorboards. "He was tailing these girls for some time."

"Revenge against me?" I shake my head. "Unless one of them told him, I don't see how he'd know I'm so involved with the girls. The way I see it, he's pissed that his family line was wiped out and buddied up with Hector to take out his anger on the only part of our world he had access to. My girls."

My stomach flips at the sheer number of pictures of the girls at Plumme. Even more alarming are the pictures of Zoe and her son. I send a quick text to her guards to ensure they don't leave her hospital room and check in with the men watching her son and mother. All are safe.

"What about these?" Stu flicks the page. Pictures from three of our other clubs, Rhinestone, Marigold, and Revenge, fill the page. "More targets?"

I drag my hand down my face, pressing my fingertips into my aching muscles. "Shit. You think he'd target someone else?"

"Fuck knows. I don't understand the mind of someone pulling sick shit like this. He's either running cause we popped Hector, or he's oblivious and our girls were a trial run."

"Alright. I'll call Rex. We'll double the weight at all of those clubs and our two others."

"You're spreading us thin. Igor's going to start asking questions."

"And?" I meet his gaze. "You want me to abandon them?"

"Not at all. I'm just warning you. Your father isn't going to care about two dead dancers."

"Yeah, well, he's never had his priorities right." As if he heard us, my phone lights up with his face and name as he calls. "Fuck. Alright, wrap up here and see if we can find out if Vinnie had ties to anyone other than Hector."

"Got it."

Outside, the wind picks up as I walk into the street and answer. "What?"

"About time," Dad snaps down the line. "Any longer and war would have broken out while I tracked down why my son can't answer his phone."

"I'm busy."

"With what?"

"Club business."

"Supply issue?"

Of course his concern is the drugs, not the girls. "Something like that. I'm sorting it out. What's up?"

"Have you come to your senses yet?" Something rustles in the background. "Is that bitch dead?"

"You mean my *wife*?"

"Don't give me that," he snaps. "You know you spat in Zak's face by marrying some slut and not his daughter?"

"Zak and I both know his daughter isn't interested in me, Dad. That was your deal."

"A deal I worked hard for!"

"So what? Now you have to pay the man a decent cut rather than us tying the knot. It's not an unsolvable problem."

"Do you have any idea what it's going to cost us?" Igor snaps. "Millions that could have been saved with two words from you."

"You're pissed. I get it. But Hollie stays."

"Why?"

"Dad. She's my wife. End of discussion. Unless you want to talk about what the fuck you did to her in the car? You might be the *Pakhan*, but that won't stop me from kicking your ass for hurting her."

"Is that a threat?"

"You taught me well, Dad. I don't make threats."

"I was saving you from making a mistake."

"Fuck off," I snap, anger igniting inside me. "I told you how things were and you went behind my back and tried to murder her. I'm sure it's reached your ears who her father is."

A deep sigh rushes against my ear. "Yes."

"You know he wouldn't have stopped until you were behind bars. So if anything, I've saved you. And you'd better crawl to her for forgiveness."

The line goes dead. Lowering my phone, I stare at the blank screen. Hollie's father, being a retired police chief, is all sorts of dangerous for career criminals like us. If anything happens to her, no bribery in the world will be enough.

Speaking of, Hollie's number flashes up on my phone a second later and I answer as calmly as I can.

"Hello?"

"Maxim?"

"Mhm. Unless you're not looking for me, in which case you called the wrong number."

"No, I am. Sorry, you just sound... different."

"It's cold. I'm tired. What's wrong?"

Hollie pauses, then her warm voice rises once more. "I want to spend some time with my mom tomorrow."

"I see nothing wrong with that."

"Just the two of us."

"I'm not invited. Got it."

"No, Maxim. I mean... without the guards. They're smothering, okay? Tiffany won't stop asking questions, and I don't want my mom to do the same, y'know? I want to pretend things are normal. Plus, if she notices, then my dad will too."

She makes a good point, but leaving her unprotected is out of the question. I study a passing car making its way down the snow-covered street. Choosing to trust her is a huge step. For all I know, this is some plan for her to escape or slip her mother the truth that could start her father digging into my life.

"Maxim?" Hope lifts her voice and my heart skips a beat.

"I'll see what I can do. Go. See your mother. You won't even know the guards are there."

16

HOLLIE

Just as promised, Maxim allows me to meet Mom for lunch and there isn't a single security guard in sight. No Toto or Stu lurking in corners, no Rex hidden behind a menu trying to blend in. There's no one but regular guests in the café, all busy in their own little worlds.

Mom sits across from me with worry etched across her brows while we share a pot of tea.

"I'm okay," I assure her quietly. "I'm not having a breakdown. I'm not on drugs. I'm not being tricked or anything like that."

Mom's brows repeatedly knit together. "It's just all moving so fast, don't you think? I'm worried about you, Hollie."

That's nice to hear after the hours we spent arguing when she and Dad first found out. For a brief moment, I consider telling her the truth. How fast would Dad get here with his cop buddies? Would they be able to take us all into protection before Maxim can make good on his threat? Or would my very action to protect them be the thing that gets them killed?

I briefly close my eyes and a flash of the dead body enters my mind, churning my gut. That's how my parents will end up if I say anything, and I'm already taking enough risks today.

My eyes flutter open when Mom's hand lands on top of mine. "Are you sure you're okay, Hollie? You don't seem like yourself."

"You're just saying that because I've never done something like this before, but aren't you always telling me to get out there and experience the world? Make mistakes and have fun?"

"Yes," she replies softly. "But I'd been talking about thinking properly about your future, getting a real job, and settling into a career that will take care of you."

"Maxim will take care of me."

"Men aren't a career, Hollie."

I snort softly, amused. "They can be."

"Hollie!"

"I'm just saying! Listen, you'll see for yourself that Maxim is a good man and that I'm happy, then everything can go back to normal, alright?" My heart flutters slightly in my chest. No part of my imprisonment with Maxim states he has to make good with my family, but he also doesn't strike me as the kind of man who will make things difficult for himself. For a man built like a truck, covered in tattoos, and rather terrifying at a glance... he's been kind so far.

If my mind wanders, I'm drawn to how tenderly he took care of my ankle rather than ordering someone else to do it. He's cooked for me. Ensured I get a good night's sleep. As far as kidnappings go, this isn't like the ones I read about on the news.

Maybe Maxim is actually terrible at what he does.

His father, on the other hand? Swallowing my tea still makes my throat throb at the memory of that hand clamping down on my neck.

My mother settles for telling me about the local community bake sale and the renovations they plan to do to the house next summer. She rambles like she usually does, and I appease her with appropriate comments and questions about design ideas, cost, and more. All the while, I keep an eye on the clock high up on the wall near the door. I need to wrap things up soon if I'm going to sneak away to the real reason I wanted some freedom today.

Mom lights up talking about fresh paint and when the conversation turns back to Christmas, there's a childlike excitement in her eyes.

"And this weekend," she continues. "I want the house to look perfect. You and Maxim are still coming, correct?" She says his name with a touch of uncertainty, like it's a word she doesn't fully understand.

"Yes," I assure her with one last glance at the clock. "Actually, speaking of. I need to slip away and meet him before I head to work. Is it alright if we wrap this up?"

Mom looks slightly disappointed as she nods and hurriedly takes a handful of dollars out of her purse, scolding me with a look when I try to pay my share. "Let it be my treat." She clutches my hand afterward and smiles strongly. "You're really okay, Hollie, aren't you?"

"Yes, Mom," I lie smoothly and lean forward, kissing her powdery cheek. "I'm fine, I promise."

After she leaves, sneaking out of the back of the cafe via the door near the toilets is terrifying. Each step down the alley echoes like a gunshot and I keep expecting Stu or Toto to jump out from behind a dumpster ready to catch me fleeing.

But there's no one. Maxim really meant it when he said there'd be no security. Of course, judging by how he operates, that likely isn't strictly true, but I'm able to give whoever is watching the cafe the slip and bolt down the street. I don't stop running until I'm a few blocks away. Once I'm certain I'm safely away, I hug a wall and breathlessly pant, willing my heart rate to decrease while my trembling fingers skim through the map on my phone seeking out the doctor I'm booked in to see.

She's a five-minute walk from here, which gives me enough time to catch my breath.

By the time I'm sitting in the office, my heart rate is almost back to normal, but the doctor still gives me a concerned glance while she checks my blood pressure.

"I ran here," I say as she looks me up and down. Sweat continues to bead at my hairline and I brush it away as the doctor sighs softly and removes the pump from my arm.

"Hollie, I can't stress enough how important these checkups are for the health of you and your baby. There are a lot of complications and problems that can be caught early, but you *need* to come and see me, do you understand?"

I nod. "I'm sorry. It's the time of year. I'm super busy all the time, and I can't afford to miss out on work. I don't make an hourly rate, y'know."

"I understand that," she says, pulling off her gloves and sitting in front of me, "but you need to make time for this if you want to ensure the health of your child. Have you had any success in tracking down the father?"

I hesitate as Maxim floods my thoughts. Nothing about him screams father, but how long can I realistically hide this from him? I already see a bump in the mirror, and I'm not sure if it's my imagination or not. A few more months and it'll be painfully obvious that I'm pregnant.

"Sort of," I lie. "But he's not going to be in the picture."

"Are you sure?" She stops scribbling on her notes and looks up at me. "Any medical information from the father can be important. If there's anything serious that runs in his side of the family that we should be on the lookout for, or any complications. Can you ask him?"

My teeth briefly sink into my cheek. "We're not exactly in communication."

She nods once. "If that changes, then his family medical history is a must."

"Yeah, sure." The thought of bringing that up to Maxim is somewhat amusing. What if all the people in his family are born as big as he is? I'll be birthing a juiced-up watermelon at this rate.

"Your heart rate is a little high even for a resting rate. How is life at home? Are you feeling stressed at all?"

It takes all my strength not to laugh in her face. Stress and I are becoming best friends at this point. The past week has been the most insane of my life. "A little. Will that affect my baby?"

"It can." She nods solemnly. "It can be detrimental to both of you, so I need you to be careful. Don't put yourself in stressful situations outside of your norms, get lots of rest, and relax, okay? I'm going to prescribe some vitamins for you just to ensure your baby is getting all the good stuff it needs. And they'll help you, so make sure you take them, okay?"

I nod slowly, watching her scribble on the pad in writing that's far too small for me to decipher. Pills. Hiding them from Maxim is going to be difficult.

What if I tell her the truth? That my baby's father is some kind of Mafia prince and I've ended up embroiled in a murder plot and forced into a marriage with no way out? Would she be able to help me?

My thoughts jumble together while the doctor moves around her office with a light smile, collecting medication from a locked cabinet and passing it to me. When our hands meet over the pill bottle, her smile wavers and her eyes widen at the sight of my ring.

"Wow!" she gasps. "You got married! Congratulations!"

"Oh." I turn my wrist and admire the ring Maxim gave me. "Thanks."

"Is he the baby's father?"

As I glance up at her, something about my expression makes her wince and she pats my hand.

"No need to answer that. Not my business. When can I see you next?"

Unable to settle on a date, I tell her I'll call her the next time I'm free, which doesn't make her happy, but it's the best I can offer, given my situation. Then, with the new pills tucked uncomfortably between my tits, I sprint all the way back to the cafe. The owner gives me an alarmed stare when I return from the back of the cafe and I watch him gaze quizzically at the bathroom as if unable to understand how I've been in there the entire time.

I've scarcely caught my breath when the cafe front door opens and Toto walks in, yawning. He catches my eye and smiles, but it falters. "You good?"

"Hm?" As I stand, I glimpse my reflection in the cafe window. My hair is ruffled, my face almost the same shade of red, and sweat gleams in the hollow of my throat. "I'm fine. Spicy food, y'know?"

"In a cafe?" Toto murmurs to himself as I move past him. "Damn."

Toto and Stu drive me back to the new penthouse and leave me at the elevator. While this elevator has the same biometric security as the previous one, Maxim added me to this system so it obeys my touch. He also showed me the access list. No one is getting up here except me, Maxim, Rex, Toto, and Stu. While it makes me feel a little safer knowing his father can't spring up here unannounced, it doesn't completely rule it out.

Maxim's nowhere to be seen when I step into the penthouse, so I beeline straight for the bathroom and hide my prenatal vitamins behind several boxes of tampons in the cupboard above the sink. As I close the door, my heart pounds and I stare at my sweaty reflection until my eyes blur.

What am I doing?

I had so many chances today to tell someone the truth or to run away. Why did I come back here? Is my presence really enough to keep my family safe from a monster like Maxim or his father? A man who kills in cold blood surely wouldn't blink twice about killing an old couple in their home.

Can I really survive under such pressure that one wrong step will destroy my family?

These thoughts plague me as I take a shower to wash off the sweat of the day, but even the amazing hot water and soothing scent of eucalyptus aren't enough to calm the racing tremor in my heart.

What if Maxim knows I left the cafe? What if he had me followed to the doctor's office and that doctor has been killed for speaking to me? What if I step out of this bathroom and meet the barrel of his gun because he knows I lied to him?

It's enough to keep me in the bathroom for what feels like hours until there's a gentle knock on the door that makes me jump.

"Hollie?" Maxim's voice drifts through from the other side. "I made chicken and gnocchi. Are you hungry?"

He sounds normal, but it does nothing to calm my panic. "Uh... yeah. Yeah, I could eat." Gently stepping forward, I press my ear to the door and close my eyes. Slowly, his footsteps retreat from the door and I release a breath trapped under my ribs.

Holy shit.

Placing one hand over my abdomen, I stroke slowly and will my heart to calm down. It's not good for the baby, right?

After a few calming breaths, I open the door and step out into the hall. My nose is immediately enticed by the creamy, smoky scents drifting down from the kitchen and I follow them as my stomach gurgles softly, alerting me to how hungry I am after a day of running around.

Maxim's in the kitchen with his back to me. Barefoot, he shuffles back and forth in time to some soft classical music rising from his phone next to him on the counter. His soft jogging pants strain around the thick muscles of his thighs and the T-shirt he wears strains at the seams as he dishes up two plates of food.

"Good shower?" he doesn't look at me, but his voice sends a wave of tension through me.

Is this a trick? Does he know what I did? "Yeah," I reply softly. "It was good."

"I hope you're hungry." Maxim turns to me with both plates in his hand. "I might have made more than we need."

"I'm starving." To his credit, the food looks amazing, chicken and gnocchi in a creamy pink sauce served with some fresh spinach mixed in at the last minute, judging by the life still in the leaves.

Maxim walks past me to the lounge, sets the plates down on the table, and then turns to me, motioning to the couch. "Sit. What do you want to drink?"

This all feels normal. Too normal. I keep expecting something to snap, or Maxim to accuse me of running, but he does no such thing. He gets me ice water at my request and sits next to me on the couch, but far enough away that his presence isn't overwhelming. Then he turns on the TV and picks an animated movie.

"Was it nice seeing your mom today?" he asks.

My heart jumps, but I can't detect any threat in his questions. He's shoveling food into his mouth, relaxed against the couch and occasionally huffing out amusement at the movie he's chosen.

He seems... normal.

Is this all in my head? I've scared myself with expectations rather than Maxim's actions, but that doesn't make me lower my guard completely. "It was, yeah. Thanks."

"No problem."

"She, uhm... she's looking forward to us helping with the house."

Maxim glances at me with a bead of sauce caught on the corner of his mouth. "I don't need to be creative, do I? Don't know if you've noticed, but I'm not exactly known for my decorating."

Considering his last penthouse and this one both look like they've stepped out from a catalog, I'm not surprised. "It'll be fine. She likes to be in control, so just do what she asks."

Maxim nods.

And that's it.

He doesn't accuse me of anything. He doesn't threaten me. He doesn't even pry into what I talked to Mom about. He just eats and laughs at his movie like he's an everyday, normal guy.

This might be the most attractive he's looked since we met.

I tuck into the meal and after several creamy, slightly spicy mouthfuls of dinner where the paprika ignites my tongue and the creamy sauce soothes it, I start to feel better. Low blood sugar must have amplified the panic running rampant in my mind, and by the time I finish my meal, I feel a little guilty.

Is it wrong for me to expect the worst from Maxim when, so far, he's done more to protect me than harm me?

I watch him slouch on the couch as tiredness weighs down his eyes, his attention locked on the movie, and the guilt within me grows.

No. It's not wrong of me.

No matter how he treats me, I can't forget what he did.

He's a cold-blooded killer, and at the drop of a hat, I could be next.

17

MAXIM

"You ready?" Hollie stands in front of me with a wide smile on her face, nervously smoothing her hands down her blouse.

Ever since her lunch with her mother yesterday, she's seemed on edge. None of the security team I stationed outside the cafe reported anything unusual, and I didn't want to press her too hard about what they talked about because I'm choosing to trust her. It's the only way something like this is going to work out long-term.

But something has definitely put her on edge. Resisting the urge to pry, I smile at her while hoping she'll tell me of her own accord. A weak hope, given how she views me.

"I'm ready," I reply. "It's only decorating, right?"

As Hollie knocks on the door of her parents' home, she gives me a tight smile. "Boy, you have no idea."

She's right, I really had no idea what I was in for. Christmas in my family is nothing more than an excuse to drink, make a few deals, and pay someone to spend the night with you. Christmas for Hollie and her family is like stepping into another world.

As soon as we've over the threshold, her father Martin thrusts an armful of Christmas lights into my arms and I'm ordered to detangle them. Toto, who accompanies us, is in the middle of laughing at me when he's dragged away to help Martin unfurl the Christmas tree. Hollie is whisked away by her mother, Susan, to get another few boxes of decorations out of the attic, and the hectic day begins.

Unfurling Christmas lights is the easiest task I'm given. As soon as I have them laid out in a straight line across the sofa and the coffee table, I'm ordered outside and up a ladder where I have to string the lights across the gutters and down the drain pipes. It takes the better part of an hour, with Toto bracing the bottom of the ladder while also weaving together a couple of dozen ribbons into miniature wreaths under Susan's guidance. Once the lights are strung up, we're painting snowflakes and rubbing Santa decals onto the windows, spraying fake snow over the flower boxes despite the flakes drifting down around us, and winding a second set of lights around the stone fence surrounding the front of the property.

My fingers are frozen numb by the time I'm back inside with a cup of hot chocolate to warm my soul. Each sip of the divine sweetness warms my soul and burns my throat, but I drink greedily. It's my last moment of warmth before I'm back outside in the snow with Martin and a gigantic tree to set up in the front yard. Through the freshly decorated window, I glimpse Toto covered in lights and tinsel as Susan and Hollie use him as a stand while decorating the tree inside.

"Hold that," Martin barks at me, leaning the tree in my direction. "Need to dig a hole for the pot."

"Do you want me to dig?" I ask, slightly concerned as Martin braces his lower back while sinking down to his knees.

"I can do it," he says briskly. "I might be old, but I'm not incapable. That goes for a lot of things." He glances up at me, his eyes narrowed with a quiet warning. "I'm a retired cop, not an invalid."

"I don't think your knees will care either way, but that's fine. I'm just here to help."

"Help," Martin scoffs. "Is that what you call it?"

I tilt my head away from the branches and watch Martin brush snow away from the ground and grasp a flat handle buried in the grass. To my surprise, the handle pulls out a large circular chunk of dirt and the resulting gap is perfect for the trunk of the Christmas tree.

"I call it help, yes," I say with a grunt, maneuvering the tree into the hole. It lands with a thunk that makes all the branches tremble. "Although if my being here is causing an issue, I'd hate to intrude."

"Hate to intrude," Martin mutters, grabbing onto the tree. He uses it as support to stand. "What exactly is it you do, Maxim?"

"For work?"

"Yes."

"I'm an accountant." The lie rolls off my tongue. "A private one, so I can't disclose who I work for."

"Sounds like you help the rich dodge their taxes."

"I help them do whatever they pay me for."

"Like a cockroach." Martin brushes the snow from his clothes and fixes me with a cold look. "You might already have a ring on her finger, but that doesn't mean I gotta like you."

"No, it doesn't," I agree. Glancing back inside, I glimpse Hollie doubled over laughing at how ridiculous Toto looks and a small smile creeps over my own face. "But I hope in time, you'll see that I care for your daughter, and it will earn me some goodwill in your book."

Martin grunts. "Hardly. She's a reckless girl who makes reckless decisions."

"You think I'm a reckless decision?" I meet Martin's eyes. There's suspicion buried in their dark depths, likely born from his years on the force, and it's dangerous for me to stand here and entertain him. I'd prefer to keep him in the dark about who I am, but a man of his caliber will dig. And he'll keep digging until he learns exactly who I am and what I do.

When that day comes, there won't be anything I can do to stop my father from *taking care* of it.

"I think you're a stranger," Martin says gruffly, sniffing against the cold. "I think my daughter disappeared and came back married, and I think there's something wrong with her."

"Is there something wrong with her?" I ask cautiously. "Or is she just happy and you've never seen that before?"

His lips part briefly, but whatever he plans to say next is silenced by Susan hurrying out of the house with two steaming mugs in her hand. "Boys! Here, drink this so you don't catch your death out here."

I clasp the cup of tea thrust into my grip with both hands and flash Susan a grateful smile. "Thank you. I like maintaining the use of my fingers."

"If this snow gets any heavier, then I want you both inside, understand?" Susan's sharp gaze darts between us. "None of this macho *I can handle it* crap."

"Honey, I'll be fine," Martin replies tiredly. This must be a common discussion they have.

"Well, Maxim won't be, and what kind of parents would we be if we let something happen to him on his first proper visit here, hmm?"

"He can take a little cold," Martin replies.

"Maybe." Susan lowers her voice. "But Hollie is here. Actually here, and not one of her usual fleeting visits. I want that to continue."

"Does she not visit you a lot?" I ask over the top of my cup.

Susan's cheek flush with embarrassment, and she shakes her head. "She's very busy in the city, I know that. I try to bring her home for things, but I imagine you know how it goes. She's so hardworking, but I miss her. Lunch yesterday was so nice, even if it was only for an hour!" Shaking her head, she waves me off. "I'm rambling. I'm just happy she's here. I suppose I have you to thank for that. I don't think she would have come by herself." With a laugh, Susan hurries back inside before the cold consumes her.

Interesting. I was under the impression that Hollie saw her parents a lot, which is why lunch yesterday was so important. A lunch that only lasted an hour while Hollie was gone for several.

Something shifts uncomfortably in my gut as I gaze through the window. Hollie stands with her back to me and her head bowed, focused on some decorations in her arms.

Did she lie to me?

The concern doesn't shift for the rest of the day as I'm in the garden helping Martin decorate the giant lawn tree. He keeps pressing me with questions about my work and my life, my family and intentions, but I dodge each one while sticking to the lie that I'm a simple private accountant. Finance is easy to hide in these days. By the time we're finished, the giant tree is covered in glittering lights, sparkling baubles, miles of tinsel, and more handmade decorations than I can ever count.

"Good job." Martin's hand suddenly lands on my shoulder, and it takes all my self-control not to draw away from him. "It looks pretty damn fine."

His sudden change in attitude is alarming, but as he flashes me a smile and trudges toward the house, I get a distinct feeling that I've just taken part in some kind of invisible test with him.

Does his change in mood mean I passed?

Martin heads into the lounge and I hurry to the kitchen, sticking my hands under hot water to revive circulation and wash off lingering glitter and dirt from the tree. Footsteps behind me make my back twitch, but I relax upon seeing Hollie.

"You and my Dad were out there for ages," she says, turning on the kettle and gathering mugs from the cabinet above her. "What did you talk about?"

"Are you nervous I told him the truth?"

She freezes and looks at me, tucking her red hair behind her ear. "You wouldn't."

"Wouldn't I?"

Her eyes narrow. "You said you wouldn't—"

"I have no intention of hurting them," I interrupt her gently as I turn off the tap. "He asked me a lot of questions and I answered them the way I always do."

"Which is?"

"I'm an accountant. And I work a lot. That's all there is to me."

Her attention returns to the cups and she starts spooning in heaps of coffee into each mug. "Is he going to be in trouble for asking questions?"

She's taken my threat on her family seriously, which is promising, but that strange weight on my chest increases slightly. After drying my hands, I massage my chest. "No.

He's just a father looking out for his daughter, and I can't fault that. And your mother seemed to have a really good time at lunch yesterday."

"Yeah." Hollie nods while the kettle boils. "It was really good."

"What did you two get up to?"

She shrugs one shoulder. "We just ate and talked."

"For five hours?"

"Mhm." Hollie doesn't look up. "My Mom can talk and talk."

She's lying to me. Right to my face. Her mother claimed she was only there for an hour and now Hollie says she was there for longer.

I could press the issue. I could scare the truth out of her. For all I know, this is part of some huge ruse to trick or trap me and she's told her parents everything. Just as my suspicions rise, she turns to me with a small smile.

"Mom wants you to stay for dinner."

"What?"

"She's ordering takeout but she wants us to go through the old cards and pick which ones to hang around the wreath on the front door."

"And she wants me to be a part of that?"

Hollie presses a hot cup of coffee into my hand and nods. "She does."

With careful balance, she picks up the other three mugs and leaves me in the kitchen in silence.

Confused emotions clash together in my chest. She lied to me but her family are working to include me. Those aren't the actions of people who know the truth. So what was Hollie really up to, and why is she keeping it a secret?

I stare down at the coffee, mapping out a couple of bubbles that remain floating on the top, and then I slowly walk through to the lounge.

Hollie is perched on the couch laughing over her mother's shoulder at a card clutched in her hand. Martin is on the couch opposite them with another card, holding it out to Toto, who snorts in amusement.

"I had a dog like that once," Toto remarks with a grin. "Poor thing outlived all my family and then one day just—" He makes a soft death sound. "She was like ninety."

"They're a good breed," Martin agrees. "I had two when I was a kid. My favorite kind."

"Look at his face!" Hollie giggles. "God, I wonder what he looks like now?"

"He shaved all his hair off, didn't you get the newsletter?" Susan swivels around to face her daughter.

"He sends a newsletter?" Hollie gapes at her mother.

"Yes! Every six months. I can't believe you never got one."

"I might have thought it was spam."

The room is warm and full of life. An array of colors gleams from the tree they all worked hard on, glittering streamers hug the ceiling, festive boots and baubles decorate the walls around a jolly Santa, and a full set of reindeer dance around the window. Outside, the tree Martin and I decorated gleams tall in the dusk, slowly disappearing under the snow.

This is family.

I feel like I'm watching through a portal at an advert for everything that makes Christmas joyful, a far cry from the cold rooms, sharp alcohol, and irritable father I'm used to. Suddenly, Hollie stands and grabs my hand. She pulls me into the lounge with a bright smile.

"Come in, silly. You need to pick the card you like the best!"

Before I can protest, she's shoved me down onto the couch and dumped a shoebox filled with Christmas cards onto my lap.

"It can be for any reason," Susan explains from nearby on the floor. "Maybe it looks goofy or makes you laugh, or makes you feel wistful. Whichever you like."

Hollie sits next to me and starts going through the box on my lap. This close, I can smell the eucalyptus she's been using and it tingles my nose. She's only this close for appearances' sake, but I can't take my eyes off her. With rosy cheeks, a soft smile, and eyes reflecting all the lights from the tree as she offers me a card with a cat on the front dressed up as Santa, my heart skips a beat.

She's beautiful.

"What about this one?" Hollie asks, completely unaware of my inner turmoil.

"I like it," I say, unable to take my eyes off her. This day, this evening, this moment... it's unlike anything I've experienced in my life, and yet for this family, it's normal. This is love. This is warmth.

"You sure?" Hollie's eyes briefly meet mine and I nod slowly, not once looking at the card.

"Yeah... I think I like it a lot."

I'm fucked.

18

HOLLIE

Performing on a Sunday is always strange. While New York City never sleeps, I'm usually hired for late-night events during the week or a party on Saturday, but the client Tiffany put me in touch with booked me for Sunday evening.

With Maxim already busy with work, I had to turn to Stu and Toto to take me to the party.

"Are you sure this is the right address?" Toto leans up from his seat and peers out the window, and Stu pulls onto a long winding drive that leads up to a gigantic square house ablaze with golden light.

"Mhm." I double-check my phone. "Yeah, this is the place. Is something wrong?"

Stu glances over his shoulder. "Does Maxim know?"

"I told him I had to work. I didn't tell him where. Why, what's wrong?"

Toto and Stu exchange a silent glance and my frustration builds. Snatching up my violin case, I hold it in my lap while glaring at Toto. "The silent treatment sucks, by the way. If there's something wrong with my being here, then you'd better tell me because I can't afford to cancel this gig."

"Money isn't the issue," Toto remarks, bringing his phone out from his pocket.

"Maybe not, but my reputation can't be bought and I don't need another cancellation on my bookings. So is there a problem?" I can't imagine what the issue could be other than the fact that we're on the outskirts of the city. If this goes against one of Maxim's secret rules that I know nothing about, then I'll be having strong words with him later.

Toto stares at his phone for a long moment, then he looks at Stu. "There's no problem?"

"You sure?" Stu's brows lift.

"Yup."

Since they refuse to clue me in, I open the door and slip from the car with a grunt. Toto's exclamation barely reaches me as I clutch my dress up to my knees and stomp up the driveway, leaving the two of them to keep their secrets while I get to work. Regardless of Maxim's influence over my life now, I'm not turning away from my music for anyone.

I climb six white stone steps to a white and gold front door that opens the moment I reach the top. A man dressed in a black suit with dark shades tilts his head at me while I place my best smile across my lips.

"Hi, I'm Hollie Wolfe. I'm booked in for three hours of music?"

"ID?" The man speaks with a waspish voice.

Digging in my purse, I locate my ID just as Toto and Stu arrive behind me, but for some reason, the man loses interest in my ID and waves me inside without a word.

"What is going on?" I murmur, stepping into an extravagantly decorated hallway with large stairs ascending up to the next floor where they split in two directions, right and left.

"Miss Wolfe?" A woman with poker-straight dark hair hurries up to me wearing a navy blue dress.

"That's me."

"Right this way, my dear. You're right on time!"

I only manage to glance at Toto before I'm whisked through to the next room and helped up onto a small black stage that surrounds a crystal Christmas tree. The lights are turned low and the woman, who introduces herself as Lara, brings me water while I get set up. Three hours of violin work is a challenge solo, but as Lara goes over the song requests with me, the room begins to fill up.

Countless men in gorgeously tailored suits and women in sparkling dresses more expensive than the mortgage on my parents' house glide in like sparkling angels, and soon, the room is filled with warmth and the gentle murmur of conversation. Lara wishes me luck and melts off the stage, leaving me to my dark corner.

So I begin to play.

Music is where I find peace. With the violin under my chin and the bow resting in my fingers like an extension of my own soul, I pour everything into my performance. I was hired to be background, but as I weave multiple songs together, a small crowd begins to grow near the stage. One woman sways back and forth, dabbing the corners of her eyes, while another clutches at her pearls as if my music keeps her on the very edge of an abyss. The crowd grows until soft applause ripples through the room each time I pause. One pause lasts fifteen minutes where Lara brings me ice water to combat the heat, an energy bar, and praise from the host, a man I haven't even met.

While chewing quickly on the sweet cherry and dark chocolate bar, I bring the water bottle to my lips... and freeze.

In the crowd, standing almost a head above everyone else, is a familiar set of deep blue eyes that lock onto me and don't waver.

Maxim.

What the hell is he doing here? Did he follow me here or something?

Just as my annoyance spikes, the crowd parts slightly and his suit is just as exquisitely fitted as everyone else's. And someone stands next to him, talking his ear off, even though his attention is clearly elsewhere.

He didn't follow me here. Maxim was invited. No wonder Stu and Toto were so concerned about this being the address.

If Maxim is here, then this is no ordinary party.

Suddenly, every pair of eyes on me becomes a threat. Handsome men morph into dangerous killers and beautiful women become cold assassins. My heart begins to race and my hand trembles as I drink.

If this party is in Maxim's world, am I even safe? Did he even know I was coming?

Judging by his calm expression, there's nothing around to visibly concern him and once he catches my eye, his lips curl up into a slight, knowing smile.

If he isn't worried, then why should I be?

My timer ends, my break is over, and it's back to the music. Only this time, Maxim stands out like a beacon in the crowd and I can't tear my attention away from him. The growing crowd melts into the shadows, the lights dim, and it feels like I'm playing just for him. So I play harder. I pour everything I have into the music, caress my violin like a lover, and lock eyes with Maxim through every flourish and accent that I bring to familiar Christmas songs that everyone loves.

He never looks away.

Somehow, that makes me feel safe, that even in this crowded room filled with likely criminals, I'm not under any threat.

As my bow glides over the strings to the final notes of my last song, a loud applause rises up from the gatherers who chose to admire my playing over dancing themselves. It's then that Maxim vanishes, swallowed by a crowd that surges forward with such loud praise that I can barely decipher any of the words. People clap and compliment my style, my poise, my playing, and my flair as I try to climb down from the stage, and just when it grows overwhelming, a rough hand suddenly glides into mine and the crowd falls silent.

Maxim.

His presence is enough to disperse the crowd within seconds, and there's not a single complaint from anyone. With flushed cheeks and sweat clinging to the back of my neck, I gratefully clutch his hand while he leads me silently through the room and out a set of glass doors onto a glittering, snow-covered patio. The chill in the air momentarily soothes my overheating skin, but just as the biting cold grows too much, Maxim's suit jacket lands heavily over my shoulders.

"Thanks," I say, finally finding my voice. Despite the clammy sweat coating my arms, his jacket is welcoming and I huddle inside it, wrapping it around my shoulder while soaking up his lingering warmth.

"I had no idea you could play like that," Maxim says as he steps down from the patio and onto a rocky path illuminated by garden lights.

"You never asked to see me play," I reply, following him carefully in my heels.

"You're right. My error." He speaks quietly, as if fearing the falling snow will steal away his words if he speaks too loudly.

"I didn't know you would be here." Stepping from smooth rock to smooth rock, I follow until my heel slips on some snow. Before I can fall, Maxim's arm is there for me to grasp and I gratefully cling to his elbow.

"I didn't know you would be, either."

Smirking softly, I glance up at him. "You never asked me where I was performing."

"It felt like prying. Given everything that's happened, I've been trying to respect what privacy you have left."

What a surprising answer. "Curiosity isn't prying. Unless you decide to force me to tell you something I don't want to."

"I don't intend for that to happen." Maxim keeps his walking pace slow after my slip. "Would you have told me if I asked?"

I squint up at the dark sky, watching the snowflakes seemingly materialize from nothing. "I don't know. Maybe not. But why are you here?"

"I enjoy parties."

"Is everyone in there like you?"

"In what way?"

"Mafia."

Maxim comes to a stop under a wooden trellis covered in vines and snowdrops that look synthetic. He turns to face me, gazing down with blue eyes so intense that they draw me in like rolling dark waves.

"Yes. Everyone in there is like me. You saw a party and I saw a meeting."

"What about?"

Maxim smirks. "Looking for dirt on me?"

My hand remains on his elbow and I shake my head. "Not exactly. But given that I have to speak to someone about getting paid, I'd like to know just exactly how much risk I'll be in."

"Risk?" His brows knit together. "I would never put you at risk."

"You didn't know I was going to be here."

"True, but as soon as Toto told me, I made sure there was no risk."

"How?" My eyes narrow. "Did you kill them like that other poor man?"

Something akin to surprise flashes in his eyes. "Why would you think that?"

"That's what you do, right? You kill the people who get in the way. Or marry them." My thumb teases the back of my wedding ring. "Just like you'd kill my parents if they became a threat, right?"

"I'm not what you think I am, Hollie."

I pout, slightly mocking. "Is this when you tell me that my kidnapper has a heart?"

There's a note of humor in Maxim's snort. "Maybe."

Snow clings to the spikes of his dark hair and in the low light, he looks... softer. Shadows ease the sharp line of his jaw. They soften the bulk of his muscles and tease out the true, almost human softness in his face. When he smiles, his eyes crinkle and there's something much softer about him.

My heart skips a beat and warmth flushes through me like a rampant fever. Here, in the snow and the dark, he's like the man who attracted me back at the bar. Right now, I see Maxim, the man so sexy that my core aches thinking about what he has between his legs.

Not the killer who upended my life.

"Hollie... come with me tomorrow."

"Where?"

"To work. Come to the clubs with me."

My mouth twists. "Why?"

"I want to show you what I do."

"Why?"

"Because what you think of me matters."

I tilt my head and huddle closer into his suit jacket. "Why do you care what I think?"

Maxim leans in closer and my heart skips up to my throat, trembling in the hollow of my neck. I glance at his lips and a sudden yearning pulls through my chest like warm taffy. Do I... do I want him to kiss me?

"I care because—"

"Miss Wolfe?" Lara's voice cuts through the dark. Maxim and I jerk apart as if we've been caught doing something we shouldn't, and my cheeks heat up as if I've been slapped. Maxim appears much more relaxed, rubbing his jaw and adjusting himself to be slightly in front of me as Lara approaches.

"Yes?" I say, fighting to keep my voice steady as the fuzzy desire for a kiss fades in my mind.

"Our host is eager to pay you so the party can end. Do you have a moment?" Lara asks.

"Uh..." I glance at Maxim, surprised to see disappointment in his eyes. "Yeah, I have time."

"Great!" Lara claps her hands together for warmth. "Let's get you paid!"

19

HOLLIE

I spend most of the day resting, tending to my violin, and talking over my schedule with Tiffany for the next two weeks while waiting on Maxim. His invitation to join him at work last night remains at the forefront of my mind throughout the day while something he won't talk about keeps him busy. By the time late evening rolls around, I'm convinced he's forgotten.

Until he calls me down to the car and we drive until we reach one of his nightclubs, Plumme. Unlike the last time we were here, music booms from inside and a queue of people lines up around the block. The neon lights flash in time to the pulsing music, and a burly man at the door moves to stop my approach until he glimpses Maxim just behind me.

Stu and Toto follow us at a distance while Rex, Maxim's head of security, walks on ahead.

"Aren't you worried?" I ask, leaning against Maxim as we walk so he can hear me over the music.

"About what?"

"That everything I see you do here will just be more ammo for me to hold over you."

"I'm not worried." Maxim takes my hand as we step out onto the upper balcony overlooking the main dance floor. He brings my hand to his lips and kisses my ring. "You're not going to tell anyone anything."

"You're sure about that?" Pulling my hand away, I cross my arms over my chest. "So, what's the big secret? What's so important about what you do at a strip club that you have to show me?" I hear the words coming out of me laced with venom, but I can't stop myself. Last night, in the snow under the trellis, I started to see him differently, like he was someone I could genuinely fall for and the crush that pulled us together hasn't faded. I almost felt like there was something real between us, so now I'm on the defensive.

"Go to the bar," Maxim replies, seemingly unfazed by my attitude. "Have a drink and relax."

I do just that but insist it's because I want to and not because he told me to. Toto follows at a distance but soon melts into the crowd of surging people hungry for the girls dancing and performing on stage. Thankfully, the bar is mostly empty other than a few skimpily dressed waitresses darting back and forth with trays filled with drinks.

"What can I getcha, chick—wait a second." The bartender pauses on her rush past me and points at me with one long, manicured finger. "I know you."

Our eyes meet and she breaks out into a wild smile.

"You're Hollie, right? Maxim's girl?"

My gut knots slightly as I nod. "Yeah. That's me."

"I'm Xena." She sticks one hand over the bar. Her wrist is covered in bracelets that jingle together in a light symphony while she waits for my hand. "I was at your wedding, remember?"

"How could I forget?" I shake her hand slightly to be polite, then press my hands together in my lap. "Could I get some water?"

She raises one perfectly penciled brow. "You came to a place like this for water?"

"Is that a problem?"

"No, we serve all sorts here, chick. But you'd be better with a soda. The water ain't exactly..." She purses her lips. "Just trust me."

"Fine. A soda." Is this what he wanted me to see? A bar where the water isn't drinkable and a building filled with half-naked women dancing and grinding for the men lusting after them?

Xena flashes me a smile and ducks under the bar, returning with an ice-cold can of soda. "Can I get you anything else, chick?"

I shake my head, welcoming the chill of the drink as the heat within the club builds. "No, thank you."

"So, what brings you back here?" She places both her hands on the bar and leans toward me. "Another wedding?" She winks.

"Do you help a lot of women get married when they don't

want to?" My eyes narrow. "Is that the business he runs here?"

"Who, Maxim?" Xena scoffs. "Listen, I may not be a lot of things but I know when someone is babbling some crazy bullshit, and you, chick, you had no idea what you were talking about."

"Are you kidding me?" Annoyance rises within me like a wave of heat. "I told you the truth and instead of helping me, you threw me back into his arms!"

"From where I'm standing, you're looking pretty okay for a woman claiming she was kidnapped." Xena's polite expression melts into one of annoyance. "Maxim did you a favor."

"A favor? You're kidding me, right? He commits God knows how many crimes, the abduction of me, for one, and you think he's done me a favor?"

"If it's so bad, why are you still here?" she challenges sharply. "The door's right there, chick."

"Don't act like you don't know," I sneer. "A man like that threatening my family? What am I supposed to do?"

Xena stares at me with wide eyes for a moment, then she bursts into loud laughter so suddenly that I jump. I don't understand. What was it I said that was so funny?"

"Oh, chick, now I know you ain't got your head screwed on right." Xena giggles.

This can't be happening. Am I the only one who sees Maxim for what he really is? Does he have all his employees so completely disillusioned about what kind of man he really is?

"What would you know," I mutter dejectedly as a chill sweeps down my arms. "You're just a—"

"A what?" Xena interrupts sharply. "A bartender? A dancer? A *stripper*? Is that what your issue is, chick? Are you too prim and proper that a woman taking her clothes off is the worst thing she can do?"

"For money? It's not exactly admirable."

"Says who, the Puritans controlling the media making you think anything sexy is bad and just for men?" Xena scoffs as if she's trying to remove something from her throat. "That's fucking bullshit. Look around, Hollie. What do you see?"

Glancing over my shoulder, I take in the heaving crowd, the sparkling stages, the gleaming poles, and the beautiful women in various states of undress and dancing and grinding like they're fucking someone invisible that I can't see.

"I see a strip club," I murmur. "I'm not judging, this just isn't my scene."

"Your scene," Xena scoffs. "You really are something. Never saw Maxim settling down with someone so stuck up."

"Maybe he shouldn't have murdered someone right in front of me, then, should he?" My heart pounds and my skin grows hot. Why do I feel like I'm the one on trial here? Like Maxim is some good person and I'm the evil one for witnessing what I did.

Xena sighs and leans her elbow onto the bar. "You see the girl in blue with the black hair?" She points, and I follow her finger. "She has three kids at home. Two years ago, she was on the streets caring more about heroin than her kids.

Maxim found her and brought her here, worked with her to get her clean. Now she works her own hours, takes home thousands of dollars a night, owns her own apartment, and got her kids back from the state. That girl in gold? She worked street corners to pay for the hospital bills drowning her sickly father. Maxim stepped in and paid for everything when he found her. Now her father's got a new lease on life and she's back in college training to be a nurse."

"So, what, Maxim is some kind of savior? Is that what you're trying to tell me?" It's difficult keeping the snark out of my tone.

"The girl in red? She was fresh out of school and spent her first night in a whorehouse. One of Maxim's guys found her and brought her here. Maxim put her back in education and paid for it all. When she graduated, she wanted to work here."

"To pay him back?"

"No, chick. Because she loves to dance and feel sexy. She has her own makeup line and never has to worry about bills ever again."

I turn back on my stool and stare at Xena. "Doing good deeds doesn't justify murder," I say. "And are these women even free?"

"Girl!" Xena laughs loudly. "We work the hours we want, we rake in the cash. I'm a shareholder in this club. What, just because this place isn't accommodating *nuns* doesn't make me any less of a businesswoman. You're judging me and them for taking our clothes off without asking if that's what we want to do. You have no idea how empowering it is to be on that stage, dancing your heart out knowing you're gonna make enough that you never have to put yourself down to afford a bill ever again."

My cheeks flame. She makes a good point, but no matter what Maxim does to help the people in his employ, what I saw doesn't change. And what he did to me doesn't change either.

"Nancy!" Xena stands on her tiptoes all of a sudden and waves over a woman dressed in a silky shawl. "Nancy, come here a sec."

Nancy joins us at the bar, languidly stretching over it and yawning. "What?"

"This is Hollie. Maxim's wife."

"Wow," Nancy drawls softly. "Lucky."

"She doesn't think so," Xena replies.

Nancy frowns at me. "What?"

"I saw him kill someone, murder him in cold blood, and then he kidnapped me and forced me to marry him to keep me quiet. Your so-called *savior* Maxim is a monster."

Nancy stares at me and then slowly smirks. "Now it makes sense."

My cheeks flare hotter. "What does?"

She points at me. "I knew Maxim would never marry someone boring out of choice."

"Choice?" Anger surges inside me. "I'm the one who didn't have a choice!"

"Bullshit," Nancy replies, unfazed. "You know who he is, which means you know who his father is. You saw something you shouldn't have and that man would have cut you up for it. But he can't, right? Because you're Maxim's girl, which means all their funny laws and rules protect you. He saved your life and you don't even see it."

Igor flashes back up in my mind, and I swallow around the memory of his hands. "The cops would have protected me from both of them," I mutter.

"Who did he kill?" Nancy looks me in the eye. "Who do you care about so much?"

"Does it matter?"

"With Maxim, it always matters," Nancy says. Xena leans over and whispers something in Nancy's ear that makes her eyes go wide and then narrow at me.

It's like I'm back at school watching people gossip about me thinking I can't hear while trying to make it obvious.

"Does she know?" Nancy looks up at Xena, who shrugs.

"Dunno."

"Did you tell her?"

Xena rolls her eyes. "Like I'd make it that easy for her after the shit she pulled." She glances at me. "Maybe she doesn't deserve to know."

"Know what?" I glance between them both.

Nancy sighs and turns in her stool until her back is against the bar and she's staring out into the dance floor. "You've no idea what you've fallen into, have you?"

"If everyone stopped being so damn cryptic, then maybe I'd know."

"A few weeks ago, there were three other women at this club. Ana, Bea, and Zoe."

Nancy speaks slowly, almost lazily, but there's something else in her tone that I can't pinpoint.

"You know Maxim is in the Mafia. He's a good man. A kind man. And he takes things very seriously. Those three women were my friends. They were good people. Ana was going to join the military soon, and Bea was saving up to open her own boutique store. Zoe's got a kid with the brightest smile you ever saw. So when men came in flashing the cash and promising the big bucks, why would they refuse? It's pretty common here, actually. Nothing makes a man show off more than a pretty woman."

Nancy speaks casually as if she's reciting something that happened at the grocery store, but Xena's silence makes me uneasy.

"So they took those two men for a private showing. And those two men kidnapped our three friends. They beat them and dragged them out the back, killed one of our security guards, and got away into the night." Nancy rubs her jaw slowly. "I've never seen Maxim so focused. He tore the city apart looking for them. No one else would do that. His father wouldn't care about three missing women. No other family in this city would give a damn. But Maxim does. He cares. So he searched."

Xena's hand lands briefly on Nancy's shoulder and squeezes.

"Those bastards took their time. Two fucking weeks. They carved Bea up so I couldn't even recognize her. They beat them, tortured them, raped them, and then when it was all over, they drowned them in a water tank. It's a sheer miracle that Zoe survived. But Bea and Ana?" Her voice quavers. "They're gone. But Maxim hasn't stopped looking." She turns to me, and her eyes shine with tears. "That man you saw Maxim kill? That bastard was one of the men who took our girls. Maxim found him, and I don't know what he did to him. I don't care. All I know is that he didn't stop until he'd torn the identity of the second bastard out of him. And then he killed him, and the only peace of mind we get is knowing that he suffered until his last, worthless breath."

Nancy's hand covers her mouth and she winces.

I'm frozen.

Not even my heart seems to beat.

I can't think.

The story laid out to me is so horrific that I can barely comprehend it. Not once did I see anything about missing women on the news, nor did Maxim give me any indication that the man he killed deserved it.

"So you see," Xena says softly, rubbing Nancy's shoulder, "Maxim is a good man. I've known him for fifteen years and he's never killed without cause. What you saw was him delivering justice to a monster who robbed us of our friends. He's the kind of man who knew what would happen to you in the hands of his family, so he got you the best protection he could by marrying you. Your yelling that he kidnapped you? We all knew there had to be a good reason. Maxim doesn't hurt people. Not intentionally."

There's still an urge to defend myself, to deny this and claim that he should have let me go to the cops or something, but if I've learned anything these past weeks, it's that his father's reach is long.

"But he's Mafia." It sounds as lame out loud as it does in my head.

Xena's smile softens. "And we're strippers. Didn't anything I say teach you not to judge someone by what they do?"

I can't think of anything to say and my head is reeling. Overwhelming sadness and sympathy for those three women clashes with disgust at what those men were capable of. No wonder that man looked beaten to within an inch of his life, and no wonder no one flinched at his death.

He deserved it.

That whole scene takes on a new light in my mind and I remain silent, staring at my unopened soda. Nancy eventually slips away and Xena returns to work, leaving me to sort through my turbulent thoughts until Maxim returns.

"Ready to go?"

His voice makes me jump. I look up at him, and it's like I'm seeing him for the first time, like when I saw him in the bar and he was just that kind, hot man with amazing muscles that made my body tremble.

Why wouldn't he tell me the truth himself?

I nod slowly and wave goodbye to Xena, then follow Maxim out of the club. In the hours that have passed, the line outside has shrunk and a fresh layer of snow coats the nearby parked cars. Toto and Stu return from wherever they vanished to, but as we reach the car and Maxim holds open the door, I stop walking.

He faces me, his brows knit in concern. "Hollie?"

"Why didn't you tell me?"

"Tell you what?"

"That the man you killed was a monster?"

20

MAXIM

My hand lingers on the car door, my attention fixed on Hollie. Snow lightly drifts through the air between us and even the thumping music seems to take a back seat while we stare at one another.

"What did you say?"

"The man you killed." Hollie lifts her chin. "He was a terrible, *terrible* person."

I lock eyes with Stu, who hovers just behind her, then steps back from the door. "Hollie, get in the car."

"Not until you give me some answers!"

"I will give you answers, just get in the car."

She rolls her eyes and for a brief moment, I think she won't. Thankfully, she relents and slides into the car with a soft grunt. I join her while Stu takes the front and Toto hangs back to take the second car with Rex.

Inside, the heater turns on and warmth quickly builds. Hollie sits with her arms crossed and the same challenge in her eyes showing she has no intention of backing down.

"Hollie—"

"Don't," she snaps. "Tell me the truth."

"I... didn't expect you to find out."

"How could I not? You left me at the bar and those girls told me everything."

"I *thought* they would tell you about the club and the charity work they do, how they own the buildings and decide their rates. I thought they would show you how I let them do things the way they want to."

Her expression wavers slightly. "I mean... they did. I learned that."

"So how did you end up talking about that night?"

A sheepish look crosses Hollie's face and she glances away. "I was pissed off and talking about how you... kidnapped me and forced me into a marriage and that I didn't care for the nice things they were saying. And then this woman, Nancy, turned up and she started talking."

"Ah." My stomach tightens briefly. Had I known Nancy was working, I would have steered clear tonight. She was attached at the hip to Bea and took her death hard.

"Ah? Did you not want me to find out?"

"I didn't want you involved any more than you already were."

"But why?" She stares at me with wide eyes. "You... you were killing the monster who hurt those women. Why did you let me think you were just some cold-blooded killer?"

My lips press together. "You wouldn't have believed me."

"Yes I would!"

"No, Hollie. You believed what you saw and any justification I gave you wouldn't have mattered. You were scared, you witnessed a horrible thing, and I had to do what I did in order to keep you safe."

Hollie slumps back in her seat. "They said you didn't kill without reason."

"I don't. I don't kill or harm innocents. The man I killed, his name was Hector, and he was a sick, twisted man trying to hurt this family because he knew all attempts at power would fail. I don't regret killing him. But I regret that you saw it because it's pulled you into a world you never needed to know about."

Her expression falls. "You let me say all those horrible things. I spent these past weeks thinking you were this horrible killer, a monster who was going to kill my parents at the drop of a hat."

"I wouldn't hurt them." Honesty might not be the best path right now, but since Hollie knows the truth, I can't lie to her anymore. "I threatened them, yes, because you already had a picture of me in your mind and leaning into that to keep you quiet was how I could keep you safe. But I don't kill innocent people. Marrying you was the only way to keep you safe. You've seen how bloodthirsty my father is. Our marriage keeps them protected by extension."

"You could have told me the truth," she whispers.

"Would you have believed me? Would you honestly have shrugged off what you saw and believed he was a monster?"

Our eyes meet and she presses her lips together while shaking her head.

"Exactly. And I had to make sure you weren't a spy."

"A spy?" Her brows dart upward and a humorless laugh escapes her. "What do you mean?"

"We met at that club two months before that night. I don't typically run into the same person twice unless they're from another family or involved in the same kind of work that I am. So seeing you twice raised all sorts of alarm bells."

"A spy," she repeats. "But you still married me?"

I shrug lightly. "Even if you were a spy, marrying you gave me unhindered access to your family and your past, so I was able to rule that out pretty quickly."

"This doesn't make sense." She settles deeper into her seat and gazes out at the passing dark streets. "Everything about you screamed... but then... and I..."

Hollie's clearly at war with herself, attempting to untangle everything she thought she knew about me.

"I don't hold it against you." My hand rests against my thigh and squeezes. "After what you went through with the wedding and my father... I think your reactions are understandable."

"How do I know you didn't just pay them all to say those

things?" Her eyes snap back to me. She talks like she's trying to find another way to justify how she feels.

"I can take you to the hospital to see Zoe if you really want me to."

Her eyes widen, then she shakes her head. "I couldn't. God..." Hollie repeatedly shakes her head. "I don't know what to think."

"Then tell me."

"I'm annoyed because how I thought things were are not how they actually are. I'm angry because killing people is still wrong, and I watched you kill him, but he was truly a despicable human being, so maybe it's justified? But who am I to decide that? Maybe real justice is at the hands of the law."

I bite back my amused scoff. "Maybe."

"And you let me say those horrible things to you and act like you were a monster when you were helping people and avenging those women, but you also didn't tell me the truth! You let me believe that so I made a fool of myself not once, but twice in front of those women at the club!"

"You said yourself that you wouldn't have believed me if I told you the truth."

"But you still should have told me!"

"Why?" I smile softly. "What difference would it really have made?"

"Were you ever going to tell me?"

"No. I wanted to keep you in the dark as much as possible so you didn't live in fear."

"Fear?" She rolls her eyes. "I'm in this world now, which means all the dangerous things here can hurt me regardless of whether I know about them or not. Were you really going to keep me in the dark?"

"Yes. Bringing you to the club was so you could see I do good in my work. Keeping you in the dark was so I could maintain some semblance of the life you lost when we married. And it's unnecessary pain."

"Why do you get to make that decision, huh?" Hollie surges forward suddenly, and within the cramped confines of the car, she ends up almost in my lap. One knee braces on the seat next to me while the other rests over my lap. She prods her finger into my chest, glaring at me. "You should have told me the truth!"

"What are you really angry at?" I ask softly, relaxing back while she hovers over me. I keep one arm tense just in case something happens that will hurt her since she abandoned her seatbelt. "I told you why I didn't tell you and it's not good enough. But it's the truth, so what are you really pissed at?"

"You let me think you were this horrible, cold man!"

"And?" My eyes narrow faintly. "Why is that a problem?"

Hollie's lips part and her words catch in her throat as she stares at me. In the depths of her gorgeous eyes, her struggles reflect back at me. There's something she can't bring herself to say, and my interest rises.

"Is it because you liked me?" I tease, taking a stab in the dark. "Was that night in the bar so memorable to you that you can't comprehend crushing on a cold-blooded killer?"

My teasing words clash with her silence and her cheeks flare a vibrant red, which causes my stomach to flip. I was only joking, choosing something that was surely so ridiculous, it would get a reaction out of her. But she doesn't argue or throw herself away in disgust.

Instead, she blushes and hesitant noises fall from her lips as she struggles to reach a defense.

My eyes widen and a lazy smirk creeps up. "I'm right, aren't I?"

"Shut up!" she snaps and tries to push away from me, but I don't let her.

I wrap one arm around her waist and pull her close, forcing her to overbalance and land fully in my lap. As her hands land on my shoulder in protest, I cradle the side of her face, slide my fingers into her thick, red hair, and drag her down for a kiss.

Hollie's body remains rigid the moment our lips meet but just as I contemplate letting her go, just when I think I've completely misread the situation, she suddenly relaxes into me.

My heart skips a beat.

"You're wrong," Hollie mutters against my lips. "You're so wrong."

"Then why are you still kissing me?" My grip relaxes and I open my eyes to meet the fire in hers.

She pushes herself away, looking almost disappointed that she can, and then her mouth is over mine once more.

Her lips cling to a fraction of the chill lingering from when we were out in the snow, and there's a sweetness from whatever gloss she chose to wear today. She's warm in my lap and her two hands resting against my shoulders suddenly turn to claws as she digs her nails in.

Something deep and warm curls inside me. Both my arms circle her and I pull her close against my chest, uncaring about the reason she's choosing to kiss me. If it's anger, frustration, or a distraction, I don't care. I just want her.

I wanted her back in the bar.

I wanted her the moment I saw her on the couch after Stu knocked her out.

I thought I would never have her.

Even if one more taste is all I'm granted, then that's what I'll take and savor.

The car lurches, sending Hollie deeper into my lap, and a soft, surprised moan lifts from her as she places her hand against the side of my neck while my tongue sweeps across her lower lip.

I want more. I want everything she'll give me, and the hunger is almost overwhelming when all that's happened is a kiss. My hands fall to her thighs, stroking from her knee to her hip and then following the curve around to the swell of her ass. I pull her against me, and she gasps against my lips, then jerks her head away.

Her face is flushed and we pant together. The tension's so thick that my head swims, and she blinks so slowly that I want to surge up and kiss every lash that brushes her cheek. Before I can move, though, the car slows to a stop.

We're home.

And I still don't understand a thing.

21

HOLLIE

ot tea warms the mug in my hands, bread toasts in the toaster next to me, and soft music drifts through the penthouse while I stare off into space.

All I can think about is Maxim.

Since learning the truth a couple of days ago at the club, everything I thought I knew has changed. As the daughter of a cop, I never considered murder justifiable growing up. Dad was always pretty clear in his beliefs as to right and wrong, and while we sometimes argued about the morality of it, I mostly agreed with him.

Until now.

Those women at the club are scared. Scared because the protection they gained from Maxim was ripped away by two monsters. The few details Nancy gave me were enough to turn my stomach, and now when I think of the man dying in front of me in the pizzeria, the guilt doesn't appear. Only disgust. And hope that he suffered more than what he put those poor women through.

Does that make me as bad as him? Maxim kissing me in the car was doubly unexpected and I can't explain to myself why I thought it was a good idea to go with it. I just... did. It felt nice. It felt right. I can't explain it.

Grumbling to myself, I bury my thoughts in my tea until my toast pops, then I aggressively butter it. Maxim hasn't mentioned the kiss since he was called away to whatever mysterious work he gets up to for the Mafia, but the few times we crossed paths like silent ships in the night, he smirked at me.

That smirk lingers in the forefront of my mind and ignites an alluring warmth up and down my bare arms.

It's ridiculous. I should hate him.

I *thought* I did.

Now he's a savior and a man who offers countless business opportunities to women in need. He protects people and refuses to harm the innocent. It explains clearer why he married me rather than just killing me like I feared.

What an odd way to move. He's almost more ethical than some of my Dad's cop buddies.

Biting into my toast, I wander through to the empty lounge and drop into one of the plush leather sofas just as music rises from my phone.

"Dad?" I say as soon as I answer. "Everything okay?"

"Hi. I thought you weren't working today?"

Another bite of my toast. "I'm not."

"Well, are you going to let me in?"

"Huh?" Sitting up slowly, I glance toward the door. "You're here?"

"Yes! I wanted to come and see you."

Confusion swirls in my chest. How does he know where to find me? I never—oh! It hits like a sharp sting where the confusion stems from, and I groan softly, almost choking on my next bite of toast.

"Wait there! I'm just at the store!"

"I can come and meet you."

"No, honestly, I'm like two minutes away. I'll be back in a sec!"

Hanging up, I abandon my tea and toast and fly into the bedroom, grab my coat, and sprint for the elevator. Toto answers my call on his second ring.

"S'up?"

"I need you to take me home," I gasp breathlessly as the elevator descends.

"Excuse me?"

"My dad came to visit me, but I never told him I'm staying with Maxim, so he's at my old apartment! I need you to drive me there right now!"

～

"Two minutes?" Dad stands at the base of the steps leading up to my apartment building as I sprint toward him. Toto dropped me off around the block so as not to raise suspicion, but it took the better part of twenty minutes to get here.

"I'm sorry," I gasp as I slide to a stop in front of him, kicking up some of the snow coating the street. "I got talking to an old friend and time just..." I wave my hands and then pull him into a hug. "It's so nice to see you."

"You got talking so intently that you forgot your groceries?" Dad hugs me back with one arm and gazes down at my empty hands. "I thought you went to the store?"

"I did!" Shit. "I, uhm... y'know, there was just nothing there I needed. I was just hungry and you know what they say. Always shop on a full stomach."

"Do they say that?" He looks at me quizzically, but I quickly brush him off and jog up the steps.

"I hope they do. Anyway, come in!" Sliding my key in the lock, I let myself into my apartment and am immediately hit by the smell of rotten food. "Oh, no," I whisper under my breath. There's a brief moment where I pray Dad won't notice, but his nose scrunches before he's even halfway through the door.

"Hollie, what's that smell?"

"Uhm... what smell?" I hurry toward the kitchen with him in tow.

"You don't smell that?"

"No, I don't smell anything. What do you smell?"

"Old takeout and off milk." He grimaces and beelines for my fridge.

I try to play off the stink and act like I'm blind to the smell, shaking my head. "I smell nothing. It must just be your nose."

"Really?" He turns away from the fridge, delicately holding some old Chinese takeout containers, very clearly long past their shelf life. "How busy are you that you don't smell this?"

"Honestly, I'm working so much, I'm barely home!" Strained laughter escapes me and together, we clear out the fridge, dispose of all food long past its edible date, and give the place a good clean.

None of this ever crossed my mind. I've been so caught up in the whirlwind of Maxim, the marriage, his father, and the club on top of my own gigs that my own apartment just faded from my thoughts. I try not to think about that even now as I turn on the kettle and gather two mugs.

"Coffee?"

"As long as there's nothing growing out of the mug."

"They're fine," I assure him with a laugh.

"You haven't decorated?" Dad settles on the stool near the island counter and glances back toward my lounge, which hasn't seen a lick of love since July 4th.

"I haven't had time."

"You always decorate."

"I know." I place a hot mug of coffee down in front of him alongside a small dish of sugar. "I've just been really busy."

"With work?"

"Mhm."

"And your new husband."

I freeze momentarily, staring down into my coffee mug and then nodding. "Yep."

"Things are moving fast there, aren't they?"

There it is. The real reason he's here. I knew he didn't just drop by to talk about decorations. Not that I can blame him. Swiveling to face him, I lean my elbows on the counter across from him and hug my mug with both hands. "When you know, you know."

"In all my years on the force, a fast marriage like that is rarely a good sign."

"You worry too much, Dad."

"Your Mom worries too. She says she saw what she thought was a bruise under your eye when you were with us for decorating."

I freeze. I'd used all the makeup I had available to cover myself up for going outside after Stu hit me and Maxim's father tried to kill me. I had no idea she noticed.

"I'm fine, Dad."

"Are you?" He squints at me. "I've been on the force for a long time, Hollie. I've seen a lot of things."

"I know you have."

"Just say the word and you'll never see him again."

His offer is as warm as his words, and my heart swells at the concern flooding his eyes. For every day my mother has volunteered or signed me up for something against my knowledge, my father has been there to help me through it and sneak me something to keep my spirits up.

He looks out for me.

But it's my turn to look out for him.

Maxim's father won't forget what I saw, and I don't doubt his reach. My marriage to Maxim extends protection to my parents, and it's the only way to keep them safe.

"I love you, Dad. And I love that you look out for me. The bruise Mom saw was from work. An unruly guest was mad at what he had to pay for drinks and I was in the firing line."

His eyes narrow. "And you didn't call the cops?"

"It was Thanksgiving. I was more concerned about having a bruise on my eye in my wedding pictures than anything else. It happens a lot, you know. New York isn't that safe."

"How often?"

"Not to me!" I assure him with a laugh, taking his hand. "I just mean in general."

He doesn't look entirely convinced, but it's enough for him to agreeably change topics. We talk about Christmas and Mom, her plans for Christmas dinner, and her not-so-subtle way of asking me to play at New Year's for her friends. She just wants to show me off. I suspect she's just trying to find ways to persuade me to stay, like she's done ever since I mentioned leaving the States.

That dream isn't dead, it's just on pause. I'm not sure where my future can lead with a Mafia prince shackled to me.

By the time Dad leaves, night has fallen. I'll need to explain all of this to Maxim and find a polite way to tell my parents where I live now. It feels like too big a bombshell to drop after the wedding.

"How is your father?" Toto asks as I approach the car.

"He's fine. Concerned."

"Why?"

"Stu gave me a black eye, remember?"

Toto winces. "That's why he avoids you."

"Is he scared of me?"

Toto shrugs. "More upset by what he did. He'll apologize when he's made peace with himself."

"Good for him." As I'm climbing into the car, my phone buzzes to life once more. This time, it's Tiffany.

"Darling!" Tiffany yells. "Listen, I know it's late, but I have an emergency booking for you!"

"Tiff—"

"I know, I know, nothing without warning, but this guy is so desperate. He needs a musician for next weekend and he's paying an obscene amount for a quick booking, and I just know you deserve this kind of money, so can you meet him?"

"Tiff, it's really late."

"I know, but think of the money!"

"I don't have my equipment with me."

"I've already sent him samples. He just wants to put a face to the name, plus, he's a fan. Please? It would be amazing for both of us. Come on, say yes!"

After a few minutes of quiet deliberation, I agree and give the change of address to Toto. He makes a call while redirecting the car, and when we arrive at the restaurant, I spot Stu parked across the street.

They take changes seriously.

With Toto lingering behind me, I head into the restaurant but before I can open my mouth to speak to the woman at the desk, a man surges up from a nearby seat.

"Miss Wolfe?"

I greet him with a smile. "Yes. You are?"

"I'm Mr. Havershire. Your agent, Tiffany, told me you'd meet me here."

"And you knew it was me?"

"I confess I'm a fan of your work. Your agent was so eager for the booking that I'm not sure if she caught that part of my request. I know who you are." He holds out his hand and smiles widely. "I won't keep you a moment."

Accepting his hand, I shake it with a smile and the small gold watch on his wrist jingles and slips, revealing a heart tattoo on his wrist.

"So, what can I do for you?"

"Well, my last musician dropped out of my event next weekend and I need someone to play a few intimate songs because I'm planning on proposing to my girlfriend. It's embarrassing, but I tried to book you initially a few months ago, but your agent told me back then that you were fully booked."

"This time of year is so hectic with bookings and cancellations so she was probably right." I chuckle. "I'd be happy to. If you tell me when and where, I'm certain I can be there."

"Excellent! I really just wanted to meet you face-to-face to make sure I wasn't being tricked. You know how it can be."

"I'd be honored if someone were trying to impersonate me." I laugh softly. "How much is your budget?"

"Fifteen thousand."

"For the whole event?"

"No." His brows lift. "That's just for you."

It's hard to remain professional in the wake of such an amount and I swallow down my shock as I reach for his hand again.

"That's... amazing! I will most definitely be there!"

22

MAXIM

P asta bubbles in a small pot on the stove, the oven warms peppers I spent twenty minutes carefully preparing, and the kitchen knife once again leaves a small groove against my palm as I carefully slice chicken breast into strips.

I haven't cooked this much in years and suddenly, Hollie's presence has me spending most of my free time in this kitchen, as limited as it already is. The other Russians are refusing to play ball on a weapons deal, my father is squeezing every last cent from the Italians, and the Irish are snapping at our heels, trying to weasel their way onto our club scene as if that's not the very landscape I crafted myself.

As stressful as it is, none of it matters when I'm back here with her.

A woman I shouldn't be getting close to.

But I can't help it. Coming home to this place knowing someone is asleep a few doors down brings me a warmth

I've never experienced before, and it plays on a loop in my mind just like the kiss I stole in the car. If we hadn't been interrupted, my hand would have ended up somewhere deeper than just past her waistband.

But a busy life and Hollie working to get back into her own schedule leaves me with limited time to see her, and no time at all to bring up what that kiss meant. Was it some-thing sweet and stolen? Or a treat from her, taunting me because she can read me like a book and knows what I want?

There's so much to unpack. So I cook and hope the meals I leave her speak loud enough for the words I never get a chance to share.

With the chicken now in thin strips, I add them one by one to a pan with minimal oil, then slather them in an array of spices and ground garlic cloves. While they fry, I check the pasta and double-check the peppers aren't burning.

I stand with cheeks warm from the gust of air from the oven and flinch ever so slightly.

Hollie stands in the doorway, dressed in the silky top and shorts she's been wearing ever since Toto brought her clothes from home yesterday. She yawns, rubbing one eye. Several hair strands stick up in an array of directions and when she catches my eye, a brief smile twitches across her lips.

"Was I too loud?" I turn down the heat under the pasta to control the boil. "Sorry if I woke you."

"You did, but it wasn't the sound, it was the smell." She approaches the counter, places both hands on it, and leans over to try and glimpse what I'm cooking. "What are you making?"

"Something my mother used to make when she knew I wouldn't be home."

"Because you'd eat it all?"

"No, so I could grab it on my way out and think of her."

"Hmm. Homey. So, what is it?"

"Just some stuffed peppers. I was making them and was going to set some aside for you when you woke up."

"How considerate."

Lifting one shoulder, I return her smile. "I'm full of surprises."

"So I'm learning." Hollie perches on the stool and yawns briefly again, sighing. "Can I have some now?"

"Sure."

"Thanks."

An amicable silence falls between us while I tend to the chicken. Hollie drums her fingers on the countertop and softly sucks on her teeth. "So..."

"If you want to ask me something, just ask."

"It's less an ask and more... I got a new client."

Was she wary of sharing good news with me? "That's great news. Toto mentioned you got a last-minute booking from Tiffany yesterday."

"Does Toto tell you everything?"

"Only when it involves deviation from the normal routes."

"Why?"

"Routes outside the norm need approval and security."

Her eyes widen. "Are you serious?"

"Did you think I was letting my wife dart around New York City without the appropriate security measures?"

Hollie purses her lips. "So that's why Stu was there."

"Mmhmm."

"I guess I never really thought about it. What else are you keeping me safe from other than your dear old dad?"

"Word spread quickly of our marriage. Unfortunately, keeping you safe this way came with the price of every enemy I have discovering my weakness."

"Oh." She straightens up slightly in her chair. "I never thought of that either."

"I don't expect you to." The chicken flips over. "You're not a criminal."

"So I'm your weakness?"

"I'd be a poor host if I married you to save your life from one maniac and lost you to another, don't you think?"

Hollie chuckles softly and gradually relaxes.

"Tell me about your new client."

"He's a fan, apparently. He's proposing to his girlfriend and the musician previously booked pulled out, so he called

Tiffany in a panic and she put him through. He seems nice, but he's paying me an obscene amount."

"How much?" As the chicken finishes, I drain the pasta while keeping a close eye on Hollie.

"Fifteen grand."

"That's nothing."

"To you, maybe." Hollie snorts. "But to me, it's enough that next year, I can send my parents away on the holiday they always talk about but never take. And maybe get a nicer apartment."

"You have access to my finances," I reply, setting the pasta pot back down. "I could pay for both of those."

"No."

"No?" I pour the homemade tomato and pesto sauce over the pasta.

"It's... I'm not in this situation to take advantage of your money. If you want to do something nice with it, consider donating it to those in need. I'm capable of taking care of my own life."

"You're shaming me for my lack of charitable deeds?"

Hollie pushes off the counter and laughs. "I'm just saying, people with money like you are never doing the right things with it. It's all penthouses and yachts, cars and clothes. It's never charity or helping real people."

"Charity will be my downfall."

"How so?" She starts to wander away toward the lounge, examining statues and decorations as she walks.

"I can't anonymously donate in the way you might expect. Hardly the safest way to maintain a criminal empire."

"Not much of an empire if some charitable deeds can end your reign."

Holly starts opening cupboards and drawers, vanishing from my sight while I remove the peppers from the oven and fill them with the chicken. By the time they're smothered in cheese and under the grill, Hollie's located a large cardboard box and set it on the couch.

"You have Christmas decorations but you don't decorate?"

My heart stills faintly in my chest while I watch her open the flaps and remove a blue and silver streamer that holds onto its glossy glint despite not seeing the light of day in years. "Those aren't mine."

She pauses and eyes me quizzically. "Then whose are they?"

"My brother's."

"You have a brother?" A red and gold streamer follows.

"I did."

Hollie pauses and her hands lower. "Oh, shit... I'm not desecrating some kind of memory, am I?"

"Not at all. This was his penthouse about ten years ago. We used to decorate it together because my father often put me to work because he was the baby. After he died... I lost the desire."

"How did he die?"

I can't answer her and instead return the meal. The silence drags on long enough that Hollie accepts it, but when I next look up, she's started taking all the decorations out of the box. A small Christmas tree rests on the coffee table, a Santa figurine balances against the wall, the streamers are draped over the couch, and she's using tape to stick them to the walls.

It's... amusing. And somewhat painful. In ten minutes, she transforms my lounge from the empty, bland pages of the catalog the furniture came from to a room full of color and life.

My heart hurts.

I don't deserve such treatment, not even in the slightest. Maybe it's her way of making herself feel at home.

"There," she declares with her hands on her hips. "Now your place looks like someone actually lives here and not like we're in a show home. Which, no offense, if minimalist is where your heart lies, then you should have expected this after we were at my parents' house.

"Ahh, so I'm the fool," I reply, spooning the pasta into two dishes and one Tupperware container.

"It's true."

Hollie moves around the lounge and adds a few more decorations. There's a rug with snow-covered boot prints which she unfurls in front of the window (because apparently, Santa would use the balcony to save his back), some white glittering boots to be hung on the wall, a sprig of holly set on the mantel and then mistletoe that she hangs above the door without missing a beat.

Mistletoe.

I turn down the grill and approach Hollie while her back is turned. I'm a foot away when she seemingly senses my presence and her shoulders raise as she turns.

I don't hesitate.

Under the sprig of mistletoe dangling precariously from the doorframe, I grasp her wrist in one hand and pull her forward. As soon as she's close, my other arm glides around her waist, and I pull her close and kiss her.

Hollie freezes up against me and squeaks in alarm just long enough for me to realize I've made the wrong call. But as I jerk away, heat flushes through my body at the wide, surprised look on her face when our eyes meet.

"Maxim, what are you doing?"

"If you have to ask me that, then I've read this situation very wrong indeed. I'm so—"

My words melt into a smothered groan as her lips crash back against my own. Her hand that's not in my grasp cups my cheek, and she pulls me down to her level while arching her body into mine with a soft, needy whine.

So I didn't misread things?

Confusion clashes with lust in my gut. She kissed me in the car because she wanted to, because perhaps she shares the same simmering feelings I felt since that night in the bar. And this crazy situation that's brought us crashing together makes a little more sense when we're together.

"You're not mad," I murmur when the kiss breaks and she gasps for air.

"No," she whispers, leaning heavily into me.

"You're...?"

"I don't know, but if you talk for too long, then I might change my mind ,so...?" She arches one brow.

I don't need her to tell me twice.

Lowering my haunches, I release Hollie's wrist in favor of grabbing her by the thighs just under the swell of her ass and sweeping her up into my arms. She squeals in delight, looping both arms around my neck for balance and winding her legs around my waist once she's high enough. Keeping her secure with one hand, my other reaches for the oven on the way past to turn it off as Hollie kisses me deeply.

She grinds so hard into me that the heat from her core presses against my abdomen and another spike of lust shoots south to my cock. Her hands graze through my hair, stroke through my beard, and clasp the sides of my neck, all while she kisses me repeatedly. I barely make it to my bedroom before my jeans have become too tight and the silky fabric of her sleepwear irritates me.

It stands between me and what I want.

Her.

Releasing her, I drop Hollie onto my bed and she wails softly and lands with a gentle bounce. Her long legs splay open as she lands but just as she tries to close them, I'm over her with my hand cupping her heat and my other grasping the side of her neck.

"Take your clothes off," I demand softly.

"Make me," she challenges, propped up on one elbow.

"Are you sure you want me to?" I ask, studying the cheeky glint in her eyes that sparkles deeper against the rosy flush rising in her face.

"If you need help taking my clothes off, then maybe you should walk out of here and leave me to take care of myself," Hollie remarks.

My pants tighten further and my blood floods with the heat of desire. "I don't need *any* help."

23

HOLLIE

Maxim doesn't hesitate. Before I can take my next breath, he tears off my silken shorts and discards them off the bed somewhere. Then he drops to his knees in front of me, drags me by the calf to the edge of the bed and buries his face between my thighs.

It's so sudden that there's no time for me to prepare for the kiss of his mouth against the outer lips of my pussy. One of his arms loops under my thigh and around to my hip while the other rests beneath me. His fingers slide through my pussy, part my outer lips and then his hot, soft tongue presses flat against me.

The shock of pleasure makes me jolt on the bed, and my abdominal muscles contract as pleasure diverts south, beading at my core.

Maxim moans as his tongue weaves back and forth through my folds like I'm the most divine thing he's ever tasted. There are no thoughts in my mind, only heated desire as ecstasy dances over my skin leaving a trail of goosebumps up my arms and down my legs. I toss my head back and forth, writhing under Maxim's talented tongue that repeatedly switches from soft and flat to firm and pointed. I grasp the sheets beneath me, whimpering and pressing my head back onto the mattress while rolling my hips up into his mouth.

He kisses me, his lips seal lightly over my clit and he sucks, sending a sharp ripple of pleasure through me.

I'm burning up. It's too much and not enough at the same time. His fingers enter me swiftly, slicked in my own juices and the slight ache from the sudden stretch of his thick digits vanishes the moment he curls them and touches a spot hidden deep inside me.

"Maxim!" I jerk one hand down and grab his hair as my orgasm erupts through me. I sink into darkness, screwing up my eyes and moaning deeply while shocks of pleasure twitch every nerve in my core and limbs, and Maxim continues to lap at my pussy like he never intends to stop.

My breath catches in my throat, my overheated skin drags against the soft sheets, and they stick to my back as I writhe back and forth. My thighs close around Maxim's head, but that only seems to encourage him because he keeps going. The intense attention of his tongue against me, his fingers inside me, and his suctioning technique continue even as I tip over the edge into over-sensitiveness. But there's no pain. Maxim's tongue becomes flatter and softer as he eats me out, occasionally shoving himself deeper between my thighs as if he's not close enough for his own desires.

He wrings a second orgasm out of me before I've even caught my breath from the first.

When he pulls away, I'm left boneless and panting on the bed with my mouth open as I gasp in deep lungfuls of air. My heart pounds fiercely and my pussy throbs in time to the frantic beats. I'm too hot and yet I miss Maxim's warmth like a craving. He stands over me, this gigantic man with long curves of muscle that dwarf me in every sense of the word. Watching him remove his shirt makes my mouth water, and even in the low light, every beautiful detail of his full-body tattoo is easy for me to follow. He drops his jeans, and then his boxers.

Propping up on one elbow, I gaze between his legs and if my mouth weren't already open then it would be now. I barely saw him in the club when we fucked all those months ago. It was a drunken, frantic mess but the ache I had the following day is something I'll never forget.

Now I see why.

His cock juts proudly out between his legs, dripping with need and my heart skips a beat. Did he get that hard just from eating me out? Did I taste that good, or does he just really enjoy being between a woman's legs? Maxim takes himself in hand and strokes from the thick base of his cock all the way up to the swollen, dark crown. As fluid swells at the tip of his cock, something pulls me forward and before I can stop myself, my lips are around that crown and I suck down the beading drops of pre-cum escaping him.

A surprised moan of desire rumbles through Maxim and a very gentle hand caresses the side of my head as I suck just on the end of his cock. The earthy, salty taste washes over my tongue but I'm far too focused on the weight in my mouth and the throbbing of my body.

I want him.

I want him more than I've ever wanted anything in my life.

But just as I shift to take more of his cock into my mouth, Maxim pulls away and an unexpected whine of disappointment escapes my throat.

"Don't fret," Maxim says, his voice low and deep. "I'm going to fuck that pretty mouth of yours."

Our eyes meet. His are as dark as the night sky and red dashes over his cheekbones. He grasps my shoulders, flips me onto my back, and drags me to the edge of the bed so my head hangs over the edge. It's unbelievably thrilling to be manhandled like I weigh nothing, and excitement bursts through my chest. Face to face with his cock, my mouth obediently falls open and I take a deep breath, then Maxim slides his cock home in my throat.

It's impossible not to choke at the stretch in my throat when he pushes past the back of my tongue, but any faint doubts in my mind turn to pride when the softest, neediest moan of pleasure reaches my ears from Maxim.

I did that.

I made him make that sound.

My eyes flutter close and I focus on the heat coursing through my body, the heady taste of Maxim on my tongue and the stretch of his thick cock each time he thrusts into my throat. He's gentle at first. A few languid thrusts to let me get used to the feeling. I curl one hand into the sheets for balance while my hips thrust with a jealous ache. I want to feel him deep inside me, to feel that stretch and ache as he fucks me with the same desperation I recall from the bar.

Suddenly, fabric tearing reaches my ears and both of Maxim's hands land on my now bare breasts. He squeezes and massages, tweaks and pulls my nipples, caresses my ribcage and then takes one of my hands in his. As our fingers lace together, his thrusts into my throat lose all finesse and melt into a desperate chase of pleasure.

Fast, sharp thrusts that rob me of my ability to breathe regularly. Each time I choke, Maxim moans and it takes every ounce of my determination to keep myself focused on sucking when I can. He grips my hand tight and teases my nipples with his other, then Maxim buries himself so deep in my throat that his thighs brush my cheeks. His free hand skims over my neck, and a strange, guttural sound escapes him as if he can't believe what he's feeling, then he removes himself in a hot rush.

I'm gasping and coughing as he hauls me upward once more, so disoriented from the rush of cool air in my lungs that I don't realize I'm in his lap until his cock impales me to the core and a strangled, desperate moan wretches out of me. I claw at his shoulders as his cock spears me open, burying so deep inside me that he can surely feel how fast my heart is beating with the tip of his cock.

"I want to look at you," he says gruffly, cupping my face with his warm hand and catching my gaze. "I want to see your face while I fuck you."

I'm speechless, reduced to moans and gasps as he does just that. He keeps one hand on my face and the other around my waist while he rests on his knees and fucks me with such power that everything is a blur. The furious pounding of his hips, the drag and stroke of his length inside me, the hot pleasure coiling in my core with every thrust, the whimpers and moans literally fucked out of me with every bounce on his cock; I'm at his mercy and drinking up every delicious second of it. He fucks me like everything about me drives him crazy, keeps me close like he can't bare an inch between us, and kisses me like it's the only thing in the world that matters.

No one in my life has fucked me like this before.

I come on his cock with a scream that mingles between our kisses and Maxim's own moans as he finds his end inside me with a sudden hot rush. I'm trembling, only able to focus on breathing as every muscle tightens, and for a long moment, I'm suspended on his cock with my pussy rhythmically pulsing and clamping down.

It's the most intense orgasm of my life.

And it doesn't end there.

Maxim gets me some water but can't keep his hands off me while I drink. He brings me to another orgasm with just his fingers and intense eye contact that makes me feel incredibly exposed, but it's one of the most erotic things I've ever experienced. While I'm twitching and quivering from the pleasure afterward, he gathers me in his arms and slides his cock between my thighs, using my own juices as lubrication. He fucks between my thighs until he's close, then I wrestle out of his arms and finish him with my mouth.

We fuck until the sun peeks over the horizon and the room turns pink from early light, falling asleep tangled in one another's arms. I don't even realize I'm asleep until a call comes through on my phone and I'm dragged from groggy, sex-filled dreams.

I'm lying on Maxim's broad chest, my head tucked under his chin, and both his thick arms around me, even in sleep. He's so warm that opening my eyes feels impossible, but my phone doesn't stop ringing.

Groaning, I lean toward the bedside table and blindly seek it out. Maxim's arms tighten around my waist, keeping me against him while I stretch until my fingertips brush the cold, vibrating device.

"Hello?" I croak, pressing the phone to my ear.

"Miss Wolfe?"

I finally open my eyes, squinting as I try to place the voice. "Mhm?"

"It's Mr. Havershire."

"Oh!" I straighten up, placing a hand on Maxim's broad chest.

He's awake now, watching me with half-lidded eyes and a light smirk across his lips.

"Is now a good time?" Mr. Havershire asks. "I'm eager for a demonstration of your skills. I know how well you play, but I'd like to hear you play the songs I've requested so I can best decide when to pop the question."

My entire lower body throbs. I'm sticky and sore and the thought of going anywhere right now is too daunting. "Does that need to happen today?"

"Your manager said today would be perfect."

"Today—" My hand flies over my mouth as Maxim suddenly rolls us over until he's on top. His face buries into my neck on the opposite side of my phone and he rolls his hips down against me, showing off his already hard cock. "I– I'm not sure I can make it today!"

"Is everything alright?"

"Yes!" I gasp as Maxim's teeth graze down my throat and his hot cock slides perfectly between my thighs. "I'm just—" His rough palm grazes up my side to my ribs, then grasps my breast and squeezes. Lust surges through me and settles hot in my core. "I'm sick, I'll call you back!"

I barely have time to end the call before Maxim's lips are locked onto mine and the thick ridge of his cock presses against my aching pussy.

"No work today," he murmurs against my lips.

"You'll need to pay me what I miss," I gasp, my eyes fluttering closed as his cock continues to tease against me.

"I'll pay you whatever you need," he murmurs, sucking lightly on my lower lip. "Just, no work."

"Mmm, okay, but I really need to shower."

"I'll help."

Maxim is true to his word. He does help me shower later, but all my efforts to get clean are erased the moment he fucks me over the counter while mourning the ruins of last night's dinner.

24

MAXIM

A sex marathon was never on the cards and yet somehow, Hollie and I spent all day yesterday fucking like we were teenagers discovering pleasure for the first time.

And it's not over.

By the time Saturday dawns, I'm still not satisfied. I want to taste her lips against mine all the time, feel her pussy gripping my cock like she never wants to let go, feel her nails rake over my tattoos like she's trying to leave her own imprint.

I want to be inside her and never leave just so I can hear those sweet, adorable moans whenever I want.

But duty calls.

"Maxim," Hollie murmurs as my arms circle her waist and I pull her close against me, distracting her from the water bottle she's trying to fill up. "I really have to go. I've postponed this guy enough and you're going to make me late."

"Who cares," I say softly, nuzzling underneath her ear. "Stay with me and fuck like rabbits like we did all day yesterday."

"My pussy can't take much more," she groans. "Trust me, she needs a break."

"Are you sure about that?" My hand glides down her abdomen and cups her core through her skirt, causing Hollie to gasp and jerk her hips back into me. "It doesn't sound like she needs a break."

"Don't listen to her," Hollie moans. "She doesn't know what she wants."

"Are you *really* sure about that?" As I talk, I gather her skirt up until it's bunched at her waist and slip my hand between her warm thighs. The heat radiating from her pussy is mouthwatering and my cock twitches in my pants.

"Don't you have somewhere to be?" she gasps, unable to stop her hips from rolling into my palm. "We're both late and I need to talk to you, but you said we don't have time!"

She's right. My father's waiting, and he's blowing up my phone with constant messages, judging by how often it vibrates in my back pocket. But Hollie's irresistible and I suspect she wants to talk about our sudden and frantic fucking. Once we bring logic into this, there's a chance I'll lose her, so I'll happily delay that *talk* as long as I can.

"I am late," I say, sucking gently on her earlobe. "And I'm starving."

"Maxim!" Hollie squeals as I scoop her up and dump her on the counter, then I fall to my knees and pull her hips off the counter and onto my shoulders while burying my face in her pussy. She's left with her shoulders and arms scrabbling for balance on the counter as I drag my tongue over her panties.

Her resistance melts away, and within seconds, her panties are soaked from my tongue and her juice. Moving them aside with my teeth, I shove my face into her pussy and soak my beard in her juices while dragging my tongue over her swollen clit to the music of her breathless moans above me. She tastes as divine as she did yesterday and I'm utterly addicted to the searing heat that warms my cheeks as I eat her out, the softness of her thighs and the silky texture as I slide my tongue inside her.

Hollie, over-sensitive from our day of fucking, comes within a matter of seconds and prods my chest sharply when I kiss her thigh and stand back up.

"You're an asshole," she pants, sweat beading her hairline. "Now I'm really going to be late!"

It was difficult to part from Hollie, but an hour later, I climb the steps to my father's brownstone and let myself in, my attention down on my phone as the tracker alerts me that Hollie's reached her destination. Toto is with her and Stu is shadowing them, so she's safe, but that doesn't stop the worried hamster from looping around my thoughts.

"Maxim?" Dad's voice cuts through my distraction as I enter his office.

"Hey."

"You're fucking late," he snaps.

I stop just shy of the door and stare at him blankly. "You're lucky I'm here at all."

"Why?" Dad's momentary confusion melts into a cold understanding. "You're not still hung up on that, are you?"

"*Hung up* on your trying to kill my wife?" Anger licks at my gut.

"She's hardly your wife. You've known her five minutes."

"That's longer than I've known the woman *you* wanted me to marry. You think I will just forgive you at the drop of a hat?"

"You, of all people, should know why she's dangerous," Dad snaps, slamming his fist down onto his desk. "We've been over this!"

"You tried to kill her. There's no excuse you can give that I'll make peace with until you look her in the eye and apologize."

Dad scoffs. "Out there in the real world, they all see you've married the daughter of an ex-police chief. How do you think that makes me look?"

"If you called me here to argue about this, then I'm leaving."

"No, I called you here because of this." Dad picks up a green folder and tosses it across the desk toward me. "We lost four shipments. Two were caught in the snow and stolen, the other two were stopped at a search and raided. The weather is fucking us up and we need a new plan."

I pick up the folder and scan the reports, noting the cost of the drugs lost due to the weather and the cops. It's an occupational hazard when it comes to traffic stops from the cops, but the weather is something else. "How behind does this put us?"

Dad sighs and takes his seat. "Given that those were to carry us through until the New Year, it's a blow. When our clients can't get what they want, who will they turn to?"

The Irish. My teeth sink into my lower lip as I set the folder down. "So we use the restaurants."

"How?" Dad meets my gaze.

"Easy. We can use the city's own shipments against them. You know how hard they work to ensure the soup kitchens are stocked at this time of year, and no one is going to interrupt a food delivery for the homeless. So we hijack a couple of their trucks, let the city do the work for us, and everyone wins."

"You think it will work?"

I shrug, crossing my arms. "Make sure you use men who can keep their mouths shut, and we're fine. I'll have Rex look into distributors. Just make sure the drugs are ready to move."

"Hmm." Dad's brow wrinkles and I see the appreciation in his eyes though he will never voice it. I had a good idea and only I will acknowledge that.

"Is that everything?"

Dad grunts and I turn to leave, but as I reach the door, he calls out to me. "Maxim."

"What?"

"You..." He hesitates and for a moment, he looks pained. Rather than entertain him, I reach for the door and he speaks once more. "Do you not see the danger you're in? What she could do to you?"

I pause, then turn to face him. "This isn't the same."

"Isn't it?" He stands abruptly. "Your brother did the same thing you're doing. He married an outsider. He cast away tradition and loyalty and married that bitch, and the next thing we know, he's dead!"

"Dad... he was killed by a drunk driver. That's not her fault. It's not *anyone's* fault."

"If it wasn't for her demanding to see her parents at Christmas, he would have been with us instead of on that road that night. Don't you see? He wasn't with the families, he wasn't in the right place because of some outsider bitch getting her claws into him and taking him away from his family!"

My heart clenches like a fist is reaching up from my gut. "He was doing something kind for the woman he loved, and if I remember correctly, they were only going to her parents' because *you* insisted that she couldn't stay here. If you want to blame someone, then blame yourself."

"That's not true." He moves around the desk. "She was welcome, just not that night. Family night. That was supposed to be just us."

"But she was part of him and you couldn't accept her."

"Inviting an outsider into a dinner of the top Mafia leaders in the city? You *know* how stupid that is. And he knew. He just wanted to make an exception, and exceptions get people killed!"

It's an argument with no end, because we will never agree, but as our eyes meet, I see a flash of the real pain inside him. A father whose son was taken from him far too soon. My anger softens.

"My situation is different. I'm trying to keep Hollie out of this life."

"For how long?" Dad rubs at his jaw. "I can't lose you, Maxim. Not you too. I'm not—" He hesitates. "If the same thing were to happen to you and I couldn't stop it..."

"Dad..." Sympathy swells inside me and I take a few steps closer. "The only thing pushing me away right now is you. Not her. For one thing, Hollie is being kept out of this life as much as I can keep her out. And she's nice. If you don't want the same thing to happen, then apologize. And mean it."

The pain in Dad's eyes melts away and he turns around, walking back to his desk. "I'll get you a list of names who won't talk."

Momentary bonding over, it seems. Staring at his retreating back, I linger for a few seconds and then leave the room. On some level, I understand him. He's preached all my life about the dangers of outsiders and I lost my brother because he was with one.

But in the end, it was a terrible accident.

Outside, the snow falls around me carrying the threat that at any moment, one wrong flake or patch of ice could bring me, or anyone I care about, to the same fate. Pulling my phone from my pocket, I head to my car but just as I'm about to text Toto about the car tires, Hollie calls.

"Hello?"

"Hey!" She sounds happy to see me and it makes my heart lift.

"How was your rehearsal?"

"It was fine. He was a little pissed at the delay and stuff, but he liked what I did so we're set. But I actually, uhm... There's something I'd really like to talk to you about. Could we do something? Maybe go shopping and talk?"

"Is everything alright?" My phone buzzes once. "Hold that thought, actually."

Checking the screen, my heart dips. It's a 911 text.

And it's from Zoe.

25

HOLLIE

"**W**here is she?" As soon as the door is open, Maxim leads the way into the apartment while I hesitate on the steps.

An elderly woman clings to the door with tears in her eyes and points down the hallway. "She locked herself in the bathroom."

"Zoe?" Maxim doesn't falter.

As I step inside, a large pair of curious, wary eyes peers up at me from behind the elderly woman. A boy. He can't be older than four and he clutches at the woman's skirt with one fist.

"Hi. I'm Hollie."

My plans to sit down and talk to Maxim have been derailed by whatever's happened here, but as soon as he explained that Zoe was the survivor of that terrible attack, nothing else mattered.

The child doesn't reply and neither does the woman, so I cautiously follow Maxim's path to the end of the hall as Toto and Stu file in behind me. Maxim stands against a locked door with one hand against it.

"Are you sure, Zoe?"

"Are you calling me a liar?" screeches a panicked voice from inside.

"No, but I want to make sure before I hurt someone who doesn't deserve it."

"It was him! I saw him! Please, Maxim, don't let him find me!"

Maxim glances at me, kisses me on the top of the head, and rushes back down the hall toward Toto and Stu. A brief discussion ensues, and then Maxim and Stu bolt out the door.

"Maxim?" Zoe calls cautiously.

"He's gone," I reply cautiously. "I think he's away to look for..." I hesitate. Not wanting to say the wrong thing, I end up remaining completely quiet.

"Who are you?" hiccups the tear-filled voice.

"I'm Hollie. I'm Maxim's... wife."

"Oh. He brought you?"

"We were going to go shopping, but he got your message and this is more important."

"Oh." The voice cracks slightly and sniffling follows. "Sorry."

"Don't be," I say softly. "Maxim is here for you." I can't fathom what this woman has been through, even from

Nancy's tale of the kidnapping. Surviving it might almost be worse than experiencing it.

"I saw him," Zoe weeps, and the door creaks as if she's leaning against it. "I swear it was him."

My chest tightens. "You saw who?"

"The man who did this to me." More sniffles follow. "I didn't think I would recognize him, but I saw him and his dark hair and that cold smirk and the heart on his wrist when he reached for me, and I just—"

"He tried to grab you?"

Zoe dissolves into tears on the other side of the door. I crouch down as her voice seems to be lower now. She cries, and my heart breaks, so I press one hand to the door. "Maxim will find him."

"What if he followed me?" she gasps. "I ran and I ran. All over. I ran for hours so he couldn't follow me home, but what if he still did?"

"I know Maxim will take care of this. He will find a new place for you and your family, I have no doubt. And he will find the man who did this to you." If the determined look on Maxim's face was anything to go by, it's only a matter of time.

"You don't know that," Zoe weeps. "He won't ever leave me alone!"

She cries until she starts to choke and Toto has to break down the door because I'm terrified something will happen to her. In the end, she's only choking on her own tears and she dissolves into frantic weeping in my arms. She cries until she has nothing left, and then she lets me gently clean her up and tend to the cuts and scrapes on her bare feet from when she abandoned her shoes because she thought they hindered her escape.

She signed herself out of the hospital against medical advice two days ago, and he already found her.

No wonder Maxim is furious. He's been searching for that bastard for weeks.

I've never seen someone look as broken as Zoe. She's covered in bandages with a few of them stained red from reopened wounds. Her breathing is labored and by the time Maxim returns, my concern is so high that he immediately agrees with me.

Zoe and her family are taken by Stu to a private hospital where she will receive medical care and round-the-clock security until that monster is found. She doesn't protest. She falls scarily quiet when being loaded into the ambulance and the sight of her confused, upset child haunts me.

"Will she be safe?" I ask Maxim as we walk together under the twinkling streetlights that capture the snow as it drifts down around us. I won the argument about being driven home while Maxim walked to process everything, insisting we should stay together.

Toto lingers somewhere behind along with a few other guards I've not been told the names of.

"Yes," Maxim replies, rubbing his eyes. "She would have been if she hadn't checked out."

"She wanted to be back with her family. I can't blame her."

"Family," Maxim murmurs. "It makes people do the craziest things."

I slide my hand into Maxim's and grip tightly. My heart lifts when he clutches me back. "Did you find him, then?"

"No. We tracked the store she saw him at and Rex was working on the security tapes, but so far, it looks like she just had a flashback and scared herself. We'll keep looking, though."

"Poor thing. The trauma and the pain she must be going through." Any lingering sympathy I held for the monster shot dead in the restaurant vanished the moment I saw Zoe's beaten face. There's no more doubt that someone capable of such cruelty doesn't deserve to live. And the second monster out there, hiding, deserves the same fate.

"She's strong," Maxim replies. "But she shouldn't have to be. My men have been working around the clock trying to—" He trails off. "I need to talk about something else before I explode."

I caress his knuckles with my thumb. "Okay, then tell me, is this sort of thing normal?" We turn into a quiet park enclosed with trees and black fence. "Do you usually kill people in pizzerias?"

Maxim snorts softly. "Not usually. In my line of work, death is rare. It's a double-edged sword. My father believes getting rid of anyone and everyone who stands in your way or threatens you is the best way."

"And you don't?"

He shakes his head and snow crunches nicely under our feet. "No. Because once you start killing those who don't deserve it to threaten those who do, you invite in those assholes who don't fear death. Then you have nothing to hold over them. A threat is a delicate thing and only works if someone has something to lose. In my world, it's hard to care and harder to put pressure on that care. But death? You feel it once and it starts to lose its effect."

"So, why does he do it? Your Dad?"

"He's from a time when dying was the scariest thing that could happen. But the world is shittier now. Death, for a lot of people, no longer feels like the worst thing. For many, it's an escape."

"That's so sad." I lean into him, cradling his hand in both of mine.

"This world is sad. So I try new things. Give people a little hope and they'll be more loyal than a threat to their family."

"Threatening their family, hmm?" I gaze up at him. "Where have I heard that before?"

"I had a role to play," Maxim replies. "I'm sorry. For people outside this world, I suppose the old school threats still work because it is the worst thing that can happen."

"It is," I agree. With no stake in this world, Maxim controls. The only thing of worth I have is my parents. And now him, to an extent, and the baby growing inside me. All of them fall under the family umbrella and would make me cave.

"Enough of that, though," Maxim says. "Tell me about your rehearsal."

"Oh! It was short, actually. He wanted me to play a few specific songs, which was fine, and he wanted my guarantee that I would be there and not cancel. I told him the money was far too good to cancel, and then he got a call and things were over."

"Does that happen a lot?" Maxim asks, his breathing becoming less tense. "People want to see you beforehand?"

"Only with private bookings. Everywhere else I've worked relies on word of mouth, and I have a good reputation. Hotels will book me without hesitation if I fit their vibe for that year. But it depends. Some years are better than others."

"And this is what you want to do with your life?"

"Actually..." I hesitate briefly. "Uhm... I was actually thinking of leaving New York. Signing on for a cruise or something. They pay well, and I'd get to travel and escape this place."

"You want to escape?"

It sounds silly now and my cheeks warm. "Before... all this, I felt stuck. My mom was always on my case, signing me up for things or volunteering me without letting me know and then getting pissed when I didn't show. My dad would have my back, but often, he'd also pull the *'You only get one mother'* card as if I were letting him down. I felt... smothered."

"Having a cop for a father must be interesting."

"Are you digging for dirt?" I tease softly.

"Maybe. Are you going to give it to me?" He meets my eyes with a light smirk. Walking through the park, we approach the exit, and a car pulls up with Stu in the driver's seat.

"My dad was distant and strict growing up. He became a *dad* after retiring early due to an injury. That and I think a heart attack scare from my mom finally put things into perspective for him."

"What did he work on?"

"He never talked about that. Other than a few morality lessons over the rare dinners he would be at. Is it weird for you? That he's a cop?"

"Well..." Maxim sighs deeply, his breath clouding out past his lips and drifting high into the sky. Our brief walk and chat seem to have relaxed him somewhat. "It certainly puts an odd spotlight on me. People talk. I have loyalties to prove. That sort of thing."

"Can't help that you helped decorate his home," I tease as we reach the car. "Which, speaking of... come to the fair with me."

Maxim's hand lingers on the door and he raises one brow. "What?"

"There's a Christmas fair I love going to. Come with me."

"I don't do fairs."

"And I don't take no for an answer," I reply with a pout, releasing his other hand. "Unless this is your way of telling me that you never want to see under this again." As sexily as I can, I smooth my hands down the thick coat keeping me warm in the cold.

"Targeting what a man holds dear... you learn fast."

I smirk and stick out my tongue. "You did say you give them hope and then threaten that, so... you're coming with me."

"Alright." Maxim chuckles as he opens the door. "I'll come to the fair with you."

26

MAXIM

"Isn't this just one of the most beautiful places you've ever seen?"

A few miles from her parents' place, Hollie stands in front of me smiling from ear to ear and splaying her arms out underneath the swirling wooden sign welcoming everyone to the Christmas fair. Just beyond her are countless stalls filled with an array of Christmas-themed goodies, with a sea of people moving between each one like the rising swell of the tide. Three days ago, I agreed to come with her, and she made sure I kept my promise.

"What exactly do we do here?" I ask, closing the gap and stepping into Hollie's space.

She stares up at me with a frown. "Damn, you weren't kidding. You really haven't ever been to a Christmas fair before?"

"I really haven't."

Her lips purse, then her gloved hand slides into mine and she pulls me under the sign. "You don't really *do* anything but experience it. You breathe so deeply that the cold invades your lungs and stays there, you admire everyone's handiwork and spend more money than you can afford on pretty items and good food, and then everything you buy ends up on the Christmas tree which, by the way..." She turns and walks backward while still leading me. "I searched that entire penthouse and didn't find a single tree, so we should pick one."

"I can buy a tree from here?"

"Of course! There should be a stall at the far end where you can purchase a ticket that will let you go and look at the trees."

"Hold on, I need to buy a ticket in order to look at the trees I might want to buy?"

"Mhm."

"Sounds like a scam."

Her eyes narrow and she turns back around. "You're only saying that because you can't fathom doing nice things for people."

She's got me there.

Hand in hand, we merge with the crowd and wander between the stalls while Toto, Stu, and the rest of my security team melt in like they belong here. There are a thousand important things I should be doing for the family right now, but none of them rise above spending time with Hollie.

She's warming to me in ways I can only dream about, and part of me watches her with slight anticipation that this is part of some ploy, but a larger part of me simply enjoys it. We pass an array of stalls carrying all sorts of items and treasures I never would have given a second glance if not for the way her face lights up.

She spends ten minutes talking to a woman who hand-weaves her own garlands, then buys a bunch and demands I put them up on all the doors. At another stall, she studies and pores over handmade jewelry created by an elderly man swathed in more layers than I can count. The wooden bracelets look carved from scratch and the beaded neck-laces sparkle even more than the ring on Hollie's finger. The love and care poured into these crafts speak wonders.

I purchase both a bracelet and a necklace, and then three wooden bird brooches for my team.

The next stall sells mulled wine served in tiny cups and the sweet, berry warmth seeps right down to my frozen toes on the first sip. Hollie passes and orders a hot orange instead, reminding me faintly of the childhood drink my mother would give me when I was sick.

After that pit stop, we continue wandering. Snow gathers in the air, but under the haze of lanterns lighting the way through the fair, it never quite seems to touch the ground. Even the cold December air is kept at bay by the crowd moving around us, but Hollie's hand permanently in mine is what warms me the most. The next stall sells wax artwork of various festive scenes, from the Nativity to falling stars, sheep, and Santa getting arrested. Toto's laughter reaches my ears from somewhere in the crowd at the sight and on our next loop past that stall, that particular painting has been purchased.

Several food stalls are the source of the sugary sweetness drifting through the air. They sell everything from meats and cheeses to Christmas cakes, puddings, and gingerbread men. Hollie purchases one and snaps the leg off, offering it to me while her lips seal around the head.

"I only get a leg?"

Hollie nods. "You're lucky you're getting anything. I love these things."

"Noted." Leaning down, I gently bite the gingerbread and take it from her gloved fingers.

Her eyes reflect the countless lights streaming above us between each stall, and I swear the pink flush on her cheeks darkens. Crunching the cookie, our eyes remained locked until a swell in the crowd spikes my protectiveness and I draw her closer to me.

"Where to next?"

She eats happily and looks around while stretching on her tiptoes, then points in one direction. "The trees should be down there, although we passed a ceramic stall that had a bowl my mom would love." She seems torn so I squeeze her hand.

"Let's get the bowl, then the tree."

"Do we have time?" Her attention dips to her phone.

"Do you have somewhere to be?"

She nods, glancing up at me. "Tiffany wanted to call me about the engagement party this weekend with that new client."

"Problems?"

"No, she's just overly cautious when it gets this close to Christmas. You've no idea how many people try to scrimp out on paying the entertainers because they don't deem us as important. Honestly, no one ever notices good music. They take it for granted. But bad music?" She rolls her eyes and stuffs her phone back into her pocket. "That'll get you struck off everyone's booking list."

"I've heard you play," I say, thinking back to the alliance party she ended up playing at. "It was beautiful." Never has a meeting between myself and the Italians been cut short because of music before, but something about Hollie's playing put everyone in a good mood that night.

Her cheeks flush and she ducks her head away from my gaze. "I try."

"If it's just a call, you have time. Come on, we can get you that bowl."

Hollie spins around and grins at me, but I barely see it.

I see him first.

His dark eyes.

His pale face.

The twist of his lips as he steels himself and pushes the last person out of his way. The knife in his hand glints like the last sparkle of a falling star, and our eyes meet as he lunges forward.

The hatred in his eyes is smothering. Rage that smolders like I'm being held over the lingering embers of a fire. He lunges. I grab Hollie by the shoulders and throw her out of his line of attack, spinning at the same time. The blade tears into the fabric of my thick sweater and sharp, hot pain flares up across my ribs.

Hollie's gasp of alarm turns into a scream of fear when she spots the crazed attacker. Keeping her safe is my only concern so the pain becomes second to ensuring I'm fully between her and the attacker.

"Maxim!" She yells and clutches at me, only for Stu to leap out of the crowd, sweep his arm around her waist, and scoop her away.

The second he has her, I spin around and block the next slash with my forearm against the man's wrist. He yells in rage, grunting as he grabs the hilt with both hands and tries to drive the knife down into my shoulder. I lash out, punching across his face, and he stumbles right to the ground. More and more of the crowd catch on to what's happening, and various screams mix with cries of alarm.

"Die!" He bellows as he climbs back to his feet, his arm swinging like it's on some kind of trigger. My hands and forearms block each rapid swing and slash of the knife. The blade catches on my clothes, nicks my skin, and sends splatters of blood across the snow with each frantic swing.

On his next lunge, I sidestep and punch him hard in the gut, grab his wrist, and drag his arm across my body as he stumbles. Kicking his knee, he goes down hard while I twist his wrist and force him to drop the knife. Then he's face down on the ground with his arm still in my grasp and wrenched up his back.

"Boss!" Toto's by my shoulder in a second with his gun aimed at the assailant, but before he pulls the trigger, I grab his wrist and lower it.

"Don't. Take him home."

"What?" Confusion melts across Toto's face until he peers over my shoulder and glimpses the face of the man swearing and cursing my existence. That confusion turns into understanding and he nods, holstering his weapon.

"On it."

Toto takes over pinning the man down as Rex appears and glances at me, concern knitting across his brows, but before he can speak, I'm scanning the crowd for Hollie.

"Where is she?"

"Stu has her by the wreaths," Rex replies. "We need to get you out of here."

His words barely reach me as I charge through the crowd toward the wreath stall several feet away. As the crowd finally parts, I glimpse Hollie in Stu's arms fighting him much like she did the first time we met. Her crimson hair flies about her face as she beats him with both her fists, though her blows are barely impactful if the look on his face is anything to go by.

They both spot me at the same time. Relief flashes across Stu's face while Hollie's mouth drops open and tears invade her beautiful eyes.

"Maxim!"

"Hollie, I'm alright."

"No, look at you!" She wrenches herself out of Stu's now relaxed grip and stumbles toward me. "What happened? What the hell was that?"

"I'm okay." My words mean nothing to her as she grabs both my arms and skims her eyes over me, then she whimpers.

"You're bleeding!"

"Boss," Stu warns. "We gotta go."

"I know. I know."

"Go? We have to take you to the hospital, oh my God!" She clutches at me repeatedly, trying to lift my arm to examine the wound, but I don't let her.

Instead, I take her by the arm and we start hurrying back through the fair to where we parked.

"This is insane," Hollie gasps. "Who was that? Was he trying to kill you? How did that even happen? Maxim, you're bleeding! Oh God, it looks so bad!"

Her frantic flurry of desperate pleas warms my heart as adrenaline pours through me like molten metal. My heart's pounding, my body's so hot that the winter chill is a distant thought, and as we approach my car parked in the vacant lot, I can't take my eyes off her.

"Hollie, I'm fine."

"Don't give me that!" She pushes against me, a single tear escaping her eye as she shoves me again. "I can see you're bleeding! You're hurt, and that man could have killed you.

What even was that? How can that happen? Why did everyone just stand around and—"

The only way to calm her, the only way to end her tirade, is to kiss her.

So I do.

As soon as we reach the car, I shove her against it, cup the side of her neck, and kiss her deeply while my heart pounds like a drum in my ears. I'm trembling. Pain doesn't exist right now. Only relief that I spotted him before he could do any real damage to me or her.

"Maxim—" Hollie groans against my lips, then her gloved hands land on either side of my neck.

She's safe.

She's fine.

Nothing else matters.

27

HOLLIE

My heart flies a mile a minute, my body burns up from fear and adrenaline while blood soaks into Maxim's white sweater, but all he cares about is kissing me.

We need to get to a hospital.

We need to get somewhere safe.

I don't want to lose him.

It's a scary thought that a man I was terrified of less than a week ago is now someone I actively want to keep in my life. The truth about him changed everything and now, on what was supposed to be a sweet night, he almost died before I could tell him my truth.

I should tell him right now.

But the words don't come because Maxim rapidly becomes a man possessed with desire. He winds one arm around my waist, pulls me away from the car, and then dumps me on the hood. The ice-cold metal seeps through my pants in seconds, a sharp contrast to the boiling heat pouring off Maxim as he presses me down with deep, desperate kisses. I slide on the hood of the car until his hips and thick, muscular thighs block me from sliding any further.

"Maxim," I gasp, quickly discarding my gloves so I can feel the warmth of his skin against my palms. "You're hurt—"

"No," he growls against me, his hips perfectly slotted in between my legs. "I'm fine."

"Don't lie to me," I gasp. "You need help, you need—"

"I need you." He cuts me off with a biting kiss that leaves my lower lip throbbing in time to my pounding heart. Then his warm hands are pulling my coat open and sliding under my shirt. He strokes over my belly and up to my breasts, grunting as he forces his fingers under my bra.

This can't be happening.

We're in public!

Stu is right there and yet Maxim doesn't seem to care. His tongue snakes into my mouth and he bites down lightly on mine while his fingers tweak both my nipples firmly enough to draw a whine of surprise from my throat.

It's hot.

The way he manhandles me is hot. The way he threw me to safety and stood between me and a crazed, armed maniac is more than hot. My core throbs as I replay that moment over and over, a safe thought now that Maxim is safely in my arms. But it's alarming. Like we're breaking some sort of rule and if I'm not careful, he'll end up in worse shape.

Maxim doesn't care.

He tweaks my nipples and gropes my breasts until I moan, he grinds his hips and his growing bulge against me until I whimper, he bites along my jawline and suckles hard on the soft juncture between my neck and shoulder, all while I rake my hands through his hair and pull hard enough to let him know how worried he made me.

Behind his head, snow drifts down from a pitch black sky and covers any bare skin in ice kisses. My forehead, my cheeks and hands, and then my belly and thighs when Maxim leans back and rips my pants down from my hips. I barely have a moment to protest before his fingers seek out my pussy and he thrusts two knuckles deep inside me.

"Maxim!"

It turns me on how much he wants me, turns me on so fast that my pussy throbs painfully with need. My thighs briefly close around his wrist as his fingers pump into me, but even those are removed swiftly once Maxim fishes his impressive, fat cock out of his pants.

He enters me with such force that I'm shoved up the hood of the car. Cold metal bites at my bare back and tangles my hair. His strong hands grip my hips and he jerks me back down, thrusting his cock deeper inside me. I barely catch my breath before Maxim's fucking into me with such speed and power that I'm utterly at his mercy.

My arms wind around his shoulders, my legs around his hips, and I cling to him as each rapid, frantic thrust punches moans, whines, and gasps right out of me. It's like he's taken control and I have no power over my own noises, my own breathing, or the insatiable lust that courses through me with each powerful stroke of his cock.

There's a constant mix of heat from his body and cold from the snow falling around us. We could get caught. People could be watching us right now, even Stu. There's no guarantee that we're even safe. My adrenaline spikes and an unexpected, delicious pull of *need* warms my core.

I need more.

I need Maxim.

"Fuck," he grunts, burying his face in my neck. His breath warms my collar and coaxes a shiver down my spine. "Fuck, your pussy's so fucking tight. So fucking hot. What you do to me is—" He cuts off with a deep grunt and his teeth latch onto my shoulder.

I dig my nails into the back of his neck, gasping repeatedly. Snowflakes land on my tongue and that sharp, bitter cold melts in an instant and Maxim suddenly devours my mouth in a sweltering kiss.

"I want to fuck you all day," he gasps, pounding into me with even more speed. "I wanna fuck you so hard you can't walk. Wanna leave my cock imprinted on you so you know you're meant only for me. *Fuck*— I wanna stay inside you always, you hear me?"

"Then do it," I gasp, my voice shuddering from the force of his fucking. "Imprint in me. Make my body never forget. Do it. Do it!"

He does. He wraps me in both his arms and holds me tight, pinning me to his broad torso, and he almost pulls me up from the hood of the car. With his knees bent and his teeth claiming the other side of my neck, he fucks me rapidly with countless short thrusts until we come together in an explosion of heat and breathless moans.

It's so intense my eyes roll back and everything briefly fades to nothing. The only thing I'm aware of is his cock splitting me open and the rush of heat inside me.

I blink, and suddenly, we're in the car with Maxim closing the door. Then he crawls over me and kisses me repeatedly.

"Holy shit," I gasp. "That was…" I'm dizzy, still floating from the sheer intensity of the pleasure that rushed through me alongside the overwhelming rush of adrenaline. "I—did anyone see?"

The car rumbles to life while Maxim continues to kiss me lazily. I cup his face, and I've forgotten everything until I caress down his body and my fingers come away sticky with blood.

Reality hits.

The man.

The knife.

Maxim's instinct to rescue me leading to that adrenaline-fueled fuck in the car.

"Maxim…" I cup his face with both hands and pull him away from nuzzling my neck. "What the fuck is going on?"

28

MAXIM

"Oh God, Maxim..." Hollie lays a gentle hand on my forearm while the other brushes under the freshly stitched wound on my ribs.

"It doesn't hurt."

"That's not the point," she mutters. "You should have gone to the hospital."

"Do you doubt Toto's stitching skills?"

"No." Her lips press into a fine line. "You got hurt and I don't understand why. And then you didn't seem to care."

"You weren't bothered while I was fucking you on the car." Flames crackle nearby as the faux fireplace sends waves of warmth washing over us where we sit on the couch.

"That was definitely the heat of the moment," she replies, unable to look away. "What happened? Who was that man?" Our eyes meet and she winces faintly. "Is he dead?"

"No. He's not dead."

Her eyes flicker. "Are you locking him up somewhere?"

"No." I bring my beer to my lips and drink slowly while she watches me until I lower it. "He'll be at home. Pissed, most likely."

"I don't understand."

"You don't need to."

"No!" Hollie suddenly prods her fingernail into my bare chest. "Don't do that. You've kept so much of your life secret and to some degree, I understand why, but you can't have me be present and then not explain something like that!"

My brows pinch together as I dwell on her words. She's right. I preach to my father that I keep her out of this life, but tonight reminded me of how that life will find a way to reach her regardless of my actions.

"Wouldn't you rather talk about what you wanted to talk about when we went to the fair?" Whatever she's been trying to tell me before life interrupts is surely more important.

"Stop. Tell me the truth." She sinks back into the cushions and crosses her arms. "Or that will be the last time we sleep together."

"Ouch." I wince playfully, then sigh. "Okay. Fine. That man... I know him."

"Is he a friend?"

"No. You know I had a brother."

She nods.

"He was younger than me. A little reckless. Didn't follow the rules the way you'd expect in this life. It's not uncommon in teenagers. Especially with our mom being gone and my dad being... well, you've seen him."

Again, she nods while tucking soft red strands behind her ear.

"He died. In a car crash. He should have been with us at Christmas like tradition dictates, but my father had a stick up his ass about his girlfriend being an outsider."

"What do you mean?"

"Typically, in this life, relationships remain in-house. Someone in this world can only find peace with someone else in this world. Everyone's already aware of the dangers and the expectations, y'know? But he... he fell for someone who wasn't part of this life. He kept wanting to include her but without going through the proper channels. There was no vetting, no investigation, no assurances that she wouldn't talk to the first cop she saw the second she got a whiff of something."

Hollie nods along while I talk, adjusting herself until her knee is resting against my thigh. "He didn't just marry her?"

I scoff softly. "What I did with you is highly irregular. I was *booked* to marry someone else, actually. It's all a business transaction at the end of the day. My father tried to talk sense into my brother and so did I, to an extent. But he was happy. And I couldn't fault that. Anyway." I take another drink. "He was supposed to be with us. We used to have a traditional dinner where the *Pakhan*, my father, hosts all the other leaders we're friendly with. As his sons, it was our duty to attend, but he brought his girlfriend and wanted to invite her family. A show of loyalty or something. It was dangerous for her and for them. My brother and dad argued and he left. He drove off with her to spend Christmas with them instead."

Hollie's mouth presses together and she reaches for me. It's not until her fingers brush my forearm that I realize I'm trembling. I've never told the whole story to anyone before.

"They were both killed when a drunk driver lost control in the snow and T-boned them. Doc said death was instant so they didn't suffer. But they died."

"Oh, Maxim..." Her hand slides down to my knuckles.

"My dad sees you as a threat. Because you're an outsider. In his own way, he fears the same thing happening to me. And that man from tonight? He's the brother of the girlfriend. I was the one who gave him the bad news back then, and ever since, he's blamed me. If anyone else did this to me?" I motion with the beer bottle toward the fresh wound on my ribs. "They would die. But with him... It's just misplaced grief. I can't fault him because what he feels for me is probably the same as what I feel for the bastard who crashed into them."

"That's awful," she breathes out softly, sliding closer. "So when your father tried to kill me, he was trying to protect you?"

"That's one way of looking at it. Our situations are different, but yes, he does see our arrangement as the same kind of threat that will ruin us."

She nods slowly. "I understand. I don't forgive, don't get me wrong. But holy shit... losing his wife and then his son. No wonder he's so intense. But that man…" She gazes up at me, her eyes darting back and forth between mine. "You just let him attack you?"

"He appears every so often, drunk and angry. It's not common and I'd praise his ability to find me if it hadn't put you in danger. But I can't bring myself to do anything to him because I know what it feels like. I spent months trapped in my own mind, wishing that the driver had survived so I could make them suffer. I can't bring them back, but I can do a little for him until his pain eases."

"That's noble." Hollie's fingers weave between mine. "And so fucked up."

"This life is fucked up. I'm sorry you had to see any of that."

"It's fine. I mean, if I have nightmares, I know where to go." A small smile creeps over her lips. "But seriously, that's intense. This whole life you lead is intense."

"And yet you don't ask about it." My head tilts. "You know I'm a criminal, yet you don't know what I do."

Her gaze falls away and she shrugs, slumping back down on the couch. "I dunno. You seem really nice so it's hard to imagine you hurting people now. Those girls at the club kept talking about how you helped them. And everything you're doing for Zoe… I guess I don't care. It feels like the less I know, the better."

"Are you sure?"

She nods slowly. "Besides, the more I know, then the bigger a threat I am."

"I don't see you that way."

Hollie locks eyes with me. "How do you see me?"

I'm about to answer when a wave of pain squeezes through my ribs. I wince and lean forward while Hollie takes the beer from my hands.

"You shouldn't be drinking."

"What are you, my doctor?"

Hollie snorts. "As good as."

"Hmm. So, what was it you wanted to talk to me about? Things have been getting in the way, but I have all the time now."

She pauses, then sets the beer bottle down on the coffee table and leans back. When our eyes meet, there's something uncertain in her eyes that I can't quite place, like something is just out of sight.

"I..."

I raise my brow slightly, trying to prompt her.

"When I was talking to Zoe, she mentioned something that I thought was kind of important. Although if it is, then taking this long to tell you is probably going to get me into trouble."

"Nonsense." Leaning toward her, I grit my teeth against a twinge of pain and take her hand. "What did she tell you?"

"Well... the person she saw in the store, or who she thought she saw... she said it was a tattoo on their wrist that scared her because she remembered one of the men who attacked her having, like, a heart on their wrist? Do you know if the guy you already caught had that?"

My phone is in my hand before she finishes speaking. "I can find out."

"I know it's common because I feel like I've seen similar tattoos, but if it's a new detail, maybe it can help?"

"Every detail helps." My thumb flies over the screen as I text Rex asking him to do some digging. If the fucker I killed has the tattoo, then I can reassure Zoe that the one she keeps thinking of is definitely dead. And if not, then it's one more detail to narrow down the search for the other cunt.

"Sorry I didn't say anything sooner. Everything was hectic and you were busy and stuff, y'know?"

"You're fine," I assure her softly. Rex replies with a thumbs up.

"Also..."

I glance at her, and her cheeks flush as she tilts her head. "Also?"

"This is going to sound so bad, but my parents want us at their Christmas party."

"When is it?"

"This Saturday."

"Isn't that when you have that engagement thing?"

"Mhm. So I was *kind* of hoping you'd say yes and go and keep my parents entertained while I work, and then I can meet you there after?" Her brows lift, hopefulness flooding her eyes.

"You think I, the Mafia prince, should spend my Saturday entertaining your parents while you work?"

She nods quickly.

"People will think I can't take care of my girl."

"Pretty please? You had a good time decorating the house with them, right? And this gig will only be a few hours, so they won't know I'm missing, *plus,* think how good it will look to them. My dad's a suspicious man, so think of it as keeping the peace."

I'd already decided my answer the second she asked me, and after texting Stu to reschedule my Saturday meetings, I nod. "Sure. It's in my best interests to keep you and your father happy."

"Yay!" Her face lights up but as I smile and lean toward her, my grimace of pain immediately erases her joy. "Right, that's it. You need to go to bed to rest."

"I'm fine."

"Bullshit. You used up all your goodwill when you fucked me on that car, so now you have to rest."

It's difficult to resist her when she looks so adorable while pouting angrily at me. As she climbs to her feet, she pulls on my hand despite our size difference, making it clear that I'm not going anywhere unless I choose. I relent quickly, though, and stand, allowing her to guide me through the apartment.

"You're bossy for a nurse, you know."

"And you're reckless for someone so apparently important, so we both have things to work on. Now get into bed and lie down."

I oblige, but as I sink down onto the mattress, I catch Hollie by the waist and drag her down with me. She lands with a squeal and a laugh while I seal both my arms around her body and pin her to my chest.

"Stay with me," I say, nuzzling into her hair and cautiously lying on my non-injured side.

She blows a few strands of hair out of her face and giggles, then cups my jaw. "Fine. But only if you rest."

"I promise."

29

HOLLIE

"I'm leaving Stu with you." Maxim grasps my thigh and leans in close for a kiss.

I return it eagerly and lightly touch his cheek, caressing down to his jaw as our lips lightly weave together. "I'll be fine."

"It wasn't a suggestion," Maxim murmurs. "It's the cost of my entertaining your parents until you get there."

"You'll have the time of your life, I promise."

Maxim rolls his eyes slightly as we part, and while his touch lingers on my thigh, sliding to my hip and then my backside as I exit the car, there's a pull of yearning in my chest. I should have asked him to come with me, and then we'd turn up to my parents' party late but together.

By the time I mull this over, the sedan has pulled away. Maxim and Toto melt into the night while Stu stands next to me, unable to look me in the eye. We've not spent much time together in the weeks I've been with Maxim. Other than his appearing to drive a car or watch from afar, the majority of our interaction came from our first night and he still hasn't apologized. If I didn't know how tough these men were, I'd assume he's scared.

"Shall we?" Treating Stu like an asshole is tempting, but I'd much rather be nice until the guilt of what he did makes him crumble. Smiling sweetly at him, we climb the steps to the manor and I knock lightly on the door.

"Invitation?" the doorman asks immediately as he opens the door.

"I'm Hollie Wolfe. I'm the entertainment."

The man grunts and glances past me to Stu. "And him?"

"My escort."

"Wait here."

The door closes in my face. Looking back at Stu, my brows pinch. "Bit rude," I murmur, clutching my shawl around my shoulders. "Making us wait out in the cold."

Stu doesn't reply but his gaze is upward as if he's studying the building. His lips twist, but just as they part to speak, the door swings open once more and the doorman returns, apparently with a new attitude.

"Miss Wolfe! Welcome, welcome. Come in, come in. Mr. Havershire has been eagerly awaiting your arrival."

"Am I too late?" I glance at my phone while stepping inside as my gut clenches. Did I get the time wrong? If I've messed up this man's engagement, I'll never forgive myself.

"Not at all. Right on time, actually," the doorman assures me. "Your escort can wait here."

Stu bristles immediately and lifts the violin case in his hands. "I stay with her," he states dryly, finally breaking his silence. "Gotta protect the lady's nails."

The doorman doesn't back down and he holds out his hand for the violin case. "I can take that."

There's a beat of tension between the two of them. Stu, under orders from Maxim, isn't to leave my side. But causing a scene risks losing me this gig, and while Maxim, the man with infinite money, wouldn't care, I do.

"It's fine, Stu," I assure him with a smile. "He's new," I say to the doorman. "But I do this all the time. I won't be long, plus, you'll still be able to hear me play."

Stu, put on the spot, is left with no choice but to hand the case over. "I'll be here," he says and locks eyes with me. "Right here, understand?"

I nod quickly, then I'm swept away by the doorman. "Your escort is intense."

"Like I said, he's new. I think he used to be a bodyguard for some celebrity so he's not used to the quieter, slower life of a musician." I laugh softly.

"Odd that your line of work involves needing an escort."

"Protecting my nails!" I waggle my freshly painted silver nails that match the silver dress I'm wrapped up in. "My hands are my most precious commodity."

"I'm sure." The doorman smiles politely and leads me into a small side room. "Mr. Havershire says you can get ready here. Someone will come and get you when it's time for the dancing, and you know the cue for his proposal?"

"Yes. He'll start making a small speech and when the rose petals fall, I switch songs."

The doorman flashes a tight smile, hands me the violin case, and then he's gone, leaving me to the quiet room that holds an odd chill in the air. Removing my shawl, I drape it over the back of the lone chair in the room and breathe deeply to calm my nerves. The faint, stale stink of smoke lingers in the air. This must have been a smoking room back in the day.

As I unpack my violin and check it over, my phone buzzes rapidly multiple times.

[Stu] You good?

[Stu] You need anything?

[Stu] What room you in?

He texts like he speaks, abrupt and to the point. Rolling my eyes, I quickly text him back.

[Hollie] Relax, I'm fine. This'll be over in no time at all.

[Stu] Didn't answer my questions.

God, he's irritating.

Turning my phone to silent, I resume checking my violin and wrap up just as a host from the party collects me for the dancing. I'm escorted through the house and into a large ballroom filled with lots of happy, lightly drunk people wrapped up in the merriment of the party. The room dazzles with Christmas decorations and a fantastical ice sculpture in the middle of the room. No wonder this place is being kept so cool. As I walk to the stage, I study the beautiful sculpture. Two dolphins surge upward on a wave, glittering like they're made out of crystal. It's stunning and even as it melts, the water drips off the wave and into a bowl below that's dyed to look like a dark ocean.

Mr. Havershire must really love this girl.

I take my place on the stage next to the piano, and the DJ fades out as I start playing. My nerves about playing in front of such a large crowd vanish within a few notes of music, and like every other time I'm on stage, it's like I'm the only one who's actually here. Everyone else melts away just like the sculpture, and I pour my heart into playing.

Forty minutes later, my fingers throb slightly but thankfully, Mr. Havershire finally begins his speech so I switch from violin to piano. He thanks everyone for coming, thanks people for their donations, and then the ceiling opens. Glittering, shimmering fabric drifts away from the ceiling, and with it come more rose petals than anyone could ever count. As instructed, I switch to the requested song. Mr. Havershire vanishes from sight as he gets down on one knee and moments later, a woman squeals in delight. Cheers follow and the crowd surges with excitement, congratulating the newly engaged couple. It's so beautiful and I pour more of myself into the performance until a light sheen of sweat clings to my skin.

By the end, I'm tired but the crowd is happy and the DJ resumes after I finish my set and quickly pack up my violin.

"Miss Wolfe?" As I'm climbing down from the stage, Mr. Havershire appears out of the crowd and smiles slightly.

"Mr. Havershire! Congratulations on your engagement."

"Thank you. Your music was delightful."

My cheeks warm as I wave him off. "It was nothing, really. I'm honored I could contribute to such a beautiful moment."

"She's happy, so I'm happy." He clasps his hands together. "If you'd follow me, we can get your payment sorted."

Tucking the violin case against my hip, I nod tiredly. "That would be amazing, thank you."

Mr. Havershire leads the way out of the ballroom, but rather than returning to the old smoking room where I left my shawl and bag, he takes me deeper into the manor. The liveliness from the party gradually fades and it's not until Mr. Havershire opens the door to his study that it hits me how quiet this part of the manor is.

"Fifteen thousand it was, yes?" Mr. Havershire asks as he holds the door open for me.

I'm forced to walk past him into the study. He closes the door behind me and then ushers me toward the desk.

"Yes," I reply. "Fifteen. A check would be perfect."

"Of course." Mr. Havershire moves around his desk and pulls a checkbook from the first drawer. "Rather old school, wouldn't you say?"

"I'd need my phone for a wire transfer," I say without thinking, then immediately kick myself. Telling him I don't have my phone? What was I thinking?

The room is silent except for the scratch of his pen against the check. It's cold here. Beyond the window, darkness spreads like an infinite, yawning abyss. While Mr. Havershire hasn't done or said anything impolite, there's a strange twitch at the back of my neck. It's like I shouldn't be here.

He writes slowly, swooping out his name letter by letter as if he can't remember how to spell it. By the time he adds all the zeros, I'm ready to leave.

"Fifteen thousand. That's a lot of money." He stands and tears the check out of the book, fixing me with a strange look.

"It's what we agreed." I smile politely as my heart ticks up faintly. He's looking at me like he knows me better than I know myself, and it's uncomfortable.

"Yes. You perform for me and I pay you." He walks around the desk and holds out his empty hand for me to shake, keeping the check just out of reach.

"Again, that's what we agreed." My smile loses all warmth, despite my efforts to keep it on my face. With the check out of reach, I have no choice but to lean for his hand. Shaking it, I reach for the check. "It was a pleasure, Mr. Havershire."

Just as my fingertips brush the check, he curls his hand and pulls it away. "What if I'm unsatisfied with the performance?"

A chill runs down my spine. "You signed a contract with my agent," I reply carefully. "Any problems should be taken up with her."

"But she's not here and you are. What if I want another performance?"

I try to jerk my hand away, but his grip remains like iron,

growing tighter and tighter until my knuckles scream and grind together.

"Mr. Havershire—you're hurting me!"

"Oh, am I?" He sounds surprised, then he suddenly lunges at me while jerking my hand toward his body at the same time.

I stumble into him with a yelp, colliding with his body. He wraps one foot around my ankle and jerks my leg, forcing me to trip. My violin slips from my grasp and within a second, he slams me face down onto the desk. His body presses down so heavily onto mine that the edge of the desk cuts into my hip.

"What—get off me, what the fuck? Get the fuck off me!"

"I'm not satisfied," Mr. Havershire growls in my ear, one large hand cradling the side of my head and forcing my cheek flat against his desk. "You're so fucking beautiful, you know that? When I heard about you, I couldn't believe it. I said there's no way someone could finally do it. But then I found your agent and I realized the easiest way to get you was to let you walk right into my trap."

I can't breathe. He leans his full weight onto me and he's too heavy. Tears sting the corners of my eyes, my heart pounds so hard I can taste iron on the back of my tongue, and none of my struggles against him or the desk do anything to help me.

"Get off!" Panic surges like a wave inside me followed by a sickly chill that crawls over my shoulders and down my back. "Get *off* me!"

"No," Mr. Havershire growls. "Like I said, I went to a lot of trouble for this!"

I'm barely able to understand what he's saying but as his body shunts and grinds against me, one of my desperately scrambling hands knocks over a paperweight. It's all I have. I grab it and throw my elbow backward, hitting something soft that forces Mr. Havershire to lean upward with a grunt.

Gasping for air, I twist my body and swing my fist, catching him on the side of his face with the paperweight. It smashes on impact, and he roars in pain as liquid and glitter rain down on his pristine suit, mingling with the blood from the glass shards now embedded in his face.

As he stumbles off me and hits the ground, I shove off the desk and sprint for the door, but his fist closes around my ankle and I fall with a scream. Twisting my body around, Mr. Havershire's bloodied face glares at me, and as I raise my other leg to kick him in the face, I see it.

The heart tattoo on his wrist.

Wait.

When Zoe mentioned it, I knew I'd seen one before.

It has to be some twisted coincidence, right? But then the things Mr. Havershire was saying? There's no time to think.

I slam my heeled shoe down into his face and his grip slips, allowing me to scramble back to my feet. Rather than leaving immediately, I turn and kick him as hard as I can in his crotch.

"You fucking rapist prick!" I scream down at him, kicking him again as hard as I can.

Then I run.

Out the door and down the corridor, trying to retrace my steps back to the ballroom. Tears flow down my cheeks, my heart pounds, and my head thumps from the surge of adrenaline, but I don't stop until I crash into someone who grabs me so tightly that a scream of fear rips from me.

"No!"

"Hollie, it's me!" Stu's face swims before me and his usually irritated face melts briefly into concern. "Holy shit, what happened?"

"We have to leave," I gasp, clutching at his arms. "Please get me out of here."

"Hollie, what—"

"Take me home!" I yell, trying to shove him away, but he refuses to let me go.

"Alright. Alright, we're leaving, but you have to tell me what happened!"

"No, no, it's... please, please, we have to go. We have to go!" Stu can't protect me, not here. If that man is who I think he is, then we both have to get out of here before he gets back on his feet.

Stu finally complies and with my purse and shawl clutched in his other hand, he whisks me right out of the manor.

It's not until I'm in the car, fighting the sobs wrenching through me that I realize I left my violin behind in that fucker's study.

30

MAXIM

"Higher... a little higher... almost... perfect!" Susan claps her hands together and cheers softly. "Oh, it looks so good there, don't you think, Martin?"

Bernard grunts from behind the Christmas tree where he's been trying to find the source of a fault with the Christmas lights for the past twenty minutes.

My shoulders ache, but it's worth it. The last of the streamers now dangle from the ceiling, the party table is set up and straining with food, the record player is set up with classical Christmas songs at Martin's request, and all that's left to do is add a dusting of fake snow to all the table decorations and ornaments set up around the home. Hollie wasn't kidding when she said her parents went overboard.

The first guests start to arrive, so I retire to the kitchen where Toto's up to his elbows in potato peels.

"Help me," he groans. "My fingers are going to wrinkle off!"

I take over and nudge him with my shoulder. "Go. Take a break. Rex is around somewhere. He might still be out back finishing the snow maze for the kids."

"I'm trading vegetable water for the cold?" Toto wrinkles his nose but grabs his coat from the hanger near the back door and vanishes out into the garden.

He approaches Rex stealthily and then announces himself so loudly that Rex jumps out of his skin and falls flat onto the portion of the maze he was working on. A fight ensues and I chuckle to myself, peeling the last of the potatoes while Rex and Toto cover themselves in snow.

"I know who you are." Martin's voice rises up from behind me and I flinch. He approached so quietly, I had no idea he was there. Glancing over my shoulder, I smile politely.

"It's me. Maxim. It's not that dark in here, is it?"

"Not that." Martin leans back against the kitchen table and crosses his arms over his chest. "Did you really think a career criminal like you could marry a chief's daughter and I wouldn't find out?"

My hands pause in the water. Potato peel floats past, following the lingering ripples from my last movements.

There was always a chance, a slight risk that Martin would be suspicious enough to do some digging. But even if he puts Hollie on trial, she can't say a thing about me, although now I don't think she'll say anything, anyway. From a woman who saw me as nothing but a cold-blooded killer at Thanksgiving, a week before Christmas and she's warmed to me.

I turn away from the sink, the peeler clutched in one hand. "I don't know what you mean."

"Is that what he trains you to say? I knew as soon as it was difficult to see Hollie's marriage certificate that there was something off about you. She never told me your last name, but when you were here helping me in the garden? I saw some of your tattoos."

Suddenly, my long-sleeved shirt doesn't feel as secure as it once did.

"There aren't many who are inked up to the degree you are. And even less with the last name Krasnov."

"I bet there's more than you think," I reply carefully.

"Don't bullshit me, Son. Your father is Igor Krasnov. It might have taken me this long to work it out, but I promise you, I won't be forgetting it."

Tension thickens in the air. Is he telling me this because he's called his buddies and I'm seconds away from being arrested on some bullshit charge? Or is this something else? Bringing this up at a Christmas party, of all places, is one hell of a choice.

"I don't know my father." An easy lie.

"I said don't bullshit me," Martin snaps. "I know who you are. You come into my home, you share dinner with my *wife*, you marry my daughter. Don't stand there and treat me like I'm stupid."

He has a point. My breath hitches, and I'm acutely aware that if Rex were to walk in right now, things could go south.

He's overly protective, but Martin isn't a threat. Not physically, at least.

"So, what is this?" I ask slowly. "You know who I am. You bring it up now? Are you expecting me to cause a scene at your party? If you think this looks bad for me, then think how it also looks to others. You, a retired police chief marrying his daughter into the Mafia. Some might question if your loyalties were always with us."

"Is that a threat?" Martin's bushy brows knit together.

"No. I'm pointing out that this can look like either thing."

He remains silent for a long minute, then his hands tighten around his elbows. "Is she in trouble?"

His question catches me off guard and for a second, my mind is blank. His concern is his daughter and I didn't see it immediately. Everywhere I look, there's a threat or someone eager to take me down, but Martin isn't one of them. Not anymore.

"Hollie," Martin repeats. "Is she in trouble?"

A lie would be easiest here. I could spin the tale that we met and fell in love so quickly, echoing the lie she told her parents back when we first met but that lie is only enough to satisfy her mother. Martin isn't going to let this go, and I get the impression he's more understanding.

"Our marriage saved her life," I say carefully. "She's not in trouble anymore."

Martin's eyes narrow. "Why would you do that? I know how marriage works for you lot. It's human trafficking and you can't tell me otherwise. Marrying people for business deals... how did this happen?" His mouth twists to the side. "She's a musician. She's floaty and reckless, but how did she end up on your radar?"

"She saw something that put her in danger and I saved her."

Martin leans away from the table. "Why?"

The complicated truth swirls in my chest like a fog, but before I can answer, Susan bustles into the kitchen.

"Martin! Stop hiding in here and go and greet our guests! The Robinsons are here, and I am not equipped to listen to Terry's debate about the ethical consumption of fish. That's your job." She pauses between us, glancing at each of us in turn. "Is everything alright?"

I meet Martin's gaze, remaining silent and waiting for him to make the choice here. Does he continue the lie or does he tell her the truth?

There's a long few seconds of silence, then Martin grunts. "It's fine. I was telling him to hurry it along or they won't be roasted in time." Clearing his throat, he vanishes from the kitchen while Susan pats my arm.

"Ignore him." She chuckles. "Honestly, we've cooked so much today that we're well over the potato quota!" She chuckles to herself, takes a bottle of wine from the fridge, and vanishes back to the party.

By the time I finish with the potatoes, Rex and Toto have finished the maze in time for a gaggle of children to head outside, and then Hollie arrives. I'm coming out of the bathroom when we bump into each other in the hallway, and I'm unable to keep the smile from my face.

She's scraped her red hair back into a ponytail and changed from her gorgeous dress into jeans and her Christmas sweater, but as our eyes meet, something cold grips my heart.

Something's wrong.

The excited light she had in her eyes when she left me in the car has truly been extinguished. She presses her lips together and struggles to meet my eye, her cheeks are flushed, and she's pulled the sleeves of her sweater over her hands, gripping them tightly.

"Hollie?"

"Maxim..." There's a note of relief in her tone, but when I reach for her, she pulls her arm away.

Something happened. "Hollie, what's wrong?"

"I thought I–I was going to be late. Too late. I can't, uhm..." She shakes her head and finally meets my eyes. They hold such sorrow that it takes all my restraint not to drag her back into the bathroom with me. Just as well because as I reach for her again, Susan comes through the hallway and squeals.

"Hollie! You came!" She throws her arms around her daughter and pulls her into a tight hug. Past her, I catch Stu's eyes and he jerks his head slightly to the side, then melts into the crowd forming in the hallway to greet Hollie.

She's swept away to greet family and friends in the lounge, surrounded by happy people and the occasional request for her to play something for everyone. Her smile, while bright, is clearly forced and uncertainty ticks through my heart.

Was her gig really that bad?

I linger for a few minutes until I can slip away, meeting Stu outside in the back garden where he stands with Toto and Rex who watch over the screaming, laughing children while they hunt the makeshift snow maze for the chocolate hidden under the snow.

I don't even need to speak. As soon as our eyes meet, Stu launches into a hurried explanation.

"She didn't tell me everything, but she was cornered after the party by the host."

"Why weren't you with her?" I cut in, unable to help myself.

"We got separated. She acted like it was normal, and I thought it was a regular party, but it wasn't. I was kept in the foyer and she told me to listen to her playing, so I did. But after it stopped, she never came back so I went looking. I found her in the hallway, and she begged me to take her home. She was flushed, crying, and worked up into a panic. She'd lost her violin. I knew we were outnumbered no matter what happened, so I got her out of there."

"Fuck." Whoever he is, wherever he is, I'll make him pay. I don't care if he just insulted her music. He won't get away with this.

"That's not all," Stu says, and he steps closer. "I did some digging while she was changing. Mr. Havershire doesn't exist."

My heart stalls in my chest. "What?"

"I dug through the sale history of that house and Mr. Havershire wasn't on the list. In fact, the building is unlisted and hasn't had an owner in over ten years."

31

HOLLIE

"I love my parents, but that party was exhausting." Slumping down onto the couch back at Maxim's penthouse, I draw the blanket over myself and try to process. I need to tell him what happened, but where to start? How to explain everything that happened, and then my determination not to ruin my parents' party?

My eyes close until the couch dips. Maxim sits beside me with his elbows resting on his knees and his hands clasped together. "Hollie, tell me what happened at the gig."

My heart jumps. Just five minutes. I want just five minutes to process and feel safe, but when Maxim's gaze locks onto mine, I realize that he already knows.

"What did Stu tell you?"

"Did you really think he would keep it a secret?" Maxim leans toward me. "Tell me."

He speaks softly and yet his words are like a command, a

demand for the truth, yet somehow, it makes me feel like refusing wouldn't be the end of the world.

"I don't know," I whisper, clutching at the blanket. "He was nice. I played music and I watched him propose to his fiancée, and then he asked me to come with him to get paid and I went. It was no different from any other booking I've had but suddenly, we were alone. And I remember thinking that it was oddly quiet with just the two of us, and then he started talking about my *performance* but it was like he wasn't talking about my music. And then he..."

I can't say it.

It sounds pathetic. Maxim faces danger every day and I've told him I can take care of myself. In the great scheme of things, it hardly seems important.

Maxim doesn't speak. He watches me intently, but his hands have twisted together so tightly that the white of his bone bleeds through the skin of his knuckles.

"He grabbed me." My voice doesn't sound like my own. "And he threw me down on the desk and he pinned me down and he... He was saying all these things about how he'd waited for me before or something, but it was easier to let me just walk into his trap, and I—" Gasping, my hand shoots over my mouth. "Oh God... I hit him. It was a paper weight, I think, but it *shattered* and he was bleeding and he fell, and I tried to run but he—"

The tattoo suddenly appears in the forefront of my mind, and the realization brings with it the weight of what could have truly happened had I not gotten away.

"He had the tattoo."

Maxim's brow lifts slightly. "The tattoo?"

I nod quickly and hold out my hand. "On his wrist. He had a heart tattoo. I knew I'd seen it before when Zoe told me about it, but I just couldn't remember where, so I thought it was nothing, but he... he had one. Right here." Pressing my fingertips against my wrist, I show Maxim exactly where the tattoo was. "I kicked him and I ran, and then—"

Maxim suddenly scoops me into his arms and draws me into his lap. The comfort of his secure hold is enough to unlock the next wave of tears and suddenly, I'm sobbing into his shoulder and clutching so hard at his shirt that my nailbeds ache.

"I'm sorry," he grunts. "I should have gone in with you."

I can't speak. On the drive to my parents' house, I kept telling myself I was fine and there was nothing really to worry about. I got away and that's all that matters. But now, after it's sunk in and I've finished performing as the perfect daughter for my parents, the pain hits.

I cry until my throat is hoarse and my eyes burn. Maxim doesn't relax even for a second. He holds me tight and close, rocking me back and forth and caressing the back of my head while murmuring things I can't decipher. Just the noise of his voice is enough to soothe me, and I cry until my phone rings for the third time in a row.

"Let me," Maxim says, reaching for my purse, but I catch his arm and shake my head.

"S'fine. Probably my mom."

"Are you sure?" There's such worry flooding Maxim's eyes, but I nod quickly and slip from his lap. "Do you think there's a connection?" I ask softly. "About the tattoo?"

Maxim doesn't reply. He stands and kisses the top of my head, then he moves out of the lounge and stands in the kitchen with his own phone pressed to his ear.

Maybe it's nothing. That tattoo is surely common, but I can't shake the feeling that there's something there.

Drying my eyes, I answer the phone while sniffling softly to control myself.

"Darling!" Tiffany's voice bursts forth. "You didn't call me after the gig, how did it go? I called the client but he didn't pick up, so I can only imagine he's celebrating his fancy new engagement and we're insanely richer, right?"

I forgot all about the money. God knows where that check ended up after we fought.

"Tiffany, hey." I try to subtly clear my throat. "Sorry I didn't call."

"Oh, honey, are you alright? You sound awful. Did you not go?"

"Uhm... I'm sorry, Tiff, there's no money."

"What? Did he stiff you? Because I swear I don't care how rich that fucker is, I'll blacklist him up and down the entire city, and he won't be able to even *eat* anywhere without feeling smothered by judgment."

"No, no, he..." I look back at Maxim. He's speaking quietly and hurriedly into his phone. "He attacked me, Tiff. So I ran. I'm sorry."

"What?" She almost blows my ear from how loudly she yells.

"I'm sorry."

"Honey, don't you dare apologize! I'm so sorry. Have you called the police? Do you need me to? I can call them right now!"

"No, no, it's okay. It's being taken care of, I just... I'm sorry. It was so much money."

"No amount is worth that, darling. Don't you dare worry about that. God, I'm so sorry. If you need anything, then I'm here, okay? I'm right here."

"Thanks."

We talk for a few minutes and then I hang up, sinking back down onto the couch. Emptiness fills me. The back of my throat burns and my head aches. In the quiet, Maxim's voice rises from the kitchen, but he's talking too low and too fast for me to make out anything he's saying. He sounds angry.

I hope he's not angry at Stu. If he'd been there, maybe it would have been different. I shouldn't have let him stay behind.

Back and forth my mind weaves, finding ways to make the attack my own fault, something avoidable and then something unavoidable. Even with the blanket on me, I still feel his weight against me and it's not the same comforting weight that comes from Maxim. This is something different and I hate it.

My vision blurs as I stare out the window where the glittering city of New York swells with light and life amid the falling snow. The longer I watch, the quieter my mind becomes until I'm so numb that even my breathing becomes hesitant.

I'm watching the snow fall as my mind loops, replaying that fight over and over again. Time is infinite, and I'm alone in this bubble of anxiety until Maxim's ridged abdomen blocks my view.

I blink and my eyes burn like I haven't blinked in hours.

"Come with me," Maxim says gently, holding out his hand.

"Don't you have calls to make?" I croak, swallowing around the cotton in my mouth.

"They can wait." Maxim takes my hand and holds me gently. "I need to take care of you first."

A protest rises in me, a declaration that I'm fine, but when our eyes meet, I can't bring myself to say it, so I let him pull me off the couch. Maxim guides me down the hall to the bathroom and once inside, the prospect of a shower sounds equal parts amazing and exhausting. But he's one step ahead of me.

He strips immediately, turns on the shower and lowers the lights to reduce the glare, then he faces me and holds out his hand. "Let me help you."

He said once that he wouldn't touch me without permission and it seems important now as he reaches out for me, but he doesn't close the gap. He leaves that choice up to me.

After an eternity of the shower running and his hand hanging in the air between us, I finally take it.

From there, Maxim takes over like it's second nature to him. He peels me out of my clothes and sets them on the counter next to the sink. As he looks me over, he pauses at my hips where a faint bruise rises from my hipbone. I want to tell him what caused it but it's like he already knows. His thumb smooths over the bruise with feather-light pressure, then he removes my underwear and scoops me up in his bare arms. In the shower, he sets me down directly under the spray, then turns me to face.

I immediately close my eyes, but not before I notice that he positions himself between me and the door as if he's protecting me from anything that could burst in and disturb us. The hot water pours over my face, washing away the salt from my tears and the ache in my brow. Maxim's hands gently scrape my hair away from my face and soon, it dangles, soaked, down my back.

Wordlessly, he lathers up his hands and starts washing me. It's strange how he knows what to do, and every time I think about saying something, the comfort that comes from his attention keeps me quiet and content. His strong, callused hands sweep up my arms, across my shoulders, and down my back, kneading and stroking with care. At my lower back, he massages into my spine and sweeps back up to my shoulders.

My head drops forward and my breathing deepens, soaking up every second of his contact. But more than that, it's what he's erasing. Maxim's hands replace that bastard's weight against my back. They replace his voice at my neck, the grip of his hands and the pressure at my hips. He doesn't stop there, either. He washes my breasts and stomach, down each leg, and around each ankle as if he knows exactly where that brute grabbed me. I never gave details and Maxim is simply being thorough, but it's welcomed.

By the time he lathers shampoo into my hair, my mind is calm and my body tingles as if every stroke of Maxim's palms renewed me. My head falls back into his hands and my next breath feels like the first real breath I've taken since I left that place.

"Why are you doing this?"

Maxim slides his lathered fingers into my hair, massaging my scalp, and I sag against him.

"I said I would protect you and I failed," he says quietly. "But I won't fail at taking care of you. And I promise, no one will hurt you ever again."

For such a large, intimidating man with miles of ink covering his muscles, he speaks with such tenderness. Like a teddy bear coming to life. I can't take his promise to heart. Being around him has taught me how unpredictable his world can be, but if this care is the care I'm destined to, regardless, then I'll take it.

I open my eyes and turn away from the spray. Squinting up at Maxim, he's focused on keeping the shampoo out of my eyes while cradling my head back so the water washes back. He's frowning slightly and his lower lip is curling faintly under his upper.

That glimpse and the warmth radiating from me because of his care births a new revelation that makes my heart skip a beat.

Shit.

I think I've fallen for him.

32

MAXIM

Hollie's hair spreads across the pillow like a spiderweb, her breathing soft and shallow but finally peaceful. After our shower together last night, I feared she wouldn't find peace after what she went through but luckily, sleep came swiftly and I spent my last hours awake doubling our security, putting a permanent car on her parents, and having Rex dig up every piece of info on Mr. Havershire.

The man's a ghost, deepening my suspicions.

Suspicions that rest on the back burner as I study Hollie's sleeping face and gently brush a few red strands away from her face. Her dark roots are peeking out now, but I like the contrast between the brown and red. Reminds me of a cinnamon candy cane at this time of year.

She turns her face toward my fingertips as if some deep part of her is aware that I'm there with her. Her lips part, and I sweep down to lightly touch her lower lip. She's become so important to me in such a short time, and I failed her when she needed me the most.

Never again.

Hollie stirs a little more and her eyelashes flutter against her cheek, then she rolls onto her back with a soft sigh. Drawing her out of slumber as gently as I can is fun, but I'm running out of time and I need to talk to her before I leave. She murmurs softly in the back of her throat and her lips part a little further, taunting me enough that I lean in and kiss her very softly.

A part of her responds with just a flicker of pressure. She's on the cusp of wakefulness, dancing that blurry line between the comfort of sleep and the lure of waking, so I continue my path. I kiss her jaw, then down to her neck and all the way down to her soft shoulder where the strap of her sleepwear rests in the crook of her neck.

Down her arm I kiss while my body gradually pushes the sheets away from her body. From her forearm to her abdomen exposed by her sleepwear rising up during her sleep, I lavish warm, gentle attention as I go until I reach the hem of her sleep shorts. She shifts under me and one leg lifts to the side, cocked at the knee. Warmth blooms through me as I pull her shorts down inch by inch until the silk rests around her knees and she's exposed to me.

Her mound makes my mouth water. I discard her shorts completely, shift under one of her legs, and very slowly press my mouth against the outer lips of her pussy. She doesn't react other than a soft, sharp intake of breath. Pressing my tongue flat against her, I press in between her folds until my tongue is against her searing heat, with her clit hardening against my tongue in seconds.

Her sweetness becomes the only thing I care about. Licking through her slowly from hole to clit, I savor her silkiness, lavishing equal attention on each of her inner lips and then focusing my pointed tongue on her clit.

That's when she wakes up, alerting me to it as her thighs suddenly tighten around my head and a louder, clearer moan rises from her throat.

I pause briefly, awaiting her decision whether to continue or pull back, and my answer comes in her legs draping over my back and fully locking me in between her soft thighs.

Message received.

Now she's awake, there's no need for me to hold back, and I surge forward voraciously, eating her out with my usual passion. Strong flicks of my tongue, hard suction of her clit and deep delves licking inside her until her juices soak my beard and every breath from her above is tinged with a moan and a whimper. I press my face as close as I can, smothering all my senses in her, and I don't stop until she comes around my fingers, quivering and moaning as if she's about to fall apart right in front of me.

"Good morning." I grin at her, my chin resting on her thigh once her last shakes of pleasure have passed.

With flushed cheeks and sparkling eyes, she gazes down at me with a cloud of pleasure drifting in her eyes. "Morning."

"I have to go out," I say softly. "I need you to stay here. And this isn't a request. You need to stay here."

She squints at me and lifts onto one elbow as if my words aren't quite making it through her sleep- and orgasm-addled mind. "Are you *telling* me I can't leave?"

"Yes."

"But... I have lunch with my mom today. She invited me yesterday at the party because Christmas is on Saturday and she still has so much to do."

"Until I know it's safe, I don't want you going anywhere." Her brows furrow so I add, "Your parents are being protected too."

Her eyes widen. "You think he would go after my parents?"

"I'm not taking any chances. Whether he's someone worth fearing or just a random asshole, I don't know. And until I know, I need you here."

Hollie seems to be debating with herself, judging by how her mouth twists to the side, but thankfully, she nods. "Okay. I'll call her and postpone."

"Thank you."

"Will you be gone long?"

Kissing her hipbone over the bruise that's darkened over the course of the night, I climb from the bed and pull the covers over her as I stand. "I don't know, but I'll leave Toto here and I'll have my phone on me. Call me if you need anything."

"Is this really the place?" Biting, icy wind whips around me, pulling at my coat and lifting my pant legs as if it's desperate to find any way beneath my warm layers. A thick coating of snow lies all around us, disturbed only by my car and Stu's footsteps. If anyone else had been here, their presence would have been erased in the snowstorm that hit a little after four in the morning.

"Yup," Stu confirms, his hands in his coat as he stares up at the building. "How did they clean everything so fast?"

When I dropped Hollie off here yesterday, this building was full of life. Christmas wreaths hung from every window, the stone pillars at the entranceway were swirled with lights, and there were several glittering wire reindeer all over the front lawn. In the cold light of day, not a single detail remains and the building looks so different, it's like we're in the wrong place.

Rex, kneeling at the front door with a lock pick in hand, grunts in surprise and stands. "Boss... It's not even locked."

The door swings open, revealing an empty foyer, and Stu's face flits between confusion and surprise. "What the hell?"

Inside, there's nothing.

Bare wooden floors stretch in every direction, open doors lead to empty rooms void of furniture, and crooked curtains hang off windows. There's not a single hint that anyone was ever here, or has been here in the last month.

"What the hell?" Stu leads the way toward the room where he found Hollie's shawl and purse. "How could they have cleaned up so fast? There were lights and decorations, Christmas trees and paintings on the wall. The entire manor looked lived in and now it looks..." He trails off and opens the door to the small room, but there's no furniture in here either.

Everything is gone.

"Find the office," I say as an uncomfortable itch crawls over my skin. "I want every room searched from top to bottom."

This is looking more and more like a setup to lure in Hollie, and the only valid reason makes my blood run cold. Hollie is my wife and she saw the tattoo, the same tattoo Zoe remembered during her triggered episode. Rex finally confirmed last night that the man I killed didn't have the tattoo which means this man, if he's the same as the fake Mr. Havershire, is my second target.

Not only does he know who I am, but he knows Hollie. And he almost had her.

It doesn't take long to find the empty office, identifiable only by a smearing of glitter on the floor and a single glass shard retrieved from between the floorboards. This is where he attacked her and she fought free with the paperweight that seems now more like a snow globe.

"Boss?" Rex joins me shortly after we clean up the glass and glitter, hoping someone can help us identify the snow globe.

"Find anything?"

"Just this in one of the upper rooms wedged behind a dresser." He hands me a crumpled flyer and grimaces. "This entire thing was a show."

"A show?" Unfurling the flyer, neon text glares up at me advertising a flash mob party.

"Basically, a group chooses an abandoned building, sets up an event, and then hosts a party to whoever turns up and then they clean it all up afterward. All within one night," Rex explains. "I remember them being viral a few years ago. My daughter was obsessed."

My brow twitches. "But the engagement?"

Rex shrugs. "Could be that he found a guest to play along with him. The whole thing is an act. No one is who they say they are. It's a night of pretend."

"Find this group." I shove the flyer back into his hands. "Hollie got this gig a few weeks ago, which means that fucker knew this was happening and chose this because there would be a crowd of strangers here to make it look real. Chances are, he knows one of them."

Rex nods quickly. "Stu's on it, Boss."

"What the fuck is this..." Gazing around the room, tension pulls across my chest as the rest of my team scurries out. "Why the fuck would he go to all this effort?"

"He's cocky. Arrogant. We reasoned that the entire reason the attack happened was that these small pricks couldn't comprehend not being important. But now you're looking into this personally... I bet he feels like he's got a fucking spotlight on him."

"So Hollie's attack was my fault?" I fix Rex with a stern gaze. "Is that what you're saying?"

"Technically, with her association to you." Rex nods. "But we did what we could to make the best of a terrible situation back then. News spread and we knew your enemies would see her as a prime target. It's just this fucker got to her first."

"I want him," I growl as my phone buzzes in my back pocket. "I want his head on a fucking platter in front of me. If he wants my attention so badly, then he's fucking got it." Anger licks at my spine as I answer the phone with a bark. "What?"

"Maxim?" Zoe's trembling voice cuts through my anger and it takes all my strength to reign it in.

"Zoe?"

"Maxim you've got to come, please! Someone tried to break in!"

33

HOLLIE

Being locked in the penthouse might mean I can't go anywhere, but that doesn't mean people can't come to me. Tiffany arrives a little after twelve with wide eyes and a bottle of champagne.

"Girl, what is with the spooky men in your lobby?" she asks in a fluster as she stumbles inside, then her eyes become saucers as she gazes from the sparkling lounge to the open-plan kitchen covered in mess from the sandwiches I made. "What the *fuck*?"

"What?" Taking the champagne from her, I set it aside in the kitchen and grab the two glasses of orange juice I prepared instead.

"This is Maxim's place?" Tiffany wanders to the lounge and gazes up at the Christmas tree, then turns and takes the glass from me. "You should have invited me sooner."

"Crazy, right?"

"Tell me." She sips her drink and drops onto the couch with a soft moan. "Oh my God it's like sitting on a cloud. But tell me, did you marry him that fast because of his money?"

"Definitely not." I chuckle, placing my own glass on the coffee table and hurrying back to the kitchen for the food.

"Is he insane in bed?"

"Yes, but also not the reason."

"Okay, so it's not the money and not the sex. He's hot for sure, but that can't be the reason you *married* him," Tiffany muses, watching me over the back of the couch.

"Did you really come here to pick apart my marriage?"

"No, honey. I came to see how you were and make sure you were okay. I put out the word that Mr. Havershire is a dick and not to be booked anywhere, so he won't be welcome anywhere in this city, that's for sure. Nowhere of note, at least."

Back in the lounge, I flop down next to her and set the plate of sandwiches and nibbles on the table. "Thank you."

"Of course. But honey, tell me what happened?" Despite her frantic way of moving through life and throwing gig after gig at me, her concern is genuine so after biting into a sandwich, I lean back and fill her in.

Every detail makes her frown deepen until her hand is on my thigh and she apologizes profusely. "I had no idea he was such a monster. I feel awful for sending you there."

"There's no way you could have known," I assure her.

"Honestly, who would do something so diabolical at this time of year? I'll never forgive myself."

"Please." Taking her hand, I squeeze gently. "I'm okay. Maxim is taking care of everything and I'm okay, I promise." As true as those words are, there's still one concern in the back of my mind. A concern that won't fade until I get a chance to speak to my doctor. While I'm sure nothing's happened to the baby, I need to be sure before I tell Maxim the truth. I can't break his heart with the truth and then find out that the attack harmed it.

"Maxim's taking care of you, huh?" She pats the back of my hand. "Well I'm glad you found a good man who does that, at least. God. You'd never expect such a thing in this line of work."

"The only thing I'm sad about is I left my violin there. God knows what happened to it."

"Well, that actually brings me to the real reason I dropped by. Not to say that I wasn't concerned about you because I absolutely am. I just have another reason."

"Oh?" I drain my glass as Tiffany busies herself in her bag.

She pulls out a blue plastic folder and hands it to me. "Here."

"What's this?"

"You know how you were always talking about leaving New York and seeing the world a little?"

"Mhm." Opening the folder, a large picture of an exquisite cruise ship takes over the first page.

"That's a private liner. They're looking for a long-term musician to cover their entire round-the-world cruise next year. From February to November, visiting thirty-seven countries with top-of-the-line guests, food, drink... everything you could ever wish for in a luxury liner. They pay more money than either of us could ever dream of, have an insurance package and a loyalty card for employees, so even if you never wanted to work for them again, you get a discount on their cruises!"

The sleek black ship is lit up with gold lighting on a deep blue ocean just in front of a gorgeous sunset. Inside the booklet details not only all the fantastical activities that you can do on board, but the beautiful countries that will be visited as well as details on perks for employees. Specifically, a dedicated hand masseuse for musicians, a personal chef for dietary needs, and bonuses every two months on board.

"Tiffany... this is insane!"

"I know!" She claps her hands together. "Apparently, the slot they need to fill is for their eighteenth musician, as the previous person has had enough sailing. Can you imagine? Anyway, I heard about this from a friend of a friend and there's a banquet on Christmas Eve for you to attend. Think of it as a dinner and interview all wrapped up in one!"

"I... I can't think what to say?" A few months ago, this would have been a dream come true. A good job that lets me live in my music while traveling the world and getting away from things for a while. Now, though... I'm not so sure I want to leave the city. Being with Maxim has shifted my perspective slightly on what's important in my life, and if I'm having this baby, could I really do that in the middle of the ocean?

"Say yes!" Tiffany clasps my hand. "You deserve this, darling. No more Christmas rushes to make enough money to last you the year, no more hotel lobbies or shitty lobbies and even shittier clients. You'd be part of a small orchestra with solo chances almost every night on top of everything else. Just tell me you'll go, please?" She looks at me with such hope. "Just attend the interview. At best, you get a dream job and at worst, you just attend a fancy party. And this one is legit, trust me. After Mr. Havershire, I checked out everything."

"I... thank you, Tiffany. This is insane."

"They don't call me a gold-standard manager for nothing." She grins, then her brow dips. "Well, if they don't, then they definitely should. Of course, full disclosure that I do get a fraction of your pay if you take this, but it's nothing compared to what they pay you. So this would benefit both of us." Her brows wiggle. "*Please* say you'll go?"

"Okay, I'll go!" Despite my uncertainty, she's hard to say no to and on some level, I'm with her. What harm could come from an interview?

"Yay!" She throws her arms around my neck and hugs me tight. "This is going to be amazing!"

Tiffany stays for another hour and we eat, drink, and discuss Christmas plans. She's flying out to see her parents on Christmas Eve, the last flight of the night, and plans to sleep the entire way through. My plans are so up in the air that I quietly assume I'll be spending it with Maxim and my parents. Soon, work calls her away and I stay in the hallway, watching the elevator descend until I'm certain she's in the lobby. After calling down to Toto to ensure Tiffany safely made it back to her car, I call Mom.

"Hi darling, you're not calling to cancel on me tomorrow as well, are you?" she says as soon as she answers the phone. "Because you know I don't like it when you cancel on short notice."

"I know," I assure her, returning to the couch. "Today just couldn't work." I dare not point out that her lunch demand at the party yesterday was also short notice because that's an argument I don't have the energy for. "I just wanted to check where you wanted to eat tomorrow so I can let my driver know."

"Your driver? Oh, la dee dah." Mom chuckles. "You can choose since your life is so fancy right now."

"Alright. And yes. You know Maxim hires drivers because it's easier in the city. It's not as fancy as you think it is."

"Sure. Back when your father was still at work and the most important man in the city, I didn't have a driver."

"Did you ever ask for one?" I slouch down until I'm prone on the couch and gaze across at the twinkling Christmas tree.

"No, but that's not the point. I don't want you to end up spoiled, dear."

I roll my eyes. "Mom. It's not a big deal."

"I'm not entirely sure I like that your husband travels with so many men. It's so... odd."

"No it's not. They all work together. It's natural."

"Well, as long as they aren't at the Christmas Eve dinner then that's fine. You'll be there, right? I don't want you bailing like you did on Thanksgiving."

"What?" Sitting upright, my gut twists. I'd forgotten all about that dinner.

"Christmas Eve? Family dinner with the family? We exchange presents? I know you like to *skip* them but since you missed Thanksgiving, I expect you to be here this year."

"I can't, Mom, I have wo—"

"No!" She snaps and cuts me off. "I won't hear it. I'm tired of you choosing work over your family at Christmas so you will be here, you understand? I've dealt with your cancellations, your silence, your sudden marriage and more, but I won't have you stand me up at this dinner, understand? I won't forgive you this time if you miss it."

I ache to tell her she can't force me, but every bitter word from her piles on the guilt until only one response slips from me. "I know. I'm sorry, Mom. I'll be there."

"Good." She hangs up without another word and I gaze back at the tree.

Fuck.

If I miss the banquet, then my dream job turns to dust. There won't be a second chance there. But if I skip Christmas Eve dinner with my parents, Mom won't forgive me and she's excellent at holding a grudge.

Family or work... How am I to choose?

34

MAXIM

"How is it looking?" I'm trying not to hover over Rex, but I can't help myself.

Ever since someone tried to break into the hospital floor Zoe's been recovering at, Rex and I have been trying to clamp down on the flow of information outside the family. I persuaded Zoe that it was just a tired doctor confused about where they were supposed to be, and it did calm her, but the security footage showed me otherwise.

A stranger dressed in black with a cap pulled down far over his eyes. Given how quickly he fled the elevator, I suspect he was simply testing my security measures, but after what happened to Hollie, I'm now utterly convinced that this fake client of hers is actually the bastard I've been hunting.

Vinnie won't be hiding for much longer.

"Not that long. Here." Rex passes me a brand-new cell-phone. "Every number there is linked to each one in the system. You can listen to anyone's calls if you need. I'm running facial recognition through every camera in the building and down the entire block. I've also got the system looped into the cameras we set up around Hollie's parents' and your father's manor. Whatever Vinnie's game is, if he pops up here or at the clubs, we'll know it."

"It doesn't feel like enough," I murmur, staring at the phone screen. "How is one man escaping us this long?"

"Because he's exactly that," Rex replies. "One man with no contacts is harder to track than an organization and he knows it. He's slotting into everyday life, but he made one mistake. One he can't hide."

My attention darts to Rex. "Which is?"

"Hollie fucked up his face with that snow globe. That shit will take weeks to heal, so he's either going to crawl into the dark and die or he'll do something big because he can't hide anymore. Either way..." Rex grunts softly and finishes his work on the keyboard. "We'll be ready for him."

After saying goodbye to Rex, I return to the small office in my penthouse and study the cameras. Down in the lobby, Toto hugs Rex and elbows him lightly in the gut, resulting in a soft brawl that ends when Rex gets a phone call. The phone in my hand supposedly can connect to any call since every call on our network routes through it, but he never actually showed me how.

I tap a few buttons and something clicks, so I lift the phone to my ear.

"I'd really prefer if you came in for a check-up," comes an unfamiliar voice. "I can't tell you much over the phone without examining you."

Is Rex sick?

"I can't do that," comes Hollie's voice, and my heart stalls briefly in my chest.

I shouldn't listen in on her conversations, but something about her tone keeps me listening, concern bleeding through with each frantic thump of my heart.

"Well, are you in any pain?" comes the stranger's voice. "Any unusual vomiting or discomfort when you lie down?"

"No, nothing. The only pain comes from my hip but he... he shoved me so hard against that desk." Hollie's voice wobbles. "I haven't told the father yet, and now I'm too scared because if something's happened to this baby, then it's all my fault and I don't know what I'm supposed to do!"

Baby?

Baby... Hollie's pregnant?

Wait... this doesn't make any sense. I haven't been fucking her long enough for her to know if she's pregnant or not, surely?

"Breathe, Hollie. Listen... I need you to come in for a scan. Preferably, as soon as possible. It's the only way I can soothe your fears and find out if there is any real cause for concern."

Hollie is silent for a long moment and then she sighs. "I have lunch with my mother today. I could maybe slip away to see you."

"Slip away?" The stranger, presumably a doctor of some kind, pauses. "Hollie, are you in an unsafe situation?"

"No, nothing like that," Hollie assures hurriedly. "It's complicated, that's all. I'm fine, I promise."

After a little back and forth, the call ends. I sit slowly, staring blankly at the security monitors in front of me.

Pregnant? Is that even possible?

Is it mine? Someone else's?

My heart races. A baby changes everything. If it's mine, even if it's not, what I feel for Hollie is almost overwhelming and it sits warmly in my chest like a hug that never lets go.

Confronting her doesn't feel like a wise move without revealing just how in-depth the new security software is, so I'll remain quiet for now. With any luck, Hollie will tell me herself when she feels ready.

But a baby?

The revelation leaves me reeling and it stays with me through the next hour until I meet Hollie in the kitchen.

"Hi," she says cheerily. "I'm just packing some water before I meet Mom for lunch. You good?"

She's so beautiful. Is she glowing because she's smiling or because she's carrying a baby? I struggle with myself, keeping my gaze locked on her eyes, refusing to look down as if I could suddenly reveal everything I wanted to know about the baby. Forcing a smile, I push a booklet toward her.

"I found this on the dresser. Are you looking to buy a private yacht?"

Hollie glances at it and groans. "No, that's the offer I was telling you about. The banquet is on Friday and it's an amazing opportunity. Tiffany thinks I'll be perfect for it, but it clashes with Mom's dinner and she's so pissed at me for missing Thanksgiving and the dinner last

Christmas. And the one before." Her brow dips as she screws the lid onto her water bottle. "I don't know what to do."

Leaning on the counter, I map out every detail of her face. The wisps of hair framing her face, the slope of her lips, the bump in her nose. I map it all out and smile. "Do you think your parents would move dinner?"

"It's in three days. There's no way," she sighs. "Plus..." Hollie stops on the other side of the counter and stares at me. "It's... kind of a huge deal, don't you think?"

"Moving dinner?"

"No. A cruise for ten months."

Is she asking me permission? It's strange to think she values my opinion here and my heart races slightly, my mind still reeling from the idea of a baby. "It is a long time. Are you sure you could handle it?"

Her brow lifts slightly and she shrugs. "I don't know. I've never been on a cruise, but it sounds nice."

"I do remember your mentioning a desire to leave New York. Is that still something you want to do?"

Her hands come together around the water bottle and her knuckles flex, then she tilts her head. "Things are... different now."

"Different how?"

"We're married."

"That doesn't equate to a loss of freedom."

"Uhm, excuse me. Yesterday, you wouldn't let me leave and

today, you're *only* letting me leave because Toto and Stu are coming with me, along with God knows who else."

"So your freedom currently involves a few shadows. I want you safe, but I don't want you imprisoned."

A soft smile creeps across her lips. "You know, back in November when you forced me down that aisle, I didn't think you had a kind bone in your body."

"And now?"

She shrugs. "I dunno. I like this version of you. The real you."

"If it makes you feel any better..." Leaning over the counter, I catch her chin and lightly kiss her lips. "I'm perfectly capable of running my business from the ocean. My father would be happy I'm no longer personally involved and I would *love* to see one of my many enemies try to catch me in the middle of the ocean."

Her lips remain slightly parted as she stares into my eyes. "You'd come with me?"

"If you wanted me to. Yes."

"I..." Her gaze breaks away and then she steps away. "I don't know. It's so much to think about. My parents are old so I don't want to miss dinner because as much as I hate it, Mom is right about how many I miss. And after you got stabbed and I got attacked, suddenly, it feels like there's not enough time with family. But also, a cruise around the world playing music would be amazing. I don't know what to do."

"You will figure it out," I assure her gently. "Either because one choice is clear and you're trying to avoid how much you want it, or things will slip into place naturally."

"Maybe." Sighing, she glances at her phone. "I'm going to be late."

As she hurries toward the elevator, my mind races.

Does this baby factor into her plans? Is that the real reason she's reluctant and she can't admit it without telling me the truth? Guilt nestles like a small ball under my ribs from accidentally eavesdropping, but I can't bring myself to influence the choice I think is best for her and the baby. No matter how I feel, I haven't known her long enough to do that.

But her talk of family sits with me.

My own father has taken a back seat since our argument and this time of year is hard for him. For both of us. With Hollie dwelling on her own family, and the baby in the air... I'm at a loss for how to support her without revealing what I know.

But I will do my best.

"Let's go dancing," I call to her as she reaches the elevator.

She spins around, causing her skirt to swirl around her legs. "Now?"

"No, tomorrow. Xena and the girls always throw some amazing parties at this time of year. I want to take you to one. Drinks and dancing. A way to properly relax after everything that's going on."

"Will it be safe?" The doors slide open behind her.

"Of course," I reply easily. "I'll protect you."

35

HOLLIE

"Are you sure about this?" The car glides to a stop outside the club and a rush of nervousness pulses through me. The last time I was here, I learned the truth about Maxim and while I don't regret gaining that insight, I can't stop thinking about that man. Vinnie is his real name, apparently, and he's still not been caught.

"I won't tell you to stop worrying," Maxim says as he takes my hand. "But I will tell you to trust me. We're here to have a good time and I want you to relax and have fun. My entire team is here, and the girls are more than aware of the situation. So if you can trust me, this night will be amazing."

He's not wrong.

Inside, the club has been transformed from the glitzy, burlesque decor I saw last time into a complete winter wonderland. White and silver glitter and tinsel wrap around the back of every chair, the legs of every table, and each pole not in use by a dancer. Large stars, candy canes, and

Christmas stockings hang from the ceiling, the fog machine hums thick and low to the floor, creating the impression of snow, and every girl is dressed up in festive wear. We pass two sexy snowmen, a nearly nude elf, and a sexy Mrs. Claus on our way to the bar. It's as if the blizzard outside has swept right in through the doors and brought with it all the beauty of snowy New York, minus the cold.

A number of patrons mingle on the floor. As we reach the bar, Toto and Stu break off and melt into the crowd with a few more of Maxim's men to check things out. Perching on a stool, my hand remains in Maxim's as Xena pops up behind the bar with a wide smile. Before I can greet her, she leans over and slides some sparkling antlers onto my head.

"There! All dressed up." She chuckles, then she looks at Maxim. "I thought you weren't coming?"

"Hollie deserves a night of fun, and what better place than this?" His grip tightens briefly around my fingers. "Two cocktails for me."

"A mocktail for me," I cut in quickly. "I think I ate something not quite right."

"Aw, chick." Hollie pouts sympathetically. "Coming right up!"

Christmas music fills the air as the lights dim and each occupied stage becomes highlighted by a spotlight. As the music swells, the girls start to dance and I watch in awe of their flexibility and sensual moves all while spinning around a pole. It would be tempting to try, but I can't.

I managed to sneak away from Mom yesterday and visit my doctor who only had time for a quick physical, but everything seems alright with my baby. Without a proper scan, though, she couldn't tell for sure. It was enough to reassure me, but I'm now overly cautious about anything that could affect this pregnancy. But the reassurance brought me to one decision. I need to tell Maxim. Regardless of how he takes the news, I need the freedom to see my doctor as often as I need.

But as much as I want to tell him right now, this night is about letting go and forgetting the stress of the past month.

I'll tell him tomorrow.

"Do you want to dance?"

I swivel in my seat to face Maxim. "You can dance?"

"Is that surprising?"

Xena snorts from behind the bar.

"Not surprising," I assure him sheepishly. "Just... you look more like you know how to dance around a boxing ring than a dance floor."

"Are you judging me?" Maxim raises his brows and slides off his stool, pulling me toward the dance floor. "I'll have you know that the real reason this place does so well is because people come to see *me* dance."

"Oh, is that right?" I giggle. "You draw in more money than these beautiful, half-naked women?"

"Definitely." Tucked into the crowd a little, Maxim's arm snakes around my waist and pulls my body tight against his. "If you have any doubts, just follow me."

"Oh, I can dance. In fact, I think you might be outmatched."

"Am I?" He doesn't hide the way his gaze roams over me as our aligned hips begin rocking from side to side in time to the music.

Despite our height difference, Maxim's crouched stature keeps our hips aligned, but he soon abandons that as we part and the music takes us. He's not wrong about his ability to dance. Every rock, sway, and bob to the music draws my eyes to his hips and his chest. He spins around me, keeping close enough that the warmth of his body envelopes me, but far enough that he doesn't disturb my own moves. It's like I'm the pole and he's the dancer the way he sways around me, his body like liquid with how he flows back and forth to the music.

My heart races. Glitter in the air clings to my skin. Strands of hair escaping my bun stick to the back of my neck, and I'm slowly overheating as the sensual rock of his body close to me ignites desire deep inside me.

I let him dance until the song changes, then I clasp his shoulders and he becomes the pole with little complaint. Where he might have the moves, I have one thing that he doesn't. He's strong and bulky enough that I can lean against him without him wavering, so I use that to my advantage. Mimicking a few of the tamer moves I've seen from the dancers around me, I lean against his back and slide down until I'm on my haunches, then I spin around to his front and climb to my feet while arched into him. My breasts drag against his body from his thighs all the way up to his chest, and Maxim's breath catches in his throat.

Determined to win, I continue my swaying dance and grind around him while occasionally stepping away from him to close my eyes and dance to the music.

It's freeing.

Within minutes, my worries melt away. Nothing exists but the pulsing music that vibrates through my bones, the soft fog caressing my bare ankles, the warmth of Maxim acting as my anchor, and the pleasant ache in my muscles that develops the longer I dance.

When did I last do this?

Just... stop and enjoy things?

No thoughts or work, family or stress. No worry about bills, the mold in my apartment, or where my next line of work will come from.

There's just me and the music, and that's all that matters.

And Maxim.

The music shifts to a slow tune and Maxim's arm returns to my waist. I open my eyes with a soft gasp as he pulls me snug against his hot torso. He leans into me until I'm arched back over his arm. Nose to nose, we breathe the same bubble of air for a few silent seconds and then he smiles and kisses me slowly.

"Maybe you win," he murmurs against my lips. "Maybe I win."

"You win?" Looping one arm around his damp neck, I tease the softer hairs at his neck. "There's no way you win."

"I get you." He leans back and our eyes meet. "So I win by default."

I roll my eyes but his affection warms my heart and a shiver moves through me. How can such an intense, intimidating man be so soft? He's like the grumpiest golden retriever I've ever met. Looking back at when we first met in that club, it must have been this energy that drew me to him in the first place. If I'd found him again in any other place than that pizzeria, maybe our relationship would have been like this from the start.

Instead, we've been through it, which only amplifies my feelings for him. Feelings that clash with a burst of reality in my mind. I don't know how he truly feels, and it can all change when I tell him the truth.

I choose my fantasy for one more night and kiss him deeply, arching into him while we sway and grind around the dance floor. The crowds seem to melt away, and it's just us under one glittering spotlight. He grinds gently against me, swaying back and forth and lightly twirling me around. As we dance, his thigh ends up between my legs as if he's helping guide me through the moves.

Sense escapes me. The pressure of his thigh against my core is enough to melt my mind and I can't stop my hips from moving like they have a mind of their own. My hands clutch the side of his neck and face, kissing him messily while his arm tightens around my waist and he supports me without a word. My hips rock, dragging my core against his thigh while chasing the rush of pleasure that sparks each time I grind a certain way and rub my clit against his firm leg.

We might as well have been alone with how desperately I'm humping his leg. Our tongues slide and weave together in a separate battle, each fighting for dominance, and while I don't give up, I adore his effort to claim me. His other hand roams over my body, caressing my hip, then up to grope at my breasts before finally settling on the side of my neck with his thumb against my racing pulse.

I'm floating, gasping and whimpering against his lips. He doesn't give me space to breathe. My air comes from him while he drinks down every sound that erupts from me, yet all of it stays secret under the thrum of the music.

I reach climax with a gasp, clutching at Maxim and losing all footing. His grip prevents me from falling and he holds me close as if we're one. When his lips curl into a cheeky smirk against my mouth, I bite his lower lip as sharply as I can while I tremble in his arms and my core clenches repeatedly.

"See?" Maxim grunts after freeing his lips from my hungry bite. "I win, no matter what. Because I have you. And the next time you want to be sassy, I'll remind you how you humped my leg in a club in front of everyone."

Heat immediately rushes to my cheeks as if I've been slapped, and reality comes crashing back. The crowd around us is none the wiser, though. Not a soul saw what we were up to and if they did, then they didn't care. The music seems louder now, and the crowd is a lot closer as I lean away from Maxim and fight to catch my breath.

"Later," I gasp softly. "You'll be debating whether this was my plan all along and I won because you're easy to trick."

"You sure about that?" He captures my lips in another strong kiss, then nudges his nose into mine. "Come on, I'm parched."

Hand in hand, we weave through the crowd back toward the bar while I adjust my clothing to account for the new dampness in my underwear. But as the crowd surges, someone's shoulder crashes into mine with such force that Maxim's hand slips out of mine as I fall to the ground with a yelp.

"Hey! Watch where you're go—"

It's him. Time slows as the man vanishing into the crowd glances back with a single, hateful look. Half of his face is covered in small cuts. It turns my blood to ice and my heart stalls in my chest.

It's *him*! Mr. Havershire— Vinnie. How is he here? How did he get in?

"Hollie!" As soon as Maxim's over me, time seems to restart and I clutch at his arm.

"Maxim, that's him! Right there! It's Vinnie!"

Maxim scoops me up into my arms and then turns, glaring through the crowd while I fight to keep pointing at the rapidly disappearing head.

"Stu! Toto!"

I'm suddenly deposited into Rex's arms and Maxim vanishes into the crowd, chasing after Vinnie.

My heart pounds as the crowd swells, swallowing them all from view. Rex carries me the rest of the way to the bar and sets me down while Xena climbs over the bar and clutches my hand.

"Was it really him?"

I nod, despite how doubt suddenly swells in my chest. What if I was wrong? What if I was so caught up in the moment that I only saw someone I thought was familiar? Xena presses water into my trembling hands as Vinnie's face flashes, then deforms in my mind. The harder I think about him, the less I'm sure of what I saw.

Did I just ruin the night?

Maxim and the others don't return until the crowd has thinned several hours later. Hours I spent fretting about something happening to them. As soon as he appears, I lunge up from my seat and throw my arms around him.

"Oh, thank God, I'm so sorry!"

Maxim hugs me tightly and buries his face in my neck for a few long seconds. "What are you sorry for?" he asks as he pulls back.

"I don't... The more I thought about it, the more I'm not sure I saw who I thought I saw."

"Don't doubt yourself. Stu saw him too and we have media of Vinnie. It was him."

"How did he get in?" Xena, back behind the bar, nearly drops her glass. "How could he get here? Better yet, did you catch him?"

I gaze up at Maxim and see the answer in his eyes immediately. "He got away."

Behind Maxim, Toto and Stu hunch over, slightly breathless. "Fucker's fast," Stu gasps.

"He's one man," Maxim growls. "One man has this entire organization chasing their fucking tails, me included. I refuse to let this continue. I want him dead, you hear me? I want him *dead*."

36

HOLLIE

"**M**om?" Knocking softly, I walk into my parents' home to the mouthwatering scents of apple pie and cinnamon.

"In the kitchen!" Mom calls.

Quickly shrugging off my coat, I glance back outside where poor Toto is forced to wait in the car with another guard thanks to my mom's insistence that she didn't want *extra* people in her home. I'll bring them some hot chocolate once I've tried to persuade my mom to let them come in.

Rubbing my hands together against the cold that seeped in through my gloves, I enter the kitchen with a smile.

"If you're here to tell me you can't make dinner tomorrow, then you just turn around and walk right back out." Mom stands over the stove, staring intently down at the compote she's cautiously stirring with a wooden spoon.

"Ironically, that is what I want to talk to you about."

"Oh, Hollie." She sighs as if my presence exasperates her. "Can't you ever arrive with good news? Maybe some excitement to spend Christmas with your family? You didn't invite us to your wedding, you missed Thanksgiving, you were late to the friends and family party last weekend. Can't you give me one thing?"

Frustration buds in the back of my mind while I lean on the island counter and watch her back. "Actually, it's my future I want to talk about. I have an interview tomorrow."

"Let me guess, it clashes with our dinner."

"Yes."

"Who interviews on Christmas Eve?"

"Do you remember at lunch on Tuesday, I was talking about what I wanted out of my work?"

"Before you left me there?"

My gut tightens. I had left, but given that it was to sneak away to my doctor, it was a worthy trip. "I told you I wasn't feeling well, but yes."

"Alright." Mom sighs and turns toward me, removing the compote from the heat. "Tell me about it."

"It's for a private cruise liner that departs in February and won't redock here until November. They're looking to fill a spot on their orchestra and I'd kind of be perfect for it."

"Ten months?" She halts her pouring of the compote over the fruit nestled into several pastry cases. "Hollie, you can't be serious!"

"I am."

"So you're just going to leave me and your father? What about your new husband? What does he think about this?"

I know she doesn't really care about what Maxim thinks. She's just using it to pile on the guilt, but Maxim is the reason I'm considering turning it down.

Until that killer is caught, no one is safe. On one hand, leaving the country might be the only way to stay safe, but I don't want to give birth on a cruise so far away from real medical care and a hospital. And I don't want to leave Maxim. Enjoying our relationship hinges entirely on how he feels about me and how he'll react to this baby, but even if he rejects me and his child, then I still don't want to have a baby in open ocean.

Leaving New York is no longer my strongest desire, but if it comes to it, then I'll go to L.A.

"Hollie?" Mom drags me from her thoughts. "What will your father say?"

I follow her gaze to the back garden where I see my father exit his shed, grab some wood, and hurry back inside to hide from the cold. I can't imagine what his reaction will be, but given how quietly he supports me, I hope he'll be happy for me. Maxim's revelation that my father knows who he is was shocking, and I keep waiting for him to speak to me about it, but he hasn't said a word. I hope that means he trusts me and in turn, he'll trust whatever I want to do for the future.

Never mind how they will both react when they find out I'm carrying their grandchild.

All the possibilities clash together in my mind and I groan softly.

Maybe I'll go home tonight and everything I'm worried about will all be over. When I left the penthouse, Maxim was on his way to meet his father. After Vinnie's appearance at the club, Maxim's been working with his father to track the bastard down once and for all.

Despite Igor's distaste for me, his protectiveness over his only remaining son gives me hope. A man like that who tried to kill me based on the possibility of hurting Maxim will surely stop at nothing now that Maxim's being toyed with.

Until then, it's a waiting game.

"Well?" Mom drags me from my thoughts again and in the time I've been thinking, she's covered all the pies with freshly rolled dough. "Are you just going to sit there and hope I'll forget what you've said?"

"No," I sigh, straightening up in my seat to ease my back. "I'm just... I need to know you support me, Mom. No matter what I decide. I can't stay here forever and having a decent, continuous income would be amazing."

"You could get that at any job," she replies bitterly. "Why one that takes you away from me?"

"Don't you see how great an opportunity this could be for me? Imagine the contacts I'll make in the music industry."

"Is that what this is about?" The pies clatter as she shoves them into the oven. "You want to be famous?"

"Not that kind of famous. I like being freelance, but yeah, I'd like to play somewhere more substantial than a hotel lobby or a restaurant."

"And for that, you need to miss dinner with your family. Again."

"I wouldn't be missing the whole thing. I'd just be late. I don't want to pass this up, but I don't want to upset you either. Please, Mom."

"Why are you here?" She faces me suddenly, scrunching a tea towel between her hands. "You've clearly already made up your mind so what's the point of discussing it. All my preparation for dinner is just useless, pointless! What's another ruined dinner, hmm?" She tosses the towel onto the counter and stomps out of the room. I rise to follow her just as Dad stumbles in the door and hurriedly closes it against the cold.

"It's barking out there," he grumbles. "Hollie! What a surprise."

"Hi, Dad."

"What brings you here?" He peels off his gloves while stamping his snow-covered boots on the mat.

"I have a job interview tomorrow and thought telling Mom face-to-face would go better than over the phone."

"Ah." He nods knowingly. "You will miss dinner?"

"Only a part of it."

"How did she take it?"

I motion to the empty kitchen. "She always acts like every Christmas is the last one we will ever have."

Dad chuckles softly. "When you get to our age, you worry it will be. It starts with missed dinners, then a call once a week, and then suddenly, you haven't seen your loved ones in a few years because everyone is just so busy. It's not personal, Hollie. She's just..."

"Moody?" I mutter.

"Your marriage scared her."

"Scared her?" I lift my gaze to his as he peels himself out of his coat. "Why?"

"It was a huge life event and you didn't include her. Now all she has is the holidays to make memories with you until you decide you'd rather make memories with your new family."

"Oh, Dad. It's not like that."

"I know. And deep down, she knows it too. But she's worried."

Before I can reply, rapid knocking at the front door draws my attention so I slip from my stool and move past my dad. "If she were honest with me, then I could tell her that."

"Your mother is anything but honest." Dad chuckles, turning on the hot tap and shoving his cold hands underneath as the door knocks again. "Could you get that?"

"Mhm." Trudging into the hall, I mull over his words. If she's really worried about missing out on other great life events, maybe it's time to tell her I'm pregnant. If she's the first to know, then it might soothe my absence tomorrow.

"Yep?" Opening the door, I expect to see Toto standing there shivering in the cold, eager for the bathroom so his dick doesn't fall off.

It's not Toto.

Vinnie's beady, dark eyes glare down at me and it takes me a second too long to recognize him. *Danger* blares through my mind as our gazes lock and despite the sharp burst of panic in my mind, only one question makes it through clearly.

How?

I slam the door closed but instead of the satisfying clack of wood on wood, the door doesn't close and Vinnie grunts in pain as his foot jams in the doorway.

"No!" I shove hard at the door again, but Vinnie throws his entire shoulder into the door and it bursts open, sending me stumbling back into the hallway. My feel catches on the rug and I fall, hitting the ground hard. I scramble up immediately but as I lunge away, his fist tangles in my hair and he yanks me backward.

"Not this time, bitch," Vinnie snarls, jerking me so hard that my entire scalp burns and I lose my footing again. This time, I fall at his feet, landing awkwardly on my knees as his fist in my hair keeps my body raised like some kind of leash.

"Hollie, what's— hey! What the fuck are you doing?"

"Dad, no!" The words don't escape in time as Dad rushes toward us both, but Vinnie snatches the gun from his hip and swings his arm out like a whip. His fist and the butt of the gun crash into Dad's face, and he grunts, collapsing back into the side table. He, the bowl of keys, and Mom's ornaments all tumble to the floor.

"Dad!"

"Outside, I don't have time for this!" Vinnie wrenches me backward and throws me out into the yard. Landing face-first in the snow, I have no time to get up before Vinnie's on me again. He hauls me up by the scruff of the neck and the bloody sight before me turns my stomach immediately.

Toto's car sits parked where I left it but the doors are open. Two dead men paint red angels across the snow and Toto lies near the Christmas tree, silent and motionless. Blood splatters the snow all around, as if someone had passed by with a hose, and as Vinnie drags me down the path, I can't get a long enough glimpse to see if Toto's even breathing.

"Stop," I gasp. "Let me go, let me the fuck go!" I lunge forward, trying to knock Vinnie off balance with my sudden movement, but he's ready for me and he drags me back with a growl.

He wrenches my head back painfully, and the barrel of the gun presses hard against the soft flesh under my chin.

"Walk," he barks down at me. "Get in my fucking truck or I'll walk back up that path and see how many bullets I need to put in your old man to stop him from following us, got it?"

Stale cigarette breath washes over me as he presents the ultimatum. Before I can reply, he throws me forward with all his strength and I land on my hands and knees in the street. My heart pounds, my head throbs, and the sight of the dead bodies littering the lawn draws a mouthful of bile up my throat. I spew onto the snow-covered ground, which pisses Vinnie off more, but as he kicks out at my stomach, I scramble out of the way and climb to my feet with a gasp.

"Alright!" Tears threaten at the corner of my eyes. "Alright. I'll come with you, just please... Please don't hurt my family!"

37

MAXIM

"He's one man!" My fist collides with the wall, sending pain lancing up my arm. "One fucking man and he's a ghost. Tell me how this makes any fucking sense?"

"That anger you feel?" My father stands behind me, a glass of Bourbon in his hand. "I understand it."

"No, you don't." That fucker was at the club, likely scouting out his next victim until he ran into us. Losing him in the blizzard weighs on me like the worst mistake of my life, and despite how we searched, he vanished into the city with another victory under his belt. "It's failure after fucking failure on a man I know more about than my own friends. I've scoured every property he's ever owned, questioned anyone he's ever associated with, tore apart that flash performance troupe looking for him, only to find out that he crashed it. He's constantly one step ahead of me and I can't catch up!"

Turning, my father's face remains passive with only a flicker of understanding in his eyes.

"I felt the same when your mother died."

"What?" Despite the fury licking at my heart, my mind stalls briefly. "How is that the same?"

"Having someone ten years younger than me telling me there was nothing they could do for her now, that her death was unavoidable... I blamed him. And I hunted him to the ends of the earth, but he kept slipping away from me because I forgot one important detail."

"What detail? The fact that he was just her doctor?"

"Exactly. He was a normal, regular person. They don't think like us. They don't plan like us. When they're running, they react. You've been chasing this Vinnie because he's from this world, but he's hardly deeply ingrained. He's a worthless cunt on the outskirts and thus, he doesn't have the same calculated mind we have. You can't catch up to someone who doesn't know where they're going."

My fists tighten and pain bleeds across my bruised knuckles. "So, what do I do?"

"He's lashing out. He's furious at you and us, which is why he and the other one attacked the girls at your club, right?"

"Yeah."

"He prolonged their pain and torture because he *could*. He wanted to show that he's in no rush, but it reveals that he doesn't fully know what he's doing. He's trying to hurt you, to fuck things up enough that someone else will take notice and think he's the key to your downfall. He's like a mosquito dancing on the edge of our web."

"So how the fuck do I ensnare him?"

"You have to act like you don't care."

"And risk more lives? Not a chance."

"Think about it, Maxim. He's returning to the scene of the first crime by coming back to the club. He's looking for his next victim and all our people are on high alert. At worst, you have to sacrifice one or two more to get him."

Shoving past him, I stalk toward the door, then turn back and angrily point at him. "How can you talk like that? What kind of loyalty does that show the people I'm supposed to lead? Telling them they're fucking expendable?"

"You can't save everyone!" he yells suddenly, then catches himself and steps back. "You can't *care* about everyone, Maxim. You can't protect everyone. You can put things in place to keep people safe but at the end of the day, the only people who truly matter are *family*. Caring for everyone means caring for no one, and the sooner you realize that, the sooner you'll be able to think about this objectively and stop this fucker."

I want to tell him he's wrong. That his words are cold and heartless, but deep down, I know he's right. There are countless businesses and families under our rule, far too many to count, and I can't keep them all safe. I can't save everyone the moment there's a lick of danger. I can't be everywhere at once.

Defeat clings to my shoulders no matter how hard I try to shrug it off. "So what do I do?"

"Protect those you care about." He brings his glass to his lips. "And Vinnie will come to you."

Hollie.

I love her.

It's the only certainty in my life and twice, that fucker has gotten too close to her. I need to get her out of his sight, especially if she's pregnant. It doesn't matter where we go, but it has to be away. Then, if Vinnie really wants to get my attention, he'll have to follow.

"Shit." I sink down onto the nearest chair. "How can one man cause all of this?"

"It feels big, but he's just a pebble in your shoe, chipping away at you. We have to make sacrifices sometimes, and then we soothe over the pain left. We kill who we need to kill, we save who we can, and we make deals that stop us from sleeping but keep us afloat. That's the cost we pay."

My eyes close and I press my fingers to the bridge of my nose. "Hollie... she has this opportunity to go—"

The sudden buzzing from my phone cuts me off and an unknown number flashes on the screen, derailing my thoughts. Exchanging a glance with my father, I answer. "Hello?"

"Maxim?" Susan's trembling voice fills my ear. "Oh, Maxim, I didn't know who else to call!"

I'm on my feet immediately as ice spreads its cold, killer fingers through my chest. "Tell me."

"It was awful, oh God, it was awful!" Susan dissolves into

tears and fabric scuffles over the phone, then Martin's voice follows.

"He's taken her," he says thickly. "I don't know who, but a man came. He's killed your men and he's taken Hollie. I've done what I can, but you need to bring my daughter back, do you understand me? I don't care what this is, but you told me you married her to save her, so you'd better fucking save her, you hear me?"

The cold spreads like a fever throughout my body and my eyes lock with my Dad's. "He's taken her."

"Move." Dad abandons his glass and we're rushing through the manor.

"I'll get her back," I swear down the phone. "Tell me everything."

By the time Martin's told me everything, I'm in the car with Stu driving and Dad in the backseat. Hearing Toto's alive is the only good thing coming out of this current disaster, and my dad mobilizes several teams to secure Hollie's parents. As the call ends, I'm about to ask Stu to take me to Rex when another call comes through.

"Hollie?" Despite barking her name, she doesn't speak and all that comes through is the hum of a car engine. I place the call on speaker and Stu pulls over to the side of the road as we exchange a glance.

"Why him?" Hollie's muffled, teary voice crackles through what seems to be a layer of fabric. "Why do you care so much?"

"Are you thick?" Vinnie's voice follows, somewhat distant. "Do you have any idea what it's like to have your family wiped out because someone leagues away from you decides it's the only way to move forward? People make mistakes but the fucking Krasnovs act like they're above all of us!"

"What's that got to do with me?" Hollie gasps. "He kidnapped me, remember? Forced me to marry him."

"I'd believe you, but I've seen the way he looks at you," Vinnie sneers.

"How did you find me?"

"I was going to take you at the cafe but when you snuck away, I got curious. Is it his baby? Are you carrying his fucking spawn?"

Stu's gaze locks on me and he mouths 'no fucking way'.

"No," Hollie gasps. "I was pregnant before I met him."

"I don't believe you."

"So that's how you found me? You followed me from the clinic?"

"Nah. I left you at the clinic and followed your mom from the cafe. Then I just had to wait. Everyone fucking loves their family at this time of year."

"And now you're taking me upstate? What's your plan, huh?"

"My plan? I'm tired. No one would give a shit if it wasn't Maxim acting like a fucking dog with a bone. But now I have you, and as long as I have you, he'll leave me the fuck alone until I'm ready for him," Vinnie snarls. "And he'll do anything to keep you safe, which buys me a new life."

"A new life where, the far side of Central Park?"

"What?" Vinnie mutters. "What are you talking about?"

"Nothing."

"What's that?"

"Nothing, Vinnie, stop—"

Their conversation dissolves into rustling and muted yells, then a thump as the phone seems to fall further away from their arguing voices. As the voices grow louder, there's a yell and my heart jumps as something akin to a gunshot blasts through the air.

Then there's a deafening screech of metal and another scream.

Then nothing but silence.

38

HOLLIE

Ow.

Everything hurts.

Despite the cushion of the snow I landed in after being flung from the car, the ground underneath is hard enough that all my bones rattled around my body for a good few seconds after impact. Sharp pain flares at the base of my skull, and my vision blurs red while I gaze up at the fat snowflakes falling around me, illuminated by the headlights from the crashed car.

I did everything I could think of.

I called Maxim, but I have no idea if the call even made it through. I tried to keep Vinnie talking so he would slip up, even tried to offer directional hints, but all of it relied on my call connecting and there's no way for me to check.

I dropped my phone before the crash. It's probably back in the car with Vinnie, wherever he ended up.

How did my life end up like this?

I lived quietly. I played music and kept to the background because that's where I belonged. All I wanted to do was live a quiet life, pursue my passion, and have a fling here and there with a hot guy. Instead, I got pregnant and tracking down the father landed me in the hot pot of the Mafia world, then married to a man I should hate.

A man I love.

Will he find me?

Will he work his magic and track me down or is he still oblivious with no idea what's happened? And my parents... Dad's face flashes through my mind, covered in blood from Vinnie's punch, and my sluggish heart squeezes.

Get up, Hollie.

I'm cold. Freezing. Icy fingers wrap around my limbs and seep through my clothes, holding me close to the ground and refusing to let me go. If I lie here long enough, the snow will cover me and I'll become one with the ice cold against my back. It's a peaceful thought and for a few long seconds, I entertain it.

Closing my eyes would be blissful and I'd let the snow bundle me up in her cotton-soft hands, carrying me into a peaceful darkness where there's no stress, no pain, and no fear.

No Vinnie either.

But I can't do that.

If Zoe can fight, then so can I. The baby inside me deserves a mother who fights.

I can't tell how long I lay there before consciousness finally fully trickled back into my mind. Wounds from the crash turn numb in the cold as I drag my frozen hands across the ground and brace them. Limbs ache and joints twinge, and my head swims as I get onto my hands and knees, then up onto my unsteady feet, and survey the damage.

Despite the bright illumination of the headlights, it takes a few seconds for the car to come into view through the thickly falling snow. The car's *above* me, caught in some warped iron fencing that Vinnie crashed through when he lost control of the vehicle. Metal creaks and groans as the car sways dangerously. With each second, the weight of the vehicle pulls against the weakening railings, bringing the car closer to collapsing down into the underpass I've woken up in.

Around me, untouched snow sparkles in the headlights, and behind me is the hole my body carved out when I was flung through the windshield. It's a miracle I'm even alive and cold tears spring into my eyes as both my hands caress my belly.

They come away sticky and warm. Glancing down, blood coats my palms, but just as panic crawls up my throat like venom, the open wound on my shoulder that's sluggishly bleeding shows itself as the source of the blood. My relief is short-lived as I stumble backward and a wave of dizziness washes over me.

I have to get out of here.

Squinting up at the car, it's empty, which means Vinnie is around here somewhere. With the car being out of reach, looking for my phone is pointless. Around me, dead trees loom out of the darkness and there's a distant trickle of water somewhere to my left. Other than that, there's silence. Pain swells from the back of my skull, clouding my thoughts as I try to recall where we were before we crashed.

"Walk," I murmur to myself, and blood sweeps over my tongue. "Gotta walk."

The miracle of surviving the crash threatens to be overshadowed by the biting cold that attacks my bare skin, exposed through my torn clothing. Vinnie didn't give me a chance to grab my coat, so I trudge through the snow in just my leggings and ruined blouse.

"Hollie!" Vinnie's voice roars out of somewhere in the darkness. I jump, nearly losing my balance. "Get back here, you fucking bitch!"

Run, Hollie, run!

Snow slips underfoot, my breath escapes in short, sharp pants, and the pain at the base of my skull swells like a ball is forming at the top of my spine. I ignore it all and I run, sprinting as fast as I can away from the wreckage. Feet pounding, arms swinging and joints screaming, I run as fast as I can.

And I don't stop.

Tree roots hidden under the snow reach through the flakes to grab my ankles and trip me up, tree branches cut my skin and pull at my clothes as I run, and the snow falls thicker to blind me in an already impenetrable darkness, but I don't stop running. I keep going even as pressure swells in my chest and forces even shorter gasps of air from me, as my gut twists and cramps and my body freezes.

Then I glimpse light.

Through the trees, an array of color welcomes me with warmth and light, and the soft hum of voices. We must be in the park, and whatever event is happening up there will save me. I just have to get there.

My heart pounds fiercely, thumping in my ears and threatening to burst with how hard I'm pushing myself, but it's all background noise. I'm almost there, I'm almost—

The thumping switches rhythm, refusing to match the pounding tremor in my chest. That noise isn't my heart.

Vinnie crashes into my back with a yell and knocks us both to the ground. A scream tears from my throat, but it's instantly muted by a mouthful of snow and pain radiates through my entire body, then a lance of fear that falling on my stomach could harm my baby.

"Where the fuck are you going?" Vinnie growls in my ear, forcing my face into the snow and then dragging my hair to one side so his lips rest against my ear. "Did you think I'd let you get away from me this easily? Did you really think I would lose my one chance to lure out that bastard? I don't need you alive and I'm more than happy to lure him with your corpse if that's how you'd prefer it!"

With my head to the side, the snow parts in our scuffle to give me a last glimpse of the light and color through the trees. From here, shadows move back and forth as regular people go about their evening. They're all so close and yet so far away, unable to hear me and unable to help. I try to scream but I can't get air into my lungs, so all that escapes me is a strangled cry.

Vinnie's weight increases for a moment and when he tightens his fist in my hair, the pain at the base of my skull becomes blinding.

"On your feet, bitch," he snarls, then something impossibly cold and sharp presses against my ribs. "Or I'll burst your lung and watch you suffocate in the snow."

What is that? A knife? Something worse?

I'm hauled to my feet and struggle to stay upright as the world spins and my knees buckle. Exhausted and pained, I meet Vinnie's eyes when he forces me to face him.

"You're insane," I gasp as snow clings to my chin and cheek. "You really think you can get to him through me?"

The crash has reopened some of the wounds on Vinnie's face from the snow globe I hit him with, and he holds himself to one side. Some of his ribs must be broken.

"It's a matter of principle," Vinnie growls, and the knife in his hand reflects the light. "He won't be able to resist, and me?" He lunges at me, breathless. "I'm going to—"

Then he's gone.

Vinnie vanishes, and I blink slowly through the haze building around my eyes. One second he was in front of me, the next he's just... gone? Did I die?

Oh.

No.

He's not gone.

Vinnie's on the ground to my left, visible briefly under the gigantic mound of Maxim who has one hand around his throat and the other smashing repeatedly into Vinnie's face.

I can't keep myself stable. The ground tips and I step to the side, then again as I struggle to keep upright.

Maxim's here?

How is he here?

Is this a hallucination?

"What...?" I stumble again and this time, I land in the arms of someone else. Before I can cry out, Stu's face swims in front of me and my heart skips a beat, then suddenly, Maxim roars out in pain.

We both look to see him land on the ground with Vinnie's knife protruding from Maxim's abdomen.

"No!" I surge forward, but Stu hauls me back as Maxim scrambles up in a flurry of snow and dirt and launches at Vinnie once more.

The fight is impossible to track in the dark and Stu's arms are like iron, refusing to let me go no matter how much I want to. If this is a dream, then I need to help, and if this is real, then I can't lose him.

Maxim hits the ground again, gasping, and suddenly, Vinnie's lunging toward me with both arms outstretched. Stu holds me so tight that the gun on his hip digs into my waist and I react without any thought. Instinct to protect fuels me.

I snatch Stu's gun from his holster as he puts himself between me and Vinnie, raise it, and pull the trigger. The first bullet hits a nearby tree with a soft thunk. The next bullet disappears into the darkness, and the third finally finds its mark in Vinnie.

He roars in pain and keeps coming, even as Maxim surges up behind him, so I keep pulling the trigger even as the kickback makes my aim wild and weak.

"Hollie!" Stu yells, finally grasping my wrist and preventing me from firing further. "Stop!"

"Did I get him? Did I kill him? Is he dead? Is it over?" A sudden full-body tremble courses through me, and Stu's arms tighten around me. The gun goes off three more times and Stu grunts in my ear.

"No, I got him. You didn't kill anyone," he says. "I got him."

Darkness swallows me for a second and the ground falls away, only for warmth to envelop me. Opening my eyes, the stars above spin faster than I can handle. Then Maxim's face swims into view and anchors me so completely that the stars finally stop moving.

"Maxim?"

"Oh, Hollie," Maxim pants. "You left me for a second there."

"I— what happened? How are you here? How am I— is he still...?"

I try to stand, but the lack of ground against my feet alerts me to the fact that I'm being carried in Maxim's thick arms.

"He's gone. He's dead," Maxim says gruffly. "I'm so sorry I didn't get here in time. I'm taking you to the hospital."

"You got stabbed," I whimper as the throbbing at the base of my skull grows. "I was so scared, I— Maxim, don't leave me, please. Please."

"I won't," he whispers, bringing his face close to mine. "I'm never letting you go ever again."

His warm lips close over my icy ones and I sink into a final, comforting darkness.

39

MAXIM

"I want to leave, you can't keep me here!" Hollie's arms cross over her chest, then she winces as the movement pulls at the stitches on her shoulder.

"Hollie, darling. I'm not trying to keep you here against your will, believe me. But the hospital is the best place for you right now."

"What about you?" She pouts up at me. "You should be in bed too."

"I wasn't thrown through a windshield."

"But you were stabbed."

"A flesh wound."

"All my injuries are flesh wounds!"

"Maybe, but you have more than me, plus some whiplash. Staying here is how I keep you healthy and safe."

"And if I refuse?" Her eyes narrow, so I sit on the edge of the bed and gently rub her thigh through the blanket.

"Why do you want to leave so badly?"

Her face crumbles slightly and she sighs. "I want to see my parents. I want to spend Christmas Eve with them, and I don't want to miss out on dinner because of that asshole."

Vinnie. He deserved a much slower death than the one we granted him, but news of his death spread quickly. While Hollie was getting checked over by the doctors last night, I spent an hour on the phone with Zoe, assuring her that the man haunting her is definitely dead. Stu will take her to see his body when she's ready so she can get the closure she needs, something I would do if I didn't need to be here with Hollie.

Finding that car and her missing was the most terrifying moment of my life. I was convinced I was too late and the only thing I'd find was her body.

Luckily, someone was watching over her.

"You're thinking about him, aren't you?" Hollie says, her expression softening.

I meet her gaze and nod. "Yeah."

"Did we do a bad thing? Killing him?"

"No, of course not. I'm thinking more about how you're right. He's taken and affected a lot of our life and I understand why you want to be with your family. So... if you can get the doctor to clear you, then I will take you home."

"Promise?"

"I promise."

"Good." She briefly closes her eyes and sinks back into the pillows. "Can we visit Toto before we leave?"

"You're so certain the doctor will let you leave."

"I have my ways. But I want to see him. When I think about him, all I see is his body in the snow." Her face crumples slightly. "So many people got hurt."

Toto's survival is thanks to the snow, ironically. It slowed down his heart enough that when the ambulance arrived for Hollie's father, they were able to tend to Toto, and he sits in the next ward with two gunshot wounds. Thankfully, he'll make a full recovery and be back on his feet by New Year's.

"But we won." My hand slides over hers. "Your father is okay, just a broken nose. Toto is going to be okay. Zoe gets to spend a Christmas with her son without being terrified. I hate that he did this to you, but I am so proud of you."

"For killing him?" Her lower lip wobbles, so I lean forward and kiss her softly.

"You didn't kill him, remember? Stu did." It was a nice touch for him to ensure he shot that bastard too. We'll never know what bullet killed him, but it helps stop Hollie from torturing herself about taking a life.

"Right." She doesn't look entirely convinced. "I, uhm..." Hollie sits up and wraps her hands around mine. "Actually... I told myself if I survived, then there would be something I would tell you."

My heart skips a beat. There's nothing she can say that will change how I feel about her, but there's apprehension in her eyes and she can't look directly at me as she speaks.

"I need you to understand that I kept this a secret at first because I was scared and I thought you were a murderer and I was terrified I'd made a mistake because you wouldn't let me leave and you had guards with me all the time. And then when I started to fall for you, I was going to tell you, but you were so busy. We both were, and I kept telling myself a perfect time would arise, but it never did, and then when Vinnie attacked me, I couldn't tell you my secret because I was so worried that it would have affected me."

Instantly, I know where she's going with this and it's almost impossible to keep the smile from growing on my face.

"And I promised myself that if I survived, then I would tell you and I really don't want you to be mad because this feels like something I should tell you, but I'm also scared because..." She trails off and glances up at me. "Why are you smiling?"

"Because you're trusting me."

She laughs briefly and rolls her eyes. "Maxim... I'm pregnant. That's why I followed you into the pizzeria last month, because I'd been looking for you for *weeks* and you were a ghost. Then I saw you and I thought fate was finally helping me, so I came to tell you that I was carrying your baby. Everything just sort of got fucked after that, but I... I'm pregnant."

Her eyes flit repeatedly up to my face as if she's almost too scared to look at my reaction. I lean forward and cup her face with my free hand, then tilt her up to look at me.

"I love you, Hollie. So much. I fell for you so fucking hard and almost embarrassingly fast, so this?" I tilt my head and glance down at her abdomen. "This is *amazing*."

"You're not mad?" she whispers. "That I hid it?"

"Not at all. If anything, I'm thankful you finally trust me," I say, kissing her softly. "A baby, Hollie. Our own little nugget is growing inside you... I can't believe this. I'm going to be a father!" Laughter bubbles up inside me and I kiss her repeatedly. There's no point in telling her that I already knew. Revealing that would likely reduce her trust in me, and I value that more than anything else.

"I'm going to be a mom." Hollie laughs, kissing me back while tears twinkle in her eyes. "It's also why I want to go to dinner with my parents and not the banquet."

Leaning back, I study her face. "Are you sure? That job is an amazing opportunity for you."

"I know, but I want this baby and I don't want to be pregnant on a cruise. My current work gives me the freedom I'd lose on a cruise, and I want to be here with my family, present while raising our baby." She slides one hand over her belly and smiles softly. "There'll be other cruises."

"Are you sure?" I squeeze her hand gently. "Your dream is important too, Hollie."

"I know. But my life back then when I wanted out of New York is so different to the life I have now. This is the one I want." Her gaze meets mine and she slides her fingers between mine, gripping tightly. "Because I love you and this is what I want."

"My life won't get any safer," I warn her gently. "I will do everything I can to keep you and our baby safe, I swear it. But I need to make sure you understand."

"I understand." Her smile wavers as her eyes sparkle. "You love me. I love you. That's all that matters."

SEVERAL HOURS LATER, Hollie's discharged from the hospital with very strict warnings that she return the *second* she feels off, and we arrive at her parents' house while they're halfway through dinner. Her mother is ecstatic to see her and her father, despite his bruises, welcomes me with a firm handshake.

"Thank you," he says firmly. "Thank you for bringing her back."

"Of course."

I watch from the doorway as Hollie sits at the table and tells her parents she's pregnant. Her mom dissolves into excited screams while her dad claps me on the back and congratulates me. Despite his knowledge of the truth, her mom still appears blissfully unaware of the truth about me and thinks Vinnie was just some crazed person high on drugs who chose a random home. That lie solidifies when she learns how far along Hollie is, which further strengthens our previous tale about how we met. She seems more accepting of our sudden wedding now.

Food is shared, music plays, and Hollie's mom chatters excitedly about the arrival of a baby. Watching her family close in around her, my heart is full. Rex and Stu are eventually invited inside, and I call Toto at the hospital to lovingly mock his absence. We'll have another party just for him when he's back on his feet. The dinner's in full swing with empty wine bottles filling the table by the time the doorbell rings a little after eleven at night.

It puts everyone on guard until I answer the door.

"Dad?"

He stands on the doorstep wrapped in a thick coat, with several of his own guards filling the front lawn. "Maxim."

"What are you doing here?"

"Rex told me you would be here. I wanted to leave some men here so you and yours can relax. And also... to bring you this." In his outstretched hand rests a small black box. Behind me, the dinner resumes once everyone is satisfied the unexpected guest isn't a danger.

"What is this?"

"Open it."

Taking the box, I pull the lid apart. A sparkling ring covered in red gems rests in a gold band. It's dainty and sparkly, and achingly familiar. "This..." I squint back up at Dad. "This was Mom's?"

Igor nods and clears his throat. "The things you have done for Hollie... I can see you are serious. I'm sorry. It will take me time, I know, to make up for what I did, but you should have this. If she really is the one for you, then I know your mother would want you to have this. It was in her family for generations and you... you deserve it. You are my future, Maxim. You and your wife should—"

He's cut off as I throw my arms around him in a very tight, very brief hug that's over as quickly as it starts. As I step back, I swallow the lump of emotion in my throat and close the box. "Thanks, Dad."

He nods once, silently.

"Do you want to come in?"

He gazes past me for a moment, then he shakes his head. "No. I have some things to tend to and until I have made up for what I did, I don't want to intrude. Next time."

As he steps away, words rise inside me and I blurt them out before I can think it through. "You're going to be a grandfather. So please, be sincere when you apologize to her."

He stops halfway down the path, caught in whatever thoughts swarm him in that moment. Then he continues down to the car and only a handful of guards follow. Given how distant he's been since my brother died, this is the warmest thing he's ever done. Closing the door, I head back inside and beeline to Hollie.

She gives me an incredible smile as I kneel next to her and she cups my face. "Hi, handsome."

"Marry me," I say quietly under the hum of activity at the table, presenting the box to her.

Her eyes widen and she gazes down at the ring while thumbing the current ring around her own finger. "We're already married."

"Marry me properly. A full wedding. Everything you could ever want. Have your family and friends there, make it as big or as small as you want. I love you, Hollie, and I never gave you the ceremony you deserve. So marry me again and let me make you proud."

Her lips part and she stares at me in quiet shock, then she takes my mother's ring and very slowly slips it on until it nestles next to her original ring. "Wow. It's heavy," she murmurs, curling her fingers. Then she cups my face and draws me up against her, kissing me hard. "Yes," she whispers against my lips. "I'll marry you again. For real this time."

Never has life been so kind, and I will spend the rest of my days earning every drop of her love.

40

HOLLIE

Sun trickles through the blinds, waking me slowly. Sleep curls its warm fingers around me, enticing me back under but the moment Maxim moves against, I'm fully awake. His firm cock presses against the crease of my ass but he still seems asleep despite how both his arms tighten around me when I move.

Every part of me tingles. We spent the whole day yesterday celebrating Christmas in all the places that are important to us. Starting with my parents', we stayed there until lunch and then visited the hospital with presents for Toto, including my deep thanks for his attempts to protect me and my family. While there, Stu finally apologized for hitting me when we first met and I happily informed him that I forgave him the moment he protected me from Vinnie in the park.

What's a slap between friends?

Dinner was spent with Maxim's father, a tense affair, but the man did seem to be making an effort. Given what I learned about his late son, I understand his urge to protect. While the actual word *sorry* never left his lips, his actions give me hope that at some point, there's a chance my baby will be born into a family without discord. After dinner, we visited Zoe and handed out some presents to her and her family, then paid a visit to the club, which is still open even at Christmas. After a mocktail with the girls, Christmas was almost over.

Then we returned home where, in our absence, Maxim had people decorating the penthouse to look like a winter wonderland, and it's here I wake up, cozy among the cushiony nest created near the Christmas tree. Cotton lies everywhere, creating the illusion of soft snow with glitter sprinkled around to add to the sparkle. Despite the weak winter sun coming in through the blinds, the room remains cozy.

The tree still covers the walls in bright colors from the lights, the dangling decorations and snowflakes spin and drift in the heat rising from the fireplace, and the soft nest we sleep in makes the thought of leaving utterly impossible.

I want to stay here forever.

"Morning," Maxim groans, tightening his arms further against me and pressing his face into the back of my neck. "You smell so good."

"I smell like you," I murmur back with a smile.

"Like I said, good."

"No complaints from me."

"Mmhmm." As he cuddles into me, his cock slides against the crease of my backside and a warm shiver curls down my spine. Stretching out some stiffness in my arm from my injured shoulder, I admire the two rings nestled together on my finger.

As soon as the baby's born, we'll have a real wedding with a real dress, proper vows, and all my family there. I can't wait.

Suddenly, Maxim rolls me onto my back and positions himself over me, his sleepy eyes locking with mine. "How did you sleep?" Concern furrows his brow. "I wasn't too rough last night, was I?"

My core throbs at the memory of his cock pounding into me and I smirk. "Not as rough as I'd like."

"You're hurt," he says softly. "I need to be gentle." The hand he's not bracing on rests against my bare ribs and the blanket shifts as Maxim fully moves over the top of me. "I don't want to do anything that sends you back into the hospital. Plus, I'm not a hundred percent either. Yet."

"If I got whiplash from your dick, I would be pretty happy," I grin, reaching up and cupping his face. "Trust me. I'm fine."

"Yes, you are." He leans down and kisses me slowly. "I say we stay here and fuck like rabbits until New Year's."

"Do you really have that kind of stamina?" I run my hand down his broad chest as he leans back up, gently mapping out the continuous swirls of his tattoos and more. "What if you get limp dick?"

His hips drop down to mine and his hot cock rubs against my thigh. "No such thing."

"Are you sure?"

"Mmhmm. I'll fuck you so hard, our little baby will get a roommate." His hand slides down to my belly and he caresses under my navel. "Fuck. I can't believe there's a baby in there."

"Right?" I lift myself onto one elbow and stare with him. "The thing that started all of this."

"Do you regret it?" Maxim looks at me earnestly as I caress his cheek. "How things turned out?"

"The journey wasn't pleasant," I admit. "But what I've gained? You. A stronger relationship with my parents. More confidence in what I want to do in my life. Surviving. Justice for Zoe... Everything like that makes it so worth it. And now we get to raise this little darling together."

"I hate to think of what would have happened had you not seen me that night." His nose brushes against mine and he kisses me, pressing me back down into the pillows. "I'm so fucking glad your car broke down."

"Me too." My giggles melt into the kiss, but just as I arch my body into Maxim's and kiss him deeper, he pulls away.

"Wait, I have one more present for you. I forgot." Maxim stretches over me to reach the tree. Discarded wrapping paper and items rustle for a moment, then he returns to my side and hands me an envelope. "Here."

"What is it?"

"Open it and see."

Settling back into his arms, I carefully open the envelope and out falls a letter. Unfolding it, I scan the words on the page and then bolt upright, reading them again and again.

This can't be real, surely?

"Oh my God, Maxim, what did you do?"

He sits up with me, his laughter brushing my bare shoulder. "I bought the company that runs those private cruise liners," he says with a grin. "Now you don't have to give up on your dream and it will be waiting for you when you're ready."

"Are you insane?"

"Maybe." He kisses my shoulder, mapping his way to my neck. "Do you like it?"

I can't comprehend the cost, nor the grandeur, of the gesture. He heard my dream, accepted my choice, and then purchased the entire company to ensure my spot would be there forever, whenever I decide to claim it. More than that, the company is in *my* name.

"Maxim, this is too much!"

"No, it's not enough." Maxim kisses my cheek and our eyes meet. "I can't tell the future. I have no idea what's going to happen, but this is yours and so is your dream, understand? It will always be yours. And you will always have the freedom to choose. Plus, it means we can take our own cruise whenever we'd like. I confess I've been fucking the CEO, and I bet she'd let us take out a liner all by ourselves."

I dissolve into laughter and discard the letter, wrapping my arms around Maxim's broad shoulders. "You're insane!"

"I'm in love." He sweeps his arm around my waist and rolls us over until I'm back on the pillows and in his arms. "There's nothing I won't do for you, Hollie."

"Oh my God." Our mouths collide as I wrap my legs around

his hips and draw him in. "I love you so fucking much, you crazy, crazy man!"

"I love you too." He grins against me. "Merry Christmas."

"Merry fucking Christmas," I groan.

This life might be insane.

But it's mine.

And I will love it forever.

ALSO BY AVA GRAY

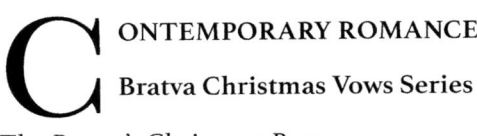

CONTEMPORARY ROMANCE

Bratva Christmas Vows Series

The Bratva's Christmas Bump

THE DUBININ BRATVA **Series**

Captive Vows

Forgotten Vows

A NEW YORK **Criminal Empire Series**

The Irish Redemption

The Russian Retribution

The Italian Reckoning

The Celtic Resolution

. . .

MAFIA KINGPINS SERIES

His to Own

His to Protect

His to Win

His to Possess

His to Claim

THE VALKOV BRATVA Series

Stolen by the Bratva

Kept by the Bratva

Captured by the Bratva

Captivated by the Bratva

Trapped by the Bratva

FESTIVE FLAMES SERIES

Silver Hills' Christmas Miracle

Holly, Jolly, and Oh So Naughty

The Christmas Eve Delivery

Valentine's with the Silver Fox

HAREM HEARTS SERIES

3 SEAL Daddies for Christmas

Small Town Sparks

Her Protector Daddies

Her Alpha Bosses

The Mafia's Surprise Gift

THE BILLIONAIRE MAFIA Series

Knocked Up by the Mafia

Stolen by the Mafia

Claimed by the Mafia

Arranged by the Mafia

Charmed by the Mafia

ALPHA BILLIONAIRE SERIES

Secret Baby with Brother's Best Friend

Just Pretending

Loving The One I Should Hate

Billionaire and the Barista

Coming Home

Doctor Daddy

Baby Surprise

A Fake Fiancée for Christmas

Hot Mess

PLAYING WITH TROUBLE SERIES:

Claiming What's Mine

Protecting What's Mine

Saving What's Mine

THE BECKETT BILLIONAIRES SERIES:

Love to Hate You

Just Another Chance

STANDALONE'S:

Ruthless Love

The Best Friend Affair

PARANORMAL ROMANCE

MAPLE LAKE SHIFTERS SERIES:

Omega Vanished

Omega Exiled

Omega Coveted

Omega Bonded

EVERTON FALLS MATED LOVE SERIES:

The Alpha's Mate

The Wolf's Wild Mate

Saving His Mate

Fighting For His Mate

DRAGONS OF LAS VEGAS SERIES:

Thin Ice

Silver Lining

A Spark in the Dark

Fire & Ice

Dragons of Las Vegas Boxed Set (The Complete Series)

STANDALONE'S:

Fiery Kiss

Wild Fate

Printed in Dunstable, United Kingdom

74982830R10214